Instead ... ***like only hours since she'd last been here.***

Since she'd last seen Rafe.

Idiot. We were kids then, childhood best friends, that's all.

There was nothing of the old feelings left. She'd been a teenager, convinced her life depended on Rafe loving her.

Liar.

She had gone. But she had left her heart and soul behind.

He's probably forgotten all about you, moved on a long time ago to someone else. Like you should have done.

She turned onto the long drive leading into ~ancho Pintada and drove down toward the ~rns, forcing back any emotion except concern ~he animals she was here to care for. She was ~ to do a job and nothing else.

~ame striding out of the barn nearest the

~d and stared.

~nt, it was yesterday again.

Dear Reader,

Ever visited a place you didn't want to leave? We're not talking Paris, Venice or Rome.

We didn't expect that the most recent place we've been to, the small fictional town of Luna Hermosa in northern New Mexico, would become so much a part of our thoughts and daily lives that we're ready to stay there until reality forces us to move on.

When we wrote our first book in the Brothers of Rancho Pintada series, *Sawyer's Special Delivery,* we knew two things: first, we wanted to write a family story about people with imperfect lives finding perfect love; and second, that story needed to be placed in a town that was alive with the things that matter to us—community, friends, fun and familiarity.

As natives of the Southwest, we saw Luna Hermosa as having all those qualities for us and the Morentes, the Garretts and the women they love. In *The Rancher's Second Chance,* you'll get better acquainted with another gorgeous member of the Garrett/Morente clan. Rafe hardly feels a part of the family that adopted him. But he's determined to prove his worth on his adoptive father's ranch. In fact, his dedication to the ranch has isolated him not only from his family but also from the Luna Hermosa community and the passion in his heart.

Then beautiful Julene Santiago, his childhood love, comes back to town to help her father with his veterinary practic When she shows up at Rafe's ranch ready to help him cure his ailing bison herd, he sees not only the spirited little girl he fell in love with, but also the impressive— and sensuous—woman she has become. His little Jule has become everything he wants in a woman, yet a he cannot have.

And Jule's best childhood friend has bec she dreams of in a man, and everything s

Nicole Foster

THE RANCHER'S SECOND CHANCE

NICOLE FOSTER

SPECIAL EDITION®

Published by Silhouette Books,
America's Publisher of Contemporary Romance

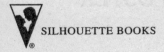

SILHOUETTE BOOKS

ISBN-13: 978-0-373-24841-4
ISBN-10:   0-373-24841-5

THE RANCHER'S SECOND CHANCE

Visit Silhouette Books at www.eHarlequin.com

Printed in U.S.A.

Books by Nicole Foster

Silhouette Special Edition

Sawyer's Special Delivery #1703
The Rancher's Second Chance #1841

Harlequin Historicals

Jake's Angel #522
Cimarron Rose #560
Hallie's Hero #642

NICOLE FOSTER

is the pseudonym for the writing team of Danette Fertig-Thompson and Annette Chartier-Warren. Both journalists, they met while working on the same newspaper, and started writing historical romance together after discovering a shared love of the Old West and happy endings. Their seventeen-year friendship has endured writer's block, numerous caffeine-and-chocolate deadlines and the joyous chaos of marriage and raising the five children between them. They love to hear from readers. Send a SASE for a bookmark to PMB 228, 8816 Manchester Rd., Brentwood, MO, 63144.

Annette Chartier-Warren:

> For my son Brandon,
> First love, dreams and forever are worth the effort.

Danette Fertig-Thompson:

> For Foster,
>
> I always wanted the chance to do something
> amazing, and then you came along,
> And now I am continually amazed at all
> that you are and all you promise to become.

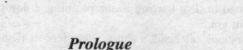

Prologue

Thirteen years ago

Julene Santiago slid off her horse, breathing quickly, heart pounding. Not from the ride; she'd made this ride countless times, though not like this, stealing up to Rancho Pintada like a thief in the midnight darkness. No. The volatile mix of fear, anticipation and bravado making her throat tight and her body tremble was because of Rafe.

She wouldn't leave Luna Hermosa without him. He'd told her he didn't want to see her again but she'd never listened to Rafe when he talked like that. Instead, she listened with her heart—she always had with Rafe.

She always would.

Letting her horse inside the corral fence out back, she stiffened her spine and went up to the door of the little adobe and frame house, not for the first time glad it was sheltered from the big ranch house by large cottonwoods. It had once belonged to Rafe's birth parents and Rafe had taken to living in it a few years ago, telling her he couldn't stomach living in the same house with his adoptive father any more.

Rafe opened the door to her, half-dressed, his black hair wild and loose. When he saw it was her, his face shuttered. But not before Jule saw the flare of hope in his eyes. "What are you doing here?"

"I had to see you. Let me in, Rafe." It was a plea for more than just entry into his house.

After a long hesitation, he stepped aside to let her pass. Inside, they stood staring at each other.

"You shouldn't have come," Rafe said finally.

"I had to. I'm leaving in the morning. I don't want to go without you."

He shook his head, a short, sharp jerk as if she'd hit him. "Don't say that again."

"Rafe…" Jule came closer, almost touching him. "I love you. I've loved you since I was eight. You're my best friend. I can't leave you."

"You can't stay. There's nothing for you here."

"You're here," she said softly.

He grimaced, pain etching his features. Familiar sorrows haunted his eyes and there was a new sorrow there now, one with her name on it. "Like I said—nothing."

"*Your* father, *my* father—they're wrong," she said.

"My father?" His short harsh laugh made her wince. "I'm not Jed Garrett's son. I'm his half American-Indian ranch hand. The only reason I have his name is because he figured it was cheaper to adopt me than hire me."

Jule didn't have an answer for him. It was an old wound she had never been able to heal, made worse by the terrible day four years ago when her father had caught her and Rafe kissing behind the barn.

Both Jed and her father insisted Rafe wasn't good enough for Jule, that he would never be more than a rough ranch hand, working on someone else's land. But Rafe's birth father's legacy to him had been a fierce love for the land of Rancho Pintada and a vow that Rafe belonged there. And so Rafe stayed, determined one day to prove himself worthy of inheriting the ranch.

And Jule stayed, too, equally determined nothing would keep them apart.

It had changed them, though. Rafe was often angry, even cruel, as if he wanted to drive her away but couldn't, and hated himself for not having the strength to let her go. She'd watched helplessly for the last four years, seeing it eat him up inside. And she'd cried for him, loved him with everything in her as if her love alone could make everything right.

"Do you love me?" she asked.

Rafe wrenched back, his expression tortured. "Jule—"

She deliberately put herself in front of him, touched his face so he was forced to meet her eyes square on. "Do you love me?"

"Yes," he ground out. "Damn you." Jerking her into his arms he kissed her with a rough, possessive passion, raw with need, telling her more than any words could ever say the depth of his feeling for her.

Jule threw herself wholeheartedly into the kiss. For ten years she'd played with him, laughed with him, whispered her secrets to Rafe and treasured his. Now she wanted to love him fully, so hard and so deep that he could never let her go.

His hands roved her body in almost reckless, frantic need. Jule tried to shake the feeling that Rafe was desperate to have her this one time before he told her goodbye. But she ignored the dark voice inside her whispering he was going to break her heart.

The fire burned between them hotly, both of them awkward and bold all at once as they moved toward a place neither of them had ever been.

Rafe pulled back from her suddenly and looked at her,

searching for the answer to a question she sensed he couldn't ask. Then carefully, as if he were afraid of hurting her, he caressed her face before gently, tenderly kissing her, taking his time, bringing tears to Jule's eyes with the sweet depth of it.

Very slowly, they began undressing each other and then Rafe carried her to his bed and made love to her as if they had forever.

This time the tears came at the rightness and the power of it. It wasn't perfect but it was right.

And for a time, Jule believed it would last forever.

Forever ended too soon.

In the cold hours before dawn, she woke up alone in a tangle of sheets. Rafe, wearing only his jeans, stood by the window, staring out at the darkness.

Not bothering to dress, she went to him, sliding her arms around him. "We can make it work. Come with me. You can find work in Albuquerque and when I finish school—"

"No," Rafe interrupted. "I'm staying." He pulled out of her embrace to look at her. "This is all I have. I can't walk away from it."

"But you can walk away from me?"

"You're the one leaving."

"Are you asking me to stay?" Jule whispered, not daring to hope.

His expression softened and she could almost touch the emotion in his eyes, a potent mix of love, need, and pain.

"Rafe—"

He turned away. "No. I want you to go."

"How can you say that, after tonight?" The words came out a hoarse croak although Jule felt as if she'd been screaming. She was cold, dying inside and suddenly overwhelmed by fear that this time he meant it.

"Tonight was a mistake," he said, looking hard at her, his jaw tight, hands fisted at his side.

"It wasn't. I love you, you love me."

"I can't—" Rafe took her by the shoulders, gripping hard as if trying to convince both of them. "I can't, Jule, I can't love you."

"Can't—or won't?"

His hands tightened almost painfully then he abruptly let her go and stepped back. "Can't, won't, it doesn't matter. Just—go. Go!" he snarled at her when she stood, frozen, desperately searching for the words to convince him they belonged together.

With a sob, Jule spun away from him, pulling on her clothes in a blind rush and then running out the door.

She heard the slam of his fist against it as she hurtled toward her horse.

But she never saw him crying with her.

Chapter One

Present day

The damned things had to be here somewhere.

Cursing himself for never taking the time to sort out the years of accumulated junk jammed into every nook and cranny of the battered rolltop desk, Rafe Garrett yanked out another drawer, rifling through papers in search of the ones he wanted.

Abran Santiago, laid up with a broken hip, was sending another vet out in his place and Rafe needed to lay his hands on the vaccination records for his bison. Another yearling had turned up sick today and if this new vet didn't have any better idea of how to stop the illness from spreading further and killing more of his calves, Rafe's little experiment with establishing a bison herd on Rancho Pintada was going to be over in short order.

As he pushed his hand to the back of the drawer to drag out the last of the papers his fingers brushed something cool and hard. Frowning, he pulled it out and found himself staring at a heart, shaped from pale-pink quartz and strung on a thin silver chain. It had been shoved in the back of the drawer for so long he'd almost forgotten it.

Almost.

Touching it with the tip of his finger, he found himself flooded with memories thirteen years old. And all of them were of *her.*

The delicate thing curved against his work-roughened hand looked wrong. Like Julene Santiago in his arms—it didn't belong.

It had been hers, of course, lost here that last night he'd held her. Holding it now opened him up to the pain he'd thought he'd finally become immune to. It exposed as lies all the times he'd told himself he'd forgotten her. That he didn't remember how her bare skin felt warm and soft against his. How it felt to tangle his hands in her hair, the dark smoothness of it. How it wound around them like a living thing when they made love.

That she didn't matter to him anymore.

You'll never be good enough for her. You're just a ranch hand like your daddy. You'll never have anything worth giving her. You'd best remember that and stay away from that girl.

He hadn't stayed away—then. And it had eaten him up inside because he knew it could never be the forever they both had wanted. Until, finally, he'd found the guts to let her go.

Except she hadn't gone. She was always with him. He'd never truly wanted another woman since. And sometimes he hated her for that.

He started to crush the necklace in his fist and throw it aside once and for all. The memories stopped him in mid gesture and instead, he very gently returned it to its hiding place, slowly closing the drawer as if by doing so he could finally lay the past to rest.

He couldn't, but he could pretend.

Forgetting the papers, Rafe grabbed up his Stetson and headed for the barns.

He deliberately took the path that kept him as far away as possible from the main ranch house. He was determined to avoid a confrontation with Jed today, rehashing the same old argument over what Jed considered Rafe's foolhardy idea to establish the bison herd along with the cattle and horses raised on Rancho Pintada. If he kept away from the house, it should be easy enough. Jed spent most of his time there these days, laid up from the chemotherapy treatments.

"Hey, Rafe! Wait a minute."

Rafe felt the tension in his neck and shoulders ratchet up a notch, immediately knowing it was his youngest brother, Josh. But he stopped short of the barns, turning to answer the call. "What now? And don't bother telling me if it's something the old man wants."

"Okay, I'll skip that part." Josh Garrett flashed a cocky grin as he strode up to Rafe.

They were family because of Rafe's adoption, but Rafe always figured that anyone who didn't know that would never believe they were brothers. Josh nearly matched him in height, but Josh was lankier, his tousled whiskey-colored hair and green eyes a sharp contrast to the dark coloring bestowed by Rafe's American-Indian heritage.

"You know, you don't always have to look like I'm gonna deliver the worst news of the day," Josh drawled, as he leaned against a fencepost. "'Course, at this point, I'm pretty much convinced that scowl is permanently engraved on your face."

"If that's all you wanted, I've got work to do," Rafe said, used to ignoring Josh's banter.

"When do you not have work to do? Wait, I know—that would be never." Josh held up his hands in mock defense when Rafe's scowl turned even darker. "Don't kill the messenger. Especially when he's come to invite you to a party."

Josh whipped an envelope out of his jacket pocket and thrust it at Rafe. Rafe eyed it suspiciously, not making any move to take it. "What is it?"

"I told you, an invitation. Sawyer's new house is finally done and he and Maya are throwing a party there this weekend."

"And you're going?"

"Sure, why not? Apart from the fact Sawyer's my brother, it's free food and beer and the chance to find out if Maya's got any single friends as hot as she is."

"Sounds like your definition of paradise. Have fun."

"You know, Sawyer's your brother, too—"

"Sawyer Morente isn't my brother," Rafe interrupted. He glared at Josh, hoping in vain to shut him up for once.

"Yeah, he is, despite your best attempts to pretend he, Cort and I don't exist." For a moment, Josh dropped his usual cavalier attitude and looked almost serious—a rarity that robbed Rafe of a ready comeback. "Maybe you should think about giving up your grudge against us—and everything human—and admit you have a family, like it or not. Now might be a good time with Dad hell-bent on tracking down his long-lost son. I know, I know," he said as Rafe started to interrupt, "you wanna pretend that he doesn't exist, too. But Dad's set on a family reunion so the rest of us gotta stick together. Besides—" serious gave way to swagger again "—if you patch things up with Sawyer and Cort, you'll probably be able to talk them into selling you the shares of this place that Dad is so dead set on forcing on them. Make nice with them and for the right price they might sell, and I might, too."

"When hell freezes over."

"Stranger things have happened." Before Rafe could push past him and head into the barns, Josh made a quick motion and shoved the envelope into Rafe's pocket. "Think about it."

Rafe didn't bother answering as he turned his back and pushed the barn door open. He'd spent enough time dredging up the past today. He had no intention of adding to it by thinking about Sawyer and Cort Morente.

They were just two more on the list of broken relationships Rafe had left behind, two more that couldn't be fixed.

* * *

"Why didn't you tell me?"

Looking at her father lying in the hospital bed, Julene Santiago stopped herself—just—from letting a surge of anger raise her voice. She turned away so he wouldn't see it in her face, looking out the window, her eyes dazzled by the early-morning sunlight. Seeing her father like this had unsettled her enough that even though she wanted to confront him over what he'd done, she couldn't bring herself to do more than ask the question. Her father, with his lean, wiry build, wasn't a big man, but confined to bed with a broken hip, his usual energetic activity curbed, he looked grayer and diminished, almost frail.

He'd talked her into coming home, into taking over his busy practice for a few months while he recuperated from his recent riding accident. He was the only vet in Luna Hermosa and he'd told her he didn't like bringing in a stranger from Taos, and who better to step in for him than his daughter? She knew the area and the people knew her. Hadn't she planned on quitting that big animal hospital in Albuquerque anyway, to set up her own practice somewhere smaller?

Her father hadn't said anything outright but Jule knew he secretly hoped once she'd been back a while, she'd get so comfortable she'd stay and take over his practice permanently. It was something he'd been hinting at for a while, implying she'd be the perfect person to take over for him when he retired.

Despite his hints, Jule had promised nothing except to stay until he was back on his feet. She'd agreed to do that partly out of love for him, but largely because she'd felt so restless lately. She always had liked working with animals but somehow, in Albuquerque, it felt so impersonal—not like in Luna Hermosa where she knew everyone, where she'd grown up.

Only her father had conveniently forgotten to tell her that she'd be spending a lot of her time at Rancho Pintada—the one place she never expected to see again.

That she'd be spending a lot of her time with Rafe Garrett. She shouldn't have come back.

"Why didn't you tell me?" she said again as she turned back to the bed.

Abran Santiago shifted with a wince then shrugged. "What was there to tell? I've been going to Rancho Pintada since before you were born. Why would you think that had changed?"

"I didn't think it had. But I didn't know about the bison and that you'd been going out there every other day for the last month." Her father had finally told her this morning that he'd been working with the bison at the ranch for the better part of a year while Rafe had apparently been trying to establish a herd. Several calves had died from an illness and Rafe was worried enough to call her father himself—out of character because he and her father had never gotten along.

Jule nearly laughed at that. Saying Rafe and her father had never gotten along was a huge understatement.

"What does it matter?" Abran said, with a touch of ill-disguised irritation. The prolonged inactivity had made him short-tempered and restless. Even Jule's mother's patience, usually endless, had been stretched thin. "Do you have something against bison?"

"It's not the bison. It's Jed Garrett I don't like." That was true, at least.

"No one likes Jed Garrett, not even his own family. What does that have to do with it?" Abran's eyes narrowed. "Don't tell me this has to do with Rafe. That was years ago. You were just a girl. Surely none of that matters now?"

Her eyes slid away from his. "Of course not."

"Which means it does, since you can't look me in the eye and tell me it doesn't. I never understood your infatuation with that boy," Abran said wearily.

Jule could feel him watching her, weighing what he wanted to say. They'd never talked about her relationship with Rafe.

Instead, they'd had flaming arguments, her father on one side, telling her all the reasons Rafe was wrong for her and her on the other, insisting none of that mattered and vowing she'd never give Rafe up. In the end it hadn't mattered because Rafe had given up on her.

She glimpsed her reflection in the window glass and she could see both the girl she'd been and the woman she'd become. Right now, they didn't feel so very different.

"No, you never did," she agreed, turning back to her father. "But it doesn't matter now."

It shouldn't matter, she told herself, and kept repeating it the whole drive from the hospital to Rancho Pintada even while she called herself a fool for being anywhere near Jed Garrett's ranch in the first place. Instead of thirteen years, it seemed like only hours since she'd last been here.

Since she'd last seen Rafe.

Idiot. We were kids then, childhood best friends, that's all. Dad was right. It was years ago.

There was no reason for the hard knot of nervous anticipation lodged in her stomach, the one that made her almost sick at the thought of seeing him again. There was nothing of the old feelings for him left. She'd been a teenager, overly dramatic and emotional, convinced her life depended on Rafe loving her. He'd thrown away their chance at love, broken her heart, and if she felt anything for him it was leftover anger at the callous way he'd cut her out of his life.

Liar.

Oh, yeah, she was so over him. That was why she was thirty-one with her vision of a soul mate still stuck at eighteen. Why she'd never had any other relationship that had lasted longer than a few months. Why she'd only made love twice in her life. With Rafe. Thirteen years ago.

"I can't, Jule. I can't love you."

"Can't—or won't?"

"Can't, won't, it doesn't matter. Just go."

She had gone. But she had left her heart and soul behind. She should never have come back.

Get a grip on yourself. He's probably forgotten all about you, moved on a long time ago to someone else. Like you should have done.

She turned onto the long drive leading into Rancho Pintada and drove down toward the barns, forcing back any emotion except concern for the animals she was here to care for. This wasn't a long-awaited reunion. She was here to do a job and nothing else. She'd see him again, realize whatever had been between them was long dead and then, maybe, finally, her heart could move on.

Jule avoided the turn to the main house. She had no desire to renew her acquaintance with Jed Garrett. What she felt for him for his treatment of Rafe still bordered on hatred.

Rafe's father and Jed had started Rancho Pintada together, but when Jed had married Theresa Morente and her family money, he'd made himself more owner than partner and Rafe's father took on the role of ranch foreman. When Rafe's parents were killed in a car crash and Jed and Theresa adopted their six-year-old orphaned son, people at first assumed it was out of respect for his partner, to ensure Rafe kept a share in the ranch.

But Jule had quickly come to the conclusion that something else was behind the adoption, although neither she nor Rafe had ever been able to understand what. Theresa never considered Rafe her child. She'd walked out on Jed two years after the adoption, taking her own two sons and leaving Rafe behind with Jed. She had died three years ago without ever seeing Rafe again. And to Jed, Rafe had never been more than a ranch hand with the Garrett name.

Jule couldn't forgive Jed or Theresa for that, so she bypassed the main house and parked her pickup truck close to the barns.

She'd climbed out of the cab and was reaching for her bag when a man came striding out of the barn nearest the drive.

Rafe.

They both stopped and stared.

And in that moment, it was yesterday again.

Chapter Two

Rafe moved first, slowly, almost stiffly, as if he were trying to remember how to take steps forward.

Jule couldn't make herself move. It was all she could do to remind herself to breathe as she watched him come toward her. All the memories rushed back and she felt eighteen again, unsure and on unfamiliar ground, as if all those years of being on her own and alone had never happened.

He'd hardly changed. The years of tough, physical work had added muscle and he looked harder, the features she'd once fancifully compared to being carved from the elements themselves now more sharply defined. He still wore his black hair long, caught back in a short tail, and her fingers flexed unconsciously with the physical memory of running her hands through it.

He stopped a few feet short of her and Jule found herself searching his eyes, wanting to believe she could see in them the boy that she'd fallen so completely in love with. Instead she saw shadows that years of bitterness had layered there.

"You—" The word sounded harsh, as if his throat hurt to say it. He shook his head as if he couldn't quite believe he was seeing her. "What are you doing here?"

"I came back—"

Because of you. To see you.

"—for the bison."

Do you remember me? Us?

"Dad couldn't come...but you know that. He said he told you he was sending—someone. And I said I would help." *Because I'm certifiably* loco. "I know about—"

Jule heard herself stammering like an idiot and stopped. Obviously, her father hadn't bothered to tell Rafe she was the replacement vet. She shouldn't be surprised, considering he hadn't told her until this morning. Taking a cue from Jed, he'd never treated Rafe with any respect. Her father had made it clear whatever unfortunate infatuation she'd had for Rafe or he for her was long over and so decided it wasn't worth warning Rafe she'd be coming.

"He didn't say anything about you," Rafe said slowly. His expression didn't give anything away, but his hands were fisted at his sides.

"I'm sorry. Dad should have told you. I thought he had."

"No. Although I guess I shouldn't be surprised." She started to apologize again but he stopped her with a sudden cutting gesture. "It doesn't matter."

"It matters to me," Jule said softly. "It always did. Rafe—" She hesitated, fumbling for something to say to him.

He watched her, studying her face as if he were memorizing it. "It's been a long time."

"Too long. I've thought about... How have you been?"

"Fine. Great." Silence, then, "You look good, Jule," he said in a voice suddenly softer at the edges. "Better than good."

"You, too."

For brief seconds Jule thought she glimpsed a flash of emotion in his eyes, something needy and vulnerable. It vanished just as quickly, leaving her to wonder if she'd imagined it.

"I heard about your—about Jed being sick," she said, to fill the uncomfortable silence. "I'm sorry."

Rafe shrugged. "If being a mean, stubborn son-of-a-bitch means anything, the old man'll live forever. He probably will anyway, just to spite me."

"Some things never change. Jed's the same." She hesitated then added, "You're still here."

"Did you think I wouldn't be?"

"No. I never thought you'd leave." The words came with a wash of sorrow and regret, tinged with an old angry hurt. Of course he'd never leave. There had been times in the past when she'd believed he was so bonded to this land that to leave would kill him.

An awkward silence fell between them again. Jule tried to think of something to say that would break the barriers between them so they could really talk as the intimate friends they'd been, instead of as strangers, skirting the edges of any meaningful conversation. But there didn't seem to be anything to say that wouldn't dredge up emotions better left buried or truths she wasn't ready to face.

"They're in here," Rafe said abruptly, gesturing sharply to the foremost barn. Apparently he'd decided their attempt at conversation was over. "I've been isolating the sick calves, but it doesn't seem to have done much toward stopping the spreading of the illness." He waited until Jule had grabbed her bag from the truck and then started striding toward the barn, not bothering to look to see if she'd follow.

He started to give her a history of how the illness had begun and the treatments her father had tried, but Jule, catching up and matching his pace, stopped him. "I looked at all Dad's records and talked to him before I came. I didn't want to waste time having you go over everything again. Dad finished an autopsy on the last calf you lost before his accident."

"Good. I hope he learned something because I'm losing more every day. I'll let you…take a look. At the calves. Here—"

As she followed him into the barn, Jule's nerves settled a little, partly because her focus turned to the calves, but more, oddly enough, because of Rafe's uncharacteristic fumbling for words. For a moment, he'd seemed as unsure and uncertain as she felt. Somehow, that was comforting, because it meant he wasn't as unmoved by seeing her as he obviously wanted her to believe.

He didn't say anything as she examined each of the sick bison calves, just watched from the shadows as she worked in close confines of the stalls. She could feel his eyes on her as palpably as a touch, finding the combination of his watching and silence unnerving.

When she'd finished with the smallest of the woolly calves, no more than a few months old, Jule sat back on her heels, rubbing at the smooth oval-shaped stone she wore around her neck. "I want to run a few more tests, but I think Dad's right and it's hemophilosis."

Rafe stared a long distant moment at the necklace, then lifted a brow. "Hemo what?"

"It's a bacterial infection that can affect the lungs, urinary tract and reproductive tracts." She paused. "If they live, it can also cause blindness. What I don't understand is why they're not responding to the usual antibiotic. This strain of the disease must have become resistant."

Rafe moved to crouch beside her, his shoulder brushing hers as he reached out to gently stroke the calf's flank. "If there's something else I need to be doing, tell me."

"Nothing, for now," Jule said. "I've got a friend in Texas who's got more experience with bison than I do. I'll give him a call and do a little research on my own. Then I'll plan on coming back tomorrow. Maybe by then I'll have a better idea of where to go from here."

She shifted to get to her feet, stumbled a little and Rafe

grasped her upper arm, steadying her as they stood up together. They looked at each other and Rafe's grip tightened.

Slowly, Jule reached up and touched his face. A shudder went through him, echoed in her.

"It's not dead, is it?" she whispered. "It never was."

"Jule—" He shook his head. "I can't do this."

Abruptly he let her go, striding out of the stall. Jule heard the barn door slam open, hinges creaking as it swung closed again, shutting out the light.

"Jule, honey, hand me a fresh dish towel, will you?" Catalina Santiago asked as she stretched on tiptoe trying to replace a dinner plate on a high shelf.

"Mom, here. Let me do that." Jule eased the plate from her mother's hand. She had five inches over her mother's five foot to help her reach a few things easier.

"Thank you." Catalina chuckled at herself. "I'm so used to your father getting all the things I can't reach around this house I never realized how short I am."

Jule smiled. Small, thin, her long black hair—dyed now to keep it that way—pulled up in an elegant bun, Catalina was still pretty, even in her late sixties. Both Jule and her father had always been proud of the way her mother kept herself up. "Petite, not short," she said, giving her mother's shoulders a little squeeze.

Catalina turned to face her daughter, her smile fading. "I miss him, you know? Crotchety old man that he is sometimes, I'd rather hear him complaining every morning over coffee about gas prices or how's he's getting too old to be dodging kicks and bites, than be away from him worrying about whether or not he's getting sick in that awful hospital."

"I know how you feel," Jule said as she handed her mother a clean dish towel. "It's hard being away from someone you love that much." The words slipped out before she realized what she was saying and she struggled to take them back. "I mean, I can imagine what it must be like." From the lift in Catalina's brow, she knew at once her attempt had failed.

Catalina clucked her tongue as she shook her head. "After all these years, it still hasn't been long enough, has it?"

Evading her mother's knowing gaze was only a delaying tactic. Jule knew the subject of Rafe Garrett wasn't about to go away. It never really had, at least in her mind. She sighed and, suddenly emotionally tired, sank into a chair at the kitchen table. "I'd tell you you're being ridiculous, but it's no use, is it?"

"Of course not," Catalina said, reaching out to stroke her daughter's smooth black hair. "I know you better than you know yourself. You're my daughter, part of me. I feel what you're feeling even when you're far away. Now that you're close, you almost don't need to speak. I feel your words before you say them."

Jule looked up at her mother, smiling a little. "So are all mothers like you, or do you possess some kind of magic I don't know about?"

Catalina shrugged, the corners of her mouth rounding in an almost catlike grin. "I don't know about others. I only know that back to your great-great-grandmother Paloma in Madrid, our women have been linked, call it magic or simply intuition. Just wait, when you have a daughter of your own, you'll know her every thought, too."

For a moment the fantasy of a beautiful olive-skinned, black-eyed baby girl, part American Indian, part Castillian, formed in Jule's imagination. It wasn't the first time she'd seen that baby in her mind's eye. But that's all it was, a fantasy.

All it would ever be.

"Maybe, but I don't see that happening anytime soon," she said, trying to sound indifferent. "With work, I have more helpless creatures to care for than I have time for now. I can't imagine juggling that with a child, too. Not to mention the fact that no one's exactly knocking my door down with an offer of marriage."

Putting her towel on the counter, Catalina took a seat next to Jule. "That's because you scare them off."

"Me? How do I do that?"

"You have a wall up around you so thick it's almost visible. You don't want men to take an interest in you, much less ever get to the point of proposing."

Jule wanted to argue, but her mother's words were too close to the truth. "It took me so long to get through school, and then to do an internship and get established at the clinic, I haven't had much time for men or relationships."

"That's what you tell yourself. But I don't believe it and I don't think you do either."

"It's the truth," she said defiantly but without any conviction behind it. She was beginning to feel uncomfortable, cornered. Her mom always did this to her and it drove her nuts.

"Honey, you're still in love with Rafe, why not be honest with yourself about that?"

Jule stared at her mother, speechless. It was one thing to silently acknowledge it, another to be confronted with it in straight words. Something caught in her throat when she tried to choke out a retort. Tears welled in her eyes and she angrily swiped them away.

"Oh, Jule." Catalina leaned forward and pulled her daughter into her arms. "Denying it is no good. All of these years, you've tried, I know, to get over him. But that obviously hasn't happened."

"It should have. Lord knows I've tried hard enough to get rid of it."

"Have you?"

"Of course I have. It just won't stay dead and buried." Extricating herself from her mother's embrace, she got to her feet and began folding the dish towel, needing some outlet for the restlessness inside her. "I know I've been a fool to let this go on for so long. I thought seeing him would help, especially if he's with someone—"

"He's not."

"How do you know?"

Catalina shrugged. "Over the years, I've heard bits and pieces about the Garretts around town. You know how people like to gossip. And when your father had his accident and people heard you were coming back…"

"That only makes it worse," Jule said. Worse because it gave strength to her feeble fantasy that one day things between her and Rafe would be right again. That they could go back to once upon a time when every dream between them seemed possible.

"You can't control your feelings," Catalina said softly. "You can only try to make peace with them. Only then can you move on and open your heart to a man who's right for you."

"Right for me?" Old memories—of her father's condemnation of Rafe, of Jed's sarcasm and demeaning attitude toward Rafe as a boy, of her mother's silent submission to her father's demands that Jule give up seeing Rafe—welled up in Jule. "Rafe was right for me. But no one ever gave us a chance to prove it. No one ever gave Rafe a chance. Not even you. You just accepted what Dad told you without question even though you knew how much it hurt me."

Catalina's eyes widened at the strike of the words. "I don't know Rafe all that well, but I've always trusted your father's judgment where you're concerned. He's always wanted only the best for you and so do I. It's what you deserve."

The hurt in her mother's voice made Jule feel guilty. She knew her mom didn't really understand how Rafe had been abused by Jed. How Jule had been the only person in his life after his parents died who'd treated him with love and respect, the only person he'd ever allowed to see inside his heart.

And she knew her mother idolized her father, which was on one hand endearing; on the other hand it made any topic where she disagreed with her father impossible to discuss with her mother.

"Rafe is so much more than anyone believes," she said softly.

"Perhaps. But you were so young and your relationship with Rafe was too intense. Even when you were children together you were inseparable, almost from the beginning. It wasn't right."

"How do you know it wasn't right?"

"Your father—"

"Oh, here we go."

Catalina rose, elongating her petite stature, all dignity and grace. "Julene, I won't argue with you about this. You've made it clear you'll only be here until your father recovers, and I won't let talk about Rafe Garrett or any of that sorry Garrett clan ruin what time we have together." With that, she turned to the sink dismissively, to finish cleaning up.

The scene reminded Jule of a lifetime of similar confrontations. It was never any use arguing with her mother or trying to change her point of view. As warm and loving as she was, her mother had lived a life sheltered beneath her father's strong wing. She would never believe anything but what her father told her about Rafe—even if her only daughter's heart was at stake.

"I'm sorry," she said finally. "I don't want to argue either." She grabbed a couple of bowls and plunged them in the hot soapy water. "Here, let me help you finish up."

"No, thank you," Catalina said. The stiff line of her back softened a little. "You've helped enough already. You must be tired. And I'd like you to get up early so you can drop me off at the hospital before you go back to the ranch. At least I'm guessing you'll be there again tomorrow?"

"Yes, I have some new medicine to pick up first after I take you to the hospital. So if you're sure you don't need any more help, I think I will turn in early."

"Of course, honey," her mother said in her usual sweet tone, as though the tension between them had never been. "Go on to bed. I turned down the sheets and the nightlight is on. I'll wake you and bring you your tea, no need to set an alarm."

Jule hugged her mother's shoulders from behind. "Thanks, Mom. See you in the morning."

"Good night, and sweet dreams."

But her dreams were never sweet because they could never be real. And that was the one ailment Jule hadn't been able to find a remedy for.

Sunlight streamed into Jule's bedroom hitting her eyes with a harsh wake-up call. Feeling as though she'd barely gotten to sleep, she rubbed her eyes and saw her mother pulling her bedroom drapes aside.

"Wake up, honey, it's a glorious fall day. A little nippy out, but bright and sunny. Your tea is there on your nightstand."

"Thanks," Jule said, still groggy from a sleep tormented by visions of the past. Of Rafe, their one night together. Of her father's and Jed's rage when she and Rafe were little more than children experimenting with a first kiss. Coming back here was even harder than she'd expected. How could she possibly do as her mother had suggested and "make peace" with her feelings? It was more about torture. She needed an exorcist to wrench it out of her.

She rose, showered and dressed in her best-fitting jeans, the ones that hugged her curves, berating herself even as she strained to yank the zipper up and paired them with a snug soft-yellow cotton T-shirt she knew flattered her figure. *I'm sure the bison will be impressed,* she told her reflection in the mirror, half aggravated for caring how she looked because she knew part of her was wondering how Rafe would see her.

After a hasty breakfast she drove her mom to the hospital and peeked in on her father, who was still sleeping soundly. She would have to visit him after work. Kissing her mother on the cheek she lingered a moment in the doorway watching her mother move her chair closer to her father's bed where she would spend her day sitting contentedly at her father's side, her palm resting atop his hand.

Whatever it is, they certainly have something that's lasted and made them both happy, Jule thought as she turned out of the room to head back into her truck, anticipating a day that promised to be anything but happy.

Jed Garrett glared down into the listless eyes of the bison calf lying in a barn stall, then at Rafe kneeling beside it. He coughed and spat out a wad of tobacco. "I say the girl's too young to know what she's doin'. Get rid of her, Rafe, and get a vet with some experience."

Josh leaned over the gate to the stall, rocking front to back on his boot heels. "You're saying that because you haven't seen her, yet. She's worth keeping around just for the view."

Rafe scowled at them both. "She's hardly a girl any more. And I'd hardly call her inexperienced after six years on the job. She's all we have right now with Doc Santiago laid up. I'm giving her a chance. If she doesn't make progress with this soon, then I'll get rid of her."

"Glad to hear it, boy," Jed said with a snort. "After all those years of pining after that spoiled little princess, I didn't think you'd have the guts."

"First, don't call me 'boy.'" Getting to his feet, Rafe put himself within a foot of Jed. "Second, if she was such a princess, she wouldn't be mucking around in stalls all day, now would she?"

Josh laughed. "Careful, big brother, or you'll have Dad thinkin' you're still carrying a torch for pretty Julene."

Rafe felt hot blood begin to pulse in his veins, but he checked his anger. His big-mouthed brother wasn't worth the effort. "Unlike you, I've got more on my mind than my next ride."

"Horse or woman?" Josh volleyed back with a wink.

"Is there a difference for you?"

"Stop it. Both of you." Jed coughed again, a harsh, raspy sound from deep in his chest. "I'm not up to hearin' your damned bickerin'." He looked hard at Rafe. "You just get this taken care of and quick. Just remember, boy, every animal that dies comes out of your pay. And the sooner that girl's gone the better. She's never been nothin' but trouble." Not giving Rafe a chance to retort, Jed stumped off toward the rear door of the barn, calling over his shoulder as he went, "Get a move on, Josh, if you're gonna show me that new filly you've been wastin' my money on."

With a shrug of his shoulders and a wicked grin for Rafe, Josh followed his father.

Rafe had failed to notice he had company again until a soft voice called out, "Good morning."

Jule was coming toward him, up the long aisle that separated the stalls; the sound of her voice momentarily paralyzed him. His heart tensed in his chest and he looked away—and caught Jed glancing back with a scowl as he recognized Jule.

The huge barn felt suddenly small, suffocating. Abruptly, Rafe turned away from Jed and strode toward Jule. Wearing an oversized denim jacket, she looked too small to be carrying the big black bag of her trade. She might be petite, but he knew all too well the strength hidden in her slender legs and arms. She'd always been a tomboy and it had paid off in adding supple muscle to a body that was otherwise all woman. As he neared her she stopped, her eyes searching his.

Seeing her face-to-face again roused old pain and bitterness that had lain dormant inside him for years, always there and festering, but pushed back into dark corners of his soul. Part of him wished she'd just turn around, walk straight back to her truck and never come back. Another part urged him to pull her into his arms and—this time—never let her go.

She was close enough he could smell the scent of sunflowers and sage that was uniquely hers, see the faint blush in her cheeks. Her lips parted slightly as if she was trying to find the voice to say something, but she just as easily could have been inviting him to kiss her.

She'd always been able to do this to him, rattle him so he couldn't think straight, couldn't think of anything but her despite all the protests his common sense could throw at him.

"Good morning," she said again, this time her voice a little tremulous.

A gruff and unwelcoming, "Yeah," was all the reply he could muster. The rush he felt from seeing her, being close to her made his head spin. Barn smells of straw, animals and dust disappeared and all he could think of were big bright sunflowers and slender sage branches swaying gently in the summer breeze, and those clear dark eyes that used to smile just for him.

Her hesitant smile vanished and she searched his face. "It doesn't sound like it's been too good for you so far."

Shaking his head, more to clear it than to deny her, Rafe backed several steps away from her. She stiffened and looked away. "Jed decided to start the morning by giving me his opinion. Good way to ruin the day."

Jule shifted the heavy bag she was holding to her other hand. "I see. Maybe I should leave. I don't want to cause you any more trouble."

Rafe reached out and took the bag from her, his rough, calloused hand brushing her soft skin. His pulse quickened. "No. You're here to do a job and I need you to get started on it, the sooner the better. I know you can handle the old man."

"It's been a long time," Jule said with a rueful smile. "I'm a little rusty." Her gaze fell to the straw-covered floor. She paused then said quietly, "Actually, I don't think I've seen Jed since…since that day."

The memories came like a vision, and he briefly closed his eyes against the pictures that rolled across his mind, playing out that scene, the one that had ultimately changed their lives forever. Himself at sixteen, high on love and lust for Jule, fourteen and the most beautiful girl he'd ever laid eyes on. They were supposed to be looking at the horses but they'd ended up behind the barn, holding each other, totally absorbed in their first serious kiss. Nothing had felt so right. Then her father had found them. And everything had gone wrong.

Shaking off the past, Rafe turned to find Jule studying him, an odd expression on her face.

"Rafe—"

"Yeah, well, like I said yesterday," Rafe hurried on, "he's the same sorry son-of-a-bitch he was back then. Only lately he's been even meaner and nastier because of the cancer. Just stay out of his way and it'll be okay."

"I doubt it. At least not for you. It's obvious he doesn't want me here."

Cursing Jed silently, Rafe struggled with an answer, deciding she might as well hear the bare truth. She probably already knew it anyway. "He wants results with the bison. Yesterday. He thinks you're too young and inexperienced to get the job done." He hesitated and then reluctantly added, "And he hasn't forgotten anything either."

"No." Jule's eyes misted. "I guess none of us has."

Chapter Three

How could he still do this to her? After all these years, how could simply being near him reduce her to a mass of needy feelings and desires? *Oh, get a grip,* she admonished herself. She wasn't a lovestruck teenager any more. Acting like one would prove what Jed Garrett accused her of—being too inexperienced, not professional enough to handle a serious problem with the bison.

A surge of self-infuriation overrode the wave of nostalgic emotion threatening to engulf her, giving her the strength she needed to shake off the past. *At least long enough to get through the next hour with Rafe.* Past that, she knew it was worthless to make herself any promises.

She lifted her chin and squared her jaw. "I don't want to waste your time."

Something made Rafe's eyes darken in that mysterious way they did whenever he didn't want her to see what he was thinking. His eyes had an odd way of turning from deep coffee-brown to almost completely black, making his gaze unreadable. Jule had often wondered if his American-Indian ancestors had passed this gift down to him, imbuing him with an ancient and secret way of protecting himself from the prying eyes of enemies.

Or the searching eyes of a past love.

"I'd like to start with the youngest calf we were looking at yesterday," Jule said.

With a curt nod Rafe turned abruptly, leaving her with a view of his broad back. "Over here."

Jule took two steps to each of his to keep up following him inside the overlarge stall built to accommodate bison. There they knelt in the straw on either side of the sleeping calf. Avoiding Rafe's intense gaze, she laid a hand on the calf's thick coat and stroked her. "Would you hand me my bag, please?"

Even though the calf was only weeks old, it was already so large that Rafe stood and walked around her to hand Jule the vet bag. When he bent on one knee next to her, Jule silently cursed him. She needed to distance herself from him to concentrate on her work. Instead of focusing on the calf, she found her attention drawn to Rafe's musky leather-and-earth scent, an aroma she remembered all too well. She allowed herself to breathe him in for a few moments, gave herself seconds to indulge in the memory of that elemental scent engulfing her as he wrapped his body around hers.

And then she stopped. Stopped thinking. Stopped breathing.

She looked at him, inches from her. He held himself taut, as though poised to strike or flee—which one, she couldn't tell from those mysterious eyes. Her fingers ached to touch him. She reached over and brushed her fingertips over once-familiar angles and planes, then gently cupped her palm to his cheek.

Rafe's eyes closed and he let out a long sigh, almost a groan. "Jule," he whispered, lifting his big, calloused hand to place over hers.

He sounded tired, as though he'd journeyed years and years,

finally arriving at his destination only to realize it wasn't where he'd intended to go. "Don't do this. To yourself. To me." His voice was low, almost a plea.

"To us?" she whispered back.

Rafe lifted her hand from his cheek and turned it palm up. He buried his lips there, long enough to leave a kiss that burned like a branding iron with his name on it through her flesh.

"There is no us," he said, turning her palm over in his then slowly laying it down on the calf. "There's only this. They need you."

"And you? What do you need, Rafe?"

"I need..." He frowned, shaking his head as if the idea of needing anything for himself had never occurred to him. "I need you to save them."

Rafe's words hit her like a fist. All these years, she'd never stopped loving him. But she wondered if his love for her had ever been as deep and unshakeable as his devotion to this land. If it ever had been, it was obvious the years had blunted whatever feelings he'd had for her.

The land was his first mistress and always had been. He needed her to make sure nothing happened to threaten his position here. That was all. No amount of wishful thinking was going to change that.

Something cold and brittle replaced the fleeting liquid warmth from his touch and Jule shifted away from him, opening her bag. "That's what I'm here to do. From now on, don't worry, it's going to be strictly business."

Bold, sensible words. She could almost believe them except for that girl inside her who wouldn't be silenced, who clung to the futile hope he would counter, telling her he cared, too.

Instead, Rafe settled back on his heels, nodding. "Right. That's all this is."

Jule didn't think her heart was capable of hurting any more, yet it did, the ache of it hitting her hard and low. But damned if she'd let him see that now. "I need to draw blood again. And I've brought a new antibiotic to try."

His expression remained flat and matter-of-fact, his tone all business. "Tell me what to do."

Boy, wouldn't I like to! No, actually, I'd rather tell you where to go. "I'm going to have to inject her in the hip. She'll wake up, so you need to be ready to restrain her."

"Will do." Rafe rolled up the sleeves of his denim shirt, exposing the hard muscles of his tanned forearms. Jule forced herself to focus on the needle in her hand.

She held up the syringe and tapped it. "I spoke to Manny Perez yesterday, the vet I told you about in Lubbock."

"And?"

"He recommended trying this. It's brand-new, so I can't guarantee anything, but apparently he's had some success with it. The old antibiotics aren't working for certain cases anymore. Okay, hold her as best you can."

With that, Jule plunged the thick needle through the heavy coat of fur and leathery skin of the calf. Instantly the calf awoke, letting out a weak cry and struggling to kick Jule away.

Rafe clamped his hands over the struggling calf, using his weight and the force of his body to restrain her until she calmed, her anxious breathing slowing to strained rasps.

"Shh, there, it's okay," Jule soothed, stroking the calf's head and nose and looking into her frightened eyes. She glanced over to Rafe. "It's in her lungs already."

"And that means what?"

Jule pushed at the sweat on her brow with the back of her hand and gave the calf a rueful glance. "It means we'd better get busy dosing every calf in the herd."

They worked side by side for the rest of the day. Except for the occasional comment on treatment or request for help from Jule, there hadn't been much to call conversation. The silence hadn't been exactly comfortable, but Rafe was thankful for it nonetheless. They'd found a rhythm, moving efficiently from calf to calf, managing to work side by side while keeping a safe distance from each other.

Rafe hoped Jule never caught on to how desperately he needed that space. Being close to her again was torture, driving him to the brink of doing or saying something irretrievably stupid. But he steeled himself against giving her even a hint of the inner hell he was in.

He'd lived there long enough in those years without her; he should be an expert at it by now.

He watched her, though, when he was sure she wasn't looking, blessing the distraction of the bison for giving him the chance. She'd grown even more beautiful with time, more poised, confident. More of all of the things that had always made her too good for the likes of him. And something else attracted him, while at the same time sending her even further out of reach. She was a consummate professional at her work. And it showed more and more with each calf she examined. She studied, prodded, listened, examined every animal thoroughly and methodically, taking meticulous notes on each one.

He'd always known she was smart, like her father, but now she had the hard-earned degree and the expertise to back it up. He found her intelligence sexy. When she talked about the sickness afflicting his bison, how it affected each calf they were treating, and how the antibiotics might help, part of him hung on every word—not because he cared for an education in bovine diseases, but because he loved the sound of her voice.

Unfortunately for his peace of mind, the voice went with the body he'd loved. He had a hard time keeping his eyes fixed on the calves, an even harder time stopping his own body from reacting to her nearness in ways that were about as far from sick bison as a man's thoughts could take him.

"That's the last one," Jule was saying, lifting the corner of her shirt to wipe the dampness from her brow.

Rafe couldn't help but glance down at the small patch of

silken flesh revealed at her slender waist. His hands burned with the memory of holding her, pulling her close as they lay together entwined, back, so far back in that other life they'd once shared.

He blew out a breath, surprised to find he'd been holding it, and on that breath the vision dissipated. Getting to his feet, he offered her a hand. "Thanks. You must be tired."

She took his hand and pulled herself up. "My back sure is," she said, rubbing at her lower back. "This was a workout." She glanced back down to where another calf lay motionless. "We still need to get this one into the barn. Is there enough room?"

Rafe tipped his Stetson back and looked out over the field they'd ridden looking for other sick animals among the grazing herd. He nodded. "We have a few stalls left. Not enough if they all come down with this, though."

"That's why I want to isolate the sick ones today. I'm hoping it'll help keep this from spreading."

"I called Josh. He's on his way out here with a couple of the hands. We can ride on back now. We'll cross paths with him on the way."

"If I can haul my body up on Blanco's back. I haven't ridden in so long."

Rafe swung a long leg easily up and over his own horse as he settled into the saddle. "You think you're sore now, wait 'til morning."

Jule gave Blanco a swift kick and headed out in front of Rafe. "Don't remind me," she called back over her shoulder.

For a moment, Rafe sat watching her. Her slender body and gently rounded backside rose and fell in perfect, graceful rhythm, her long braid bouncing against her back the way it had when she was a wild little girl riding bareback at his side. At the same time, now as a woman, he could see her riding just as effortlessly, only sidesaddle in a flowing gown, as naturally as a lady from a medieval castle or a princess on her royal steed.

Get real. Someday she'll find her prince. That's what she deserves. And, hombre, you ain't no prince.

* * *

Josh, riding a few paces behind two of the ranch hands, pulled up short next to them as they neared the barns.

"'Bout time you two made it back. Mom says dinner's at six, sick bison or no sick bison." He flashed Jule a wide, flirtatious grin. "I had an extra place set for you. Bonnie's making a special dinner just for you."

"Oh, thanks, but no," Jule said quickly. The idea of spending more than five minutes with Jed Garret was enough to kill her appetite. Simultaneously with that thought, her stomach rumbled to spite her and she realized she hadn't eaten since breakfast. "I really couldn't."

Rafe scowled at his brother. "She's been at it all day. She wants to get home."

Jule shot Rafe a look she hoped told him she could speak for herself. He didn't have to make it so plain that he'd had enough of her for one day. "It sounds nice, but I smell like bison and I don't have any clean clothes and I need to do some write-ups on the calves tonight."

"Not an excuse. Mom keeps all kinds of extra clothes in the guest room. You can shower and change there." Josh turned a smug smile on Rafe. "Besides, Dad wants a full report on the bison."

Rafe leaned over his saddle toward Josh. "I can give him that."

Josh leaned harder. "She can do it better."

Just keeping herself from rolling her eyes, Jule resisted riding off and leaving the two of them to their male posturing. *For heaven's sake, do you both have to act like ten-year-olds trying to outdo each other on the playground?*

"Fine, since you went to the trouble of getting me invited, I'll come to dinner," Jule told Josh.

He grinned broadly at Rafe, who in turn had his hands fisted around the reins and looked as if he wanted to wipe the taunt off Josh's face by knocking him out of the saddle. Baiting Rafe seemed to be a form of entertainment for Josh. Jule felt like kicking him.

She touched Rafe's shoulder to draw his attention to her. "It might be easier if I told Jed about what we're doing with the bison. I'm the one responsible if the treatment doesn't work."

"No. You're not," Rafe said shortly. He looked hard at her a moment, then jerked his hat down lower over his face and started his horse in the direction of the barn. "You do what you want."

What she wanted right now was to never have come back. But it was too late for that.

All heads turned as Jule entered the rustic but formal dining hall of the rambling Garrett ranch house. She wore a borrowed turquoise knit dress, the only one that came close to fitting her, but it hugged her breasts and hips a little too tightly. She wished more than ever she'd stuck to her first instinct and refused Josh's offer.

Josh, his laughing eyes making it clear he liked what he saw, was the only one with a welcoming smile on his face. He motioned to her. "Got you a seat over here next to me."

Across from Josh, Rafe, cleaned up and freshly shaved, his long black hair neatly pulled into a tail at his nape, looked as darkly handsome as she'd ever seen him. His mood matched his appearance; he seemed in a black temper, scowling at anyone with the misfortune to catch his eye. He didn't smile at her and Jule returned the favor.

"Why, hello, Julene." Josh's mother Del nodded as Josh pulled out Jule's chair for her. Del's hair was piled just as high and dyed just as yellow as it had been the last time Jule had seen her. But the lines that used to show only when she smiled were now etched deeply into her forehead, the corners of her made-up eyes and bright-pink mouth.

"My, it has been a long time," Del was saying. "Look at you, all grown up. But then she always was a pretty thing, wasn't she, Rafe? No wonder you had such a crush on her."

Jule winced inwardly, avoiding eye contact with Rafe. Rafe ignored his stepmother.

Oblivious, Del kept on. "I hope you found everything you needed." She gave Jule a sharp-eyed onceover, lifting a brow at the snug-fitting dress.

"Yes, thank you," Jule returned coolly, willing herself to at least appear unruffled and confident. "I appreciate you letting me get cleaned up and for lending me this dress. I'll have it laundered and bring it back the next time I check on the bison."

When Bonnie Cooper, who'd been the Garretts' cook and housekeeper for as long as Jule could remember, began serving the salad, Jed turned on Jule. "So what's going on with my animals?"

Rafe snapped a glare at Jed. "Those would be *my* animals."

"You may've bought 'em, but as long as they're livin' on *my* ranch that makes 'em *my* animals."

Jule saw the whites of Rafe's knuckles show where he gripped his fork.

Before Rafe could retort, Josh stepped in. "*How* long or *if* they're livin' seems more important to me. You're the expert, Jule. Where do we stand?"

It was obvious Josh had spoken up to try to deflect another confrontation between Rafe and Jed. After Josh's earlier antics, Jule was surprised. She'd half believed that Josh would be more likely to encourage fireworks between his brother and father than act as the buffer. "Well, Rafe knows about as much about this as I do now," she answered him, "but basically we're trying out a new antibiotic."

Jed coughed, wheezing too hard afterward to speak for a moment.

"Jed, honey, now don't you go and get all worked up," Del said, patting her husband's arm. "You just eat your meal and go right on back up to bed."

"Stop your naggin', woman. I'll stay here as long as I damned well please." He looked pointedly at Rafe. "Until I get some satisfyin' answers, that's for sure. Am I going to lose the herd or not? That's what I want to know."

"We can't answer that yet," Rafe said tightly.

Jed gave a derisive snort. "Well, don't that figure. I told you from the start we should have stuck with cattle and horses. I warned you those bison would be nothin' but trouble and wind up bein' a waste of my money."

"You haven't spent a dime on those animals since the day I brought them in. Cattle get sick, too. A couple of winters back you lost nearly half the bulls in your herd."

"It's too soon to draw any conclusions," Jule quickly added, hoping to avert a blow-up. She could tell Rafe was close. If he gripped the silverware any harder, it wasn't going to survive. "If you can just let me—" she turned to Rafe "—*us* keep treating them and monitoring them. We've isolated all of the sick calves as of today. We'll know a lot more in a couple of weeks."

Josh leaned back in his seat while Bonnie cleared his salad plate, replacing it with fresh stoneware for the main course. "Tell you one thing. Many more calves come down with this and we'll have to build a new barn."

"We'll do whatever we have to," Rafe said, with a frowning glance at Josh. "I didn't waste years of my life and the last of my savings to let this fall apart now."

"Your call, big brother." Josh held up his hands in surrender. "This is your thing, not mine. So enough already about the humpbacked rugs. Jule's a guest and I for one plan to get to know her a little better tonight."

Jule smiled, grateful for the change of subject, although she worried what Josh's next topic might be. From what she'd seen so far, Josh might be over six feet of wickedly handsome cowboy, as fast with his mouth as he was with his killer smile, but a good part of him was still that wild boy she'd known who could get into trouble faster than blinking. Of course, he'd wriggled out of it just as quickly; even as a kid, Josh could charm or talk his way out of anything.

"The last time I remember seeing you," she told him, "you were caught trying to lasso the neighbor's sheep. Practice, you said, although I don't think Felix Ramos saw it that way."

For the first time that evening, a hint of a smile tugged at Rafe's mouth. "He hasn't changed much. Except his aim's a little better. And once in a while he gets a paycheck for it."

"I'd call it more than once in a while. And the last time I remember seeing Jule she was hightailing it out of town to get away from you. Folks still ask me what went wrong with you two. Everybody thought you were inseparable."

Rafe shoved back from the table and started to stand. "It's nobody's business, and that includes yours."

"Whoa, hey, didn't mean to hit a sore spot. Come on and sit down. You can't leave when we still have a guest at the table."

Jule's heart was pounding so hard she was sure Rafe could see it through the thin fabric of her dress. She looked at him, her eyes imploring him to stay.

Reluctantly, Rafe sat back down, though the effort to keep his temper reined in cost him in the tension tightening the muscles in his shoulders and neck. "You were too young to know what the rest of us were doing. Cort, Sawyer, Maya, Jule and I were all in high school when you were still trying to figure out how to take your training pants off."

Everyone laughed, even Josh. Well almost everyone, Jule realized. Given the sudden downturn on Del's lips, apparently his mother failed to find the comment amusing.

"Hey, I'm only a few years younger than Jule." He leaned into her slightly. "You know the older woman/younger man thing is hot right now."

"Sorry, but I've heard all about you," Jule said, putting a hand to his shoulder to gently push him back into his own space. "Everyone warned me you'd grown into the town bad boy. Now I can believe it."

"I'll wager you haven't heard the half of it," Rafe added.

"That's enough of that," Del said, flinging her napkin on the table. She stood and took Jed's arm, urging him from his chair. "It's late and you need to take your medicines."

"Better than listening to these boys snipe at each other," he grumbled. He shot a parting glance at Jule. "You'll be back tomorrow to check on my bison?"

"Yes."

"When's your daddy coming back?"

"I don't know. He's still in the hospital."

"Getting old is hell. Tell him to hurry up and get well. I need him here."

"I'll do that. Thank you both for the lovely dinner."

Del nodded and slowly led Jed out of the dining hall.

As soon as his parents had rounded the corner and were out of view, Josh kicked back in his chair and put his boots up on the table. "So, Miss Julene, since you already know I enjoy the company of beautiful women, I hope you won't mind me asking if I might have the pleasure of your company for Sawyer and Maya's housewarming party. All your old friends will be there."

"I—I really didn't…" She darted a quick glance at Rafe, realizing her mistake at once. His face had turned to a mask of barely concealed rage and for some reason part of it was aimed at her. "I'm not sure they'd appreciate an uninvited guest."

"Darlin', half the town will be there, one more won't make any difference. And you aren't uninvited. You'll be with me."

"I don't think that's the same thing," Jule protested. She knew Maya and Sawyer Morente, although she'd been a little surprised when her mother had told her that Sawyer, high-school golden boy turned hometown hero, had married Maya Rainbow, the daughter of Luna Hermosa's resident hippies. She didn't know them well enough, though, to quite believe Josh's claim that she'd be welcomed as an old friend.

"Too bad our *new* brother won't be there for you to meet," Josh added. "For all of us to meet, right, Rafe?"

"You don't know when to quit do you?"

"Aw, come on," Josh drawled, linking his hands behind his head. "I'm rarin' to meet Cruz, aren't you?"

"Cruz?" Jule asked, looking from Rafe to Josh in confusion.

With a short sharp gesture in Josh's direction, Rafe muttered, "Go ahead. Since you seem to be hell-bent to tell it."

"Well, it seems Dad sowed more than his share of wild oats in his young days," Josh said. "He had a son before any of us with his first housekeeper, Rosa Dèclan, which knocks Sawyer and Rafe out of the top spot as the oldest. Although Sawyer's got six months on you," he added, flicking a grin at Rafe.

Jule inwardly winced. The slight age difference between him and Sawyer had been another sore spot with Rafe because, since he couldn't lay claim to being the oldest son, in his eyes it lessened his claim on the ranch. Now, with this revelation about Cruz Dèclan, it apparently didn't matter anymore.

"Still leaves you at the bottom," Rafe threw back at Josh.

"Maybe. With Dad, you never know. Anyway, unfortunately for Rosa, Dad was engaged at the time to marry Sawyer and Cort's mom, Theresa, and all that Morente money. So he sent Rosa on her way with a 'so sorry' and a nice payoff."

"That's terrible," Jule blurted out, then thinking it was Josh's father she was talking about, added, "I mean, I don't know what to say."

Rafe let out a snort of disgust. "I do, but I won't in mixed company."

"So you two haven't met Cruz yet?"

"None of us has," Josh said. "Not even Dad. He got this idea, though, after he found out about the cancer, that he wanted to find his long-lost son and give him a share of the ranch along with the rest of us."

"Yeah, that ought to make up for a lifetime of not knowing his father." Rafe shifted in his seat, swinging his long legs out beside the table. "Then again, maybe Cruz is the lucky one."

"Where's Cruz now, do you know?" Jule asked.

Josh nodded. "In Iraq. He's some kind of big-shot engineer.

Cort tracked him down when Cruz was working on some new hospital in Australia. But Cruz is in the army reserve and he got called up before Cort or Sawyer could give him the good news about Dad."

Whether or not this Cruz Dèclan would call it good news remained to be seen, Jule thought. One thing she was certain of, Rafe wouldn't consider it anything resembling good news, since it meant another contender for his share of the ranch. "So, I guess that makes five of you now?"

"There might be five of us, but I got all the charm," Josh said, favoring her with that wicked smile that was meant to dazzle her off her feet. "Cruz sounds dull as dirt. Sawyer and Cort are too busy being action heroes and Rafe never stops working long enough to realize there's life beyond bison. That's why I'm the one you should be going to that party with. So, what time should I pick you up?"

"Ah, thanks, but I don't know whether I can go. As I said, my dad's still in the hospital. And with working at the clinic and spending so much time here, I don't have the energy for much else." She was rambling but couldn't stop herself. What she wanted was Rafe to step in and help her out, but he did nothing but sit back in his chair, arms crossed over his chest, and glare at her and Josh. She was tempted to tell Josh yes just to get a reaction from him. Except it probably wouldn't be the one she wanted and would inevitably make things worse. "Well, this has been a wonderful evening—" *liar* "—and please thank Bonnie for the amazing meal, but I need to be going so I can see my father before visiting hours are over."

"Hey, slow down," Josh said oh-so-innocently the moment she stood up to leave. "I didn't mean to scare you off."

"You didn't. I do appreciate the offer. I just need to get going."

"I'm telling you, you won't want to miss this. Half the town will be there."

Rafe shoved back out of his chair. "Are you deaf or just stupid? She said she doesn't want to go with you."

A flicker of annoyance crossed Josh's face but Jule suspected it was hardly the first time he'd had to deal with Rafe's temper.

"I haven't heard her say that," Josh retorted, flashing a conspiratorial look at Jule, inviting her to share in his game.

She realized this was his way of needling Rafe in return for Rafe's harshness, but she had no intention of playing along. "I'm not planning on going with anyone," she said firmly, the words for Josh but her eyes locked with Rafe's.

I don't want to, I shouldn't, but I'm still waiting for you, she thought at him as hard as she could. *I'm still waiting for you.*

Chapter Four

Rafe leaned back in the corner booth of the diner, nursing a beer, trying not to think.

He usually avoided this place. Any time he stopped by it seemed like half of Luna Hermosa was there and usually the half he took pains to avoid. Tonight, though, after a long, frustrating day that had started before dawn with another bison calf turning up sick and that ended in a shouting match with Jed, the diner had seemed a kind of haven. Not up to sitting through dinner listening to Jed's bitching, Josh winding him up about anything that happened to occur to him, and Del complaining about him always upsetting Jed, Rafe had decided to combine a trip into town to pick up a new saddle with a stop for a quick meal.

The problem was, without the distraction of his so-called family, the effort to not think was failing miserably. Despite trying to push her out of his head every way he could, his thoughts kept circling back to Jule. Worse, his body obviously hadn't gotten the message that what was forbidden to him thirteen years ago was even more out of his reach now. Just the memory of that moment of weakness when he'd given into his consuming desire to touch her and had kissed her palm was enough to make him burn with wanting her.

Wanting what he couldn't have. Jule was everything he wasn't and would never be. And nothing was going to change that.

"Is the chili that bad? Your scowl is worse than usual." Nova Vargas stood next to his table, one hand on her hip, eyeing him with the look that meant whatever was going to come out of her mouth was aimed at provoking him. In her pink waitress garb, snug in all the strategic places and hemmed inches higher than the other servers to showcase a pair of mile-long legs, she always looked like trouble.

"It's not the chili, it's the company," Rafe muttered, hoping she'd get the hint, drop his bill and leave.

Nova didn't even blink. "Oooh, we are in a temper tonight. You know what your problem is, Rafe?"

"No, but I'm sure you'll tell me."

"You need some real company. And I don't mean those bison of yours. Then again—" pursing up her pretty mouth, Nova looked at him in all innocence "—I did hear that Julene Santiago was back in town. So maybe, problem solved?"

"Maybe you should mind your own business," Rafe said low and hard.

"I'm not very good at that," she easily returned with a wink and a smile. "I'll get you another beer. You look like you could use it." She'd swiveled to go back toward the kitchen when she stopped, killing Rafe's relief that he'd finally gotten rid of her for a few minutes at least. "Well, speak of the devil. Look who's here."

Rafe looked up as the diner door swung open and Jule walked in.

"You didn't have to take me to dinner, too," Catalina said as she and Jule walked into the diner. "Especially after coming with me to the hospital today. I know how busy you've been. I don't mind cooking for you."

Jule smiled and touched her mother's arm. "You've got enough to do right now. And I've been much busier than this. Don't worry so much. Besides, I wanted to see Dad, too."

"Yes, but you look…" Catalina paused a moment, searching Jule's face as if she were trying to come up with an appropriate—or maybe the most diplomatic—phrase. Finally, she settled on, "Tired. Maybe this wasn't a good idea."

"I don't think Dad would agree with you," Jule said lightly, deliberately misunderstanding. "You know how upset he was just thinking about turning over his practice to a stranger."

She used the words as a buffer against the real meaning behind her mother's concern. No, it hadn't been a good idea, coming here. But it was too late to go back now. Jule was at least glad of the work that had kept her occupied the last few days because the sheer amount of it had distracted her from obsessing about Rafe.

When she thought about him all she could envision was how close they'd come to being in each other's arms. And she was sure that if they had, then neither of them would have been able to pull away.

She wanted him, so badly it felt like an ache that never left her. She'd told Rafe that the feelings between them weren't dead and it was true. They were not only alive, they were kicking and screaming, demanding to be noticed. But Rafe was determined to ignore them, as if he believed that if he shoved them away hard and often enough, then they would eventually leave.

In her better moments, Jule tried pushing her feelings away, too. She didn't want to be hurt again and so maybe this distance between them was for the best. She wasn't sure she could survive letting herself love Rafe and having to leave him again.

"I think it's been years since I last saw you in here," Nova Vargas greeted Jule as she ushered her and Catalina to a table.

"But you sure picked the right night to come back. Or maybe the wrong one." Nova nodded behind her and winked.

Confused, Jule looked in the direction Nova indicated—and straight into Rafe's eyes.

For a few moments Rafe felt paralyzed, unable to do anything except stare at her. He didn't realize her mother was with her until Catalina, with a frown his way, touched Jule's arm, urging her to sit down.

Jule immediately buried her nose in the menu, giving Rafe time to indulge himself watching her. She looked tired, fine lines at her eyes and a slight droop to her shoulders, the smile she gave Catalina to some query her mother made barely lifting the corners of her mouth. Rafe knew she was unhappy. And he was the reason. He was sure of that.

He told himself to stop gawking at her; she kept staring at everything but him. Neither of them, though, seemed to be able to control where their eyes strayed and Rafe found himself locking gazes with her more than once.

The fourth time, he forced himself to focus on the rest of his dinner. That stopped him from seeing her but he was close enough that he kept catching scraps of her conversation with her mother.

"...doctor says he's doing better. I hope he can come home soon."

"...forgot to ask him about the Davidson's dog."

"...working too hard. You need to take some time for yourself while you're here."

"I've got a lot to keep up with...don't know how Dad managed all these years without a partner."

Rafe listened to her voice, but didn't hear the words, remembering instead other words she'd spoken to him. Words said softly, breathless with passion and need; vibrant with laughter, breaking with sorrow. Words of love spoken only in dreams.

Dreams he'd dreamed so hard and for so long that they almost seemed real.

Cursing himself, he tossed back the rest of his beer, threw some bills on the table, and steeled himself to walk past her as if it didn't matter.

She stopped him with a simple glance upward. He didn't even try to fight it, knowing it was a lost cause.

"I didn't expect to see you here," Jule said huskily. "You never used to—"

"Still don't," he answered shortly. "Except when I need a break from Jed or my own cooking." He hesitated then added, "I didn't expect to see you here, either."

"We were visiting Dad." Jule seemed to suddenly remember her mother and slid a guilty glance in the other woman's direction. "You remember my mother, don't you?"

Rafe nodded curtly in Catalina's direction. He hadn't paid her much attention when he and Jule were together, largely because it appeared to him that Catalina Santiago followed her husband's lead when it came to having opinions. Since Abran's opinion was that Rafe wasn't and never would be good enough for his daughter, Rafe figured it was a good bet Catalina felt the same.

"I'm sorry to hear about the trouble you've been having with your bison," Catalina said. The words were polite but there was a stiffness in her tone and the way she held herself. "I suppose it must be quite serious. Jule has been spending so much time out at the ranch."

Rafe started to come back with some comment about how it was Abran's doing, not his, but Jule, her eyes flicking to his, forestalled him by saying quickly, "That's what I'm here for, Mom. It's what Dad asked me to do."

"I'm sure he didn't mean you to be out there every day."

"He did," Jule said shortly.

She started to get that look in her eyes, the one that said Catalina was pushing the wrong buttons. Jule, normally even-tempered, could flare up given sufficient provocation and Rafe didn't want to be the cause of an argument between her and her mother. The problem was he wasn't very practiced at being a peacemaker and didn't quite know what to say.

"Jule is very good at what she does," he settled on. "If it weren't for her putting in so many hours, I'd stand to lose more than half my herd by now."

A delicate flush stained Jule's cheeks. Rafe chose to call it embarrassment at being complimented in front of an audience. "You're the one doing all the work. I'm just trying to make it a little easier." She turned to her mother. "You should hear Rafe's plans for the ranch. He's got some really innovative ideas."

Rafe couldn't help but feel touched by her sticking up for him. She'd always done it before and she was doing it now. He wanted to thank her but the words caught in his throat and stayed there.

"I need to get going," he said gruffly. "I want to check on those calves one more time tonight."

"How about I come out later?" Jule asked. Her whole attention focused on him.

Rafe wanted to say yes. The urge welled up so strongly he hesitated a fraction of a second before making himself tell her, "You said you'd be out in the morning. That'll be soon enough." He quickly said his goodbyes, not missing the obvious relief on Catalina's face at his leaving or the thoughtful look in Jule's eyes. He'd hoped she'd missed his brief moment of indecision. But even after all these years, she knew him too well.

Outside, for a moment he leaned straight-armed, his palms resting on the side of his truck, head bowed. Why was it so damned hard to put her behind him? Seeing her again felt like the recurrence of an illness he couldn't shake.

One from which he was unlikely to ever recover.

It didn't matter what he'd said.

Jule kept telling herself that on the drive back out to Rancho

Pintada although her common sense argued otherwise. Rafe was right, she didn't need to go back out to the ranch tonight; he'd call if there were any urgent problems with the calves. She'd had a long day and could do with a few extra hours of sleep. And she could definitely do without her mother's blatant disapproval. Catalina hadn't said a word, but the disappointment following her out of the house was so heavy she could almost feel it on her back.

She would have listened to her common sense if it hadn't been for that moment when Rafe hesitated at her offer to come back tonight. He'd wanted to say yes. She knew it. And that crack in his walls was enough to convince her he wasn't as hardened against caring as he wanted her to believe.

She hadn't bothered calling ahead to tell Rafe she was coming, knowing he'd try to talk her out of it. Instead, she parked her truck near the barn, grabbing up her bag and a flashlight, and started inside, intending to check the calves before she went looking for Rafe.

He saved her the trouble. He and Josh met her at the barn door, starting out just as she was going in.

"What are you doing here?" Rafe asked. In the glow cast by the security light above the barn door, she could see he looked a little taken aback to see her there.

Jule blessed the darkness that hid her flushed face. "I wanted to check on the calves. I've been so busy the last few days, I haven't been able to spend as much time as I'd like working with them. I'd have called first but I didn't want to bother you—"

She broke off when Josh laughed and Rafe frowned, clearly skeptical.

"That'd be a little more convincing, darlin', if you didn't look so guilty," Josh drawled. "Sure you weren't thinking of a midnight rendezvous with more than just the bison?"

"Shut up," Rafe growled, "before I do it for you."

Far from intimidated, Josh shrugged and shot Jule a wink. She pretended not to see and, trying to scrape together her dignity, walked past them into the barn. "I need to check those calves."

Rafe and Josh followed her in, Josh moving to lean against the inside wall of the stall as Jule knelt to check the first calf; Rafe stayed outside, arms crossed over his chest, watching her in silence.

"You know, you're too much like Rafe, always working," Josh said. "You need a break. A woman as pretty as you shouldn't be spending her nights with animals—at least the non-human type."

"I'm guessing there was a compliment in there somewhere," Jule returned lightly. He was flirting with her but she knew it wasn't serious. With Josh, flirting seemed to come as naturally as breathing and she guessed he did it with anything female. She was five years older than he was, nothing flashy to look at, and dedicated to her work, so Jule doubted he would honestly consider her as a potential conquest. No, he was doing it to rile Rafe and it was working only too well.

The way Rafe glared at his brother, if looks could hurt, Josh would be undergoing some serious torture about now.

"Besides," she added as she finished with the calf and sat back on her heels, "the bison are at least quiet and well-mannered."

"Ouch, that hurt." Josh grinned. "I'm only saying you need to relax every now and then. And tomorrow night's party would be the perfect time to start. It's not too late to tell me yes. I haven't got a date yet."

"I that find hard to believe," Jule said, but she looked at Rafe. His expression appeared to be darkening by the second. Getting to her feet, Jule picked up her bag and came out of the stall. The moment she did, Rafe shifted in her direction. The motion was slight but there was possession in it, a clear warning to Josh to back off.

"You know, if you're waiting for my brother here to ask you, it's never gonna happen," Josh said, relentless in his pursuit. "Rafe's idea of socializing is a heart to heart with his horse."

"Sounds like me except I prefer dogs," Jule returned lightly. "We workaholics are like that."

"All the more reason you should go with me."

"Has anyone ever told you no?"

Josh flashed that cocky smile again. "Not often. And if they do, I usually ignore 'em."

"So I've noticed," Jule said, half amused, half exasperated by Josh's antics. Rafe still said nothing. Jule knew Josh was right and he wouldn't be going to any party. And she had no real reason for being there. "I haven't made up my mind if I'm even going," she told Josh firmly. "I probably won't have the time, and even if I do, I'll just drop in on my own. I wasn't really invited, except by you and—"

Jule glanced at Rafe, the expression on his face stopping her in mid-sentence. A small smile of satisfaction, almost smug, flicked up his mouth, the smile of a man confident of his claim on a woman.

Anger rushed through Jule. All this time, he'd been hell-bent on pushing her away and now he was posturing like she belonged to him and was determined to warn away any man who came within touching distance.

Instead of satisfaction, his reaction perversely made her want to prove to him that he couldn't have it both ways. Abruptly she turned to Josh. "On second thought, I've changed my mind. I'd like to go with you."

She almost took it back when Josh flashed a triumphant grin Rafe's direction. "I knew I could wear you down."

Rafe continued his silence but there was no satisfaction in his face now. He stared at her in disbelief.

Jule only half listened to Josh's plans to pick her up. She was already regretting her impulsive action but her pride wouldn't let her back down now. Telling Josh she'd see him tomorrow, she turned and beat a hasty retreat back to her truck, forgetting the rest of the calves and wishing she'd listened to her common sense and stayed home.

She'd reached for the door handle when a large hand on her arm turned her around and Rafe's angry face confronted her. "What the hell do you think you're doing?"

"Apparently going to a party. I can't spend all my time in your barn."

"That's crap. You know Josh isn't serious. He's only doing this to mess with me."

"Even if that's true, why do you care what I do? You don't care, do you Rafe?" Jule's throat constricted and she swallowed hard. "You've told me enough times."

Rafe's hand tightened around her arm. He opened his mouth, shut it and finally shook his head as if trying to clear it. "I do care," he finally forced out, his voice a husky breath of sound. "I care like hell. And I wish I didn't."

He stepped close to her and for one crazy, dizzying moment, Jule thought he would pull her into his arms and kiss her. She leaned into him, all but begging him to touch her.

Very gently, Rafe brushed the stray hair back from her face, tracing his fingertips over her cheekbones, her mouth.

Then, with a suddenness that startled her, he let her go, whipped around and stalked away into the darkness, not looking back.

Chapter Five

As she stood paralyzed in the spacious entryway and living room of Sawyer and Maya's new hacienda, Jule felt as though she was stuck in one of those bad dreams where you walk into a party, then realize you're buck naked.

The place was already filled with people mingling and chatting. Until she and Josh appeared, that was. Then everyone suddenly turned eyes toward her and fell silent. Nova Vargus practically had her jaw in her lap.

Since Jule doubted she could provide that much entertainment on her own, she guessed it was very likely because it was Josh—not Rafe—who had his hand protectively at the small of her back. She'd grown up with many of the people here and most of them knew about her and Rafe's past. Or were going to know before the night was over.

Worse, her impulsive decision to spite Rafe by coming with Josh was going to have consequences she hadn't stopped to consider. Not only was everyone going to be speculating about her and Rafe, she'd made herself the gossip of the week by appearing in public on the arm of his brother, a younger man who reputedly liked his women as wild as he was.

"This was a bad idea."

She realized she'd given voice to the one dominant thought in her head when Josh laughed. Tossing his head back slightly and shoving his fingers through the wave of hair falling over one eye, he drawled, "Darlin', they're only staring because you're the most drop-dead-gorgeous woman in the room."

Jule glanced down at her simple long-sleeved shift then rolled her eyes at him. "Oh please…" She'd deliberately worn something on the conservative side so as not to send the wrong message to Josh. "They're staring because I'm here with you and they know everything about Rafe and me. I'd almost forgotten how small this town is."

"Don't be paranoid. That was a long time ago." He flashed her a sassy grin. "It might be a small town, but there's been plenty of action over the years to take the busybodies' minds off you and Rafe. Hell, I've stirred up enough trouble since then to make them forget all about you and my brother."

"That I can believe." Jule turned from him to place her housewarming gift on a beautifully hand-carved table already piled high with brightly wrapped presents. "Really, Josh, I don't want to stay long. I can get myself home. I don't want to ruin your night."

Josh took her by the hand then and practically dragged her over to where Maya and Sawyer were greeting newcomers. "Relax, honey. We're all friends here. You'll have fun," he said, giving her a flirtatious wink. "I promise."

"Jule, Josh, we're so glad you could come," Maya said, reaching out to give them each a hug.

Being welcomed as an old friend caught Jule off guard since she'd never been particularly close to either Maya Rainbow or Sawyer Morente. She and Sawyer's brother Cort were the same age, but growing up, most of Jule's time and focus had been absorbed by lessons and studying in an effort to live up to her parents' expectations for their only child. The only person she'd ever truly opened up to, shared her hopes and dreams and laughter with, had been Rafe.

Something in Maya's unaffected manner, the warmth she exuded, though, put Jule at ease and made her think the night might not be a total disaster after all.

"Sawyer, you remember Jule, of course," Maya was saying.

Sawyer held out his hand. "Sure I do. It's good to see you back in town. I don't know what Rafe would have done if you hadn't been available to fill in for your dad."

At the mention of Rafe's name, Maya quickly glanced at her husband and then back at Jule. "How is your father?"

"He's improving, but very slowly," Jule answered, grateful for the change of subject. She had the sinking feeling regular reminders of Rafe were going to be impossible to avoid tonight. She only wished she could do something about the painful twist of her heart that went along with them. "They moved him to a nursing home about two weeks ago and we're hoping the therapy he's getting there will help."

Maya laid a gentle hand on her arm. "We'll keep him in our thoughts. Please let me know if there's anything I can do."

"Thanks, I'll do that."

"Maybe Maya can help you out with Rafe's walking rugs," Josh put in. "You know, with those magical weeds and whatever she does at the clinic. Then Rafe would have one less excuse for not moving off the ranch."

The comment left Jule looking at Maya in confusion.

"My baby brother is trying to be clever," Sawyer said. "Maya's an alternative healer. But even she couldn't come up with a miracle cure for Rafe's terminal bad attitude." He shrugged off Maya's disapproving look. "You know it's true."

"I know the two of you are evenly matched when it comes to being hard-headed," Maya said.

Jule had the impression this was part of a discussion they'd had many times before. But Maya let it drop and Josh took the opportunity to jump in.

"Rafe's married to the ranch and those animals of his. Hell'll freeze over before he decides there's anything more important than that."

"He's just worried about the bison right now." Jule felt compelled to defend Rafe, although she knew Josh had struck on the truth. "They're not responding to treatment too well yet."

"I'm sorry to hear that," Maya said. "It would do Rafe good to get away from the ranch once in a while."

"Speaking of someone who needs to get away from work and enjoy himself," Josh interrupted, "here comes Cort. Without a date as usual." He put a hand on Sawyer's shoulder and leaned toward him as if confessing a secret. "I think that black-leather-and-chains, big-bad-biker look scares the women off."

"Nova doesn't look too scared. Give her ten minutes and she'll be doing her best to back Cort into a dark corner."

Jule couldn't blame Nova as she watched the other Morente son crossing the room with long-legged strides. Black jeans hugged his muscular thighs, a black T-shirt formed his chest and he carried a black leather jacket and motorcycle helmet in one arm. He might look dark and dangerous, but he also looked incredibly hot. His looks were darker than Sawyer's but not as dark as Rafe's. She couldn't help but notice, though, that even though Rafe didn't share blood with his brothers, they all had one thing in common: an elemental magnetism that went beyond the obvious physical attraction and had every woman around glancing their way.

As Cort neared, Josh crossed his arms over his chest and eyed him up and down. "Working undercover again with the bad guys, bro, or are you auditioning for *Terminator IV?*"

Cort smiled and flicked Josh's cowboy hat hard enough to jostle it from his head.

"Hey!" Josh scrambled to catch it before it hit the floor.

Sawyer threw his head back and laughed outright. Jule and Maya exchanged a glance and a smile.

"Well, little brother, I'd have tried out for *Howdy Doody* instead, but you've got that role sewn up tight."

"Funny, Cort, real funny," Josh shot back.

Looking satisfied he'd won that round, Cort's eyes settled on Jule. "It's been a long time, Julene, and you've grown up." She felt her cheeks flush as he took a slow assessment. "Nicely, very nicely, I have to say."

"I could say the same for you, Cort. It's good to see you."

"You, too. I hope this is a permanent move home."

Jule looked away. "Only for now. I'm just filling in for my dad."

Before anyone could question Jule further about another topic she wanted to avoid, an elderly but spry woman came up to them carrying a tray of drinks.

"Give me that, Reggie," Sawyer said, taking the tray. "You aren't supposed to be playing waitress."

"I'm not so old I can't still carry a tray now and then," the woman admonished. "Besides, I haven't seen this boy in so long—" she turned to Cort and tapped him on the shoulder "—that I was beginning to think the only thing living at his apartment were the cats."

Cort draped his arm around her shoulders. "I'm there enough to appreciate your care packages. If it weren't for you, I'd be surviving on microwave burritos."

"Cats?" Josh's eyes sparked with wicked laughter as he stared in mock disbelief at Cort. "You have cats?" Cort shrugged and Josh laughed. "I hate to break it to you, but cats and black leather clash."

Smiling, Maya turned to Jule offering her a glass. "What would you like to drink? Regina has made her famous sangria but we have everything else, too."

While Jule was deciding what she was thirsty for, Maya leaned over to touch a kiss to the older woman's cheek. "Regina was Sawyer and Cort's nanny and now she helps us with Joey once in a while. And, she's about the most amazing cook this side of the Rio Grande."

Jule smiled and nodded at Regina, thinking how lucky Maya was to have her. "That sangria looks irresistible. I'd love to try it."

"All right then, everybody grab a drink and I'll take you on the grand tour. We thought this house would never be finished and now that it finally is I'm dying to show it off!"

Jule took a sip of fruity sangria. "Delicious," she said and Regina beamed before excusing herself to make her way over to an older couple at the far side of the room. To Maya, Jule said, "I'd love to see the rest of it. The entryway and living room are just beautiful—and unique."

Sawyer parked the tray on a nearby table, took a couple of beers and handed them to his brothers. "I want to talk a little shop with Cort and Josh first. You ladies go on ahead."

A pretty pout puckered Maya's lips. "Oh, Sawyer, not tonight."

Her husband wrapped an arm around her waist and leaned down and kissed her soundly. "I'm on the clock. Ten minutes, promise."

Jule's heart twisted with a pang of envy as she watched Maya melt into Sawyer's arms. "I'm setting the timer."

Sawyer popped a playful pat on her backside as she turned and took Jule's hand to lead her away from the trio of men.

"Do you mind if we check on Joey first? Val Ortiz is keeping an eye on our Joey and her Johnnie—they're best buddies. She's got her twins and the Gonzales boys in there, too, so I'm sure she could use a break by now."

"Val has another baby?"

Maya led Jule down a wide, elegantly tiled hallway, giving Jule a glimpse of bedrooms and what appeared to be a study. "She and Paul had Johnnie a couple of months before Joey was born."

They passed by a smaller room, and Jule glanced in. It was obviously a child's room, decorated in bright blues and yellows. Thinking it belonged to Joey, she turned slightly to go inside but Maya shook her head. "No one in there yet." She opened the door a bit wider and Jule could see it was a nursery. "We're not quite finished with it yet, but we've still got four months or so." Jule smiled and Maya added, "I guess you've figured out Sawyer and I are expecting another baby—another boy. I'm going to be seriously outnumbered here. It's one of the reasons we built the house. The house we had before was barely big enough for two, let alone a family."

Congratulating her warmly, Jule glanced around the nursery and a wave of loneliness, mingled with the shadows of past regrets, washed over her. "All of you have families now. I feel like the odd woman out."

"Nonsense. You were in school so many years and then you had to set up your practice. Trying to start an ambitious career and a family at the same time is a lot harder than some people seem to think. Your time will come."

"I suppose," Jule answered absently as she followed Maya out of the nursery and into the adjacent room. Her thoughts had drifted to the "what ifs" with Rafe. What if Rafe had wanted to marry her all those years ago? Would she have gone on to school or settled down to have children? Would she have tried to do both, knowing her parents would never have forgiven her if she hadn't finished veterinary school?

Futile questions, she decided. He didn't want to marry her then. He certainly didn't now. Except she hadn't ever been able to envision herself happily married, raising a family, with anyone other than him.

Her heart surged as she saw two toddlers—one with big blue eyes and Maya's red hair and the other black-haired and dark-eyed—delightedly playing with oversized blocks in a brightly decorated room at end of hall. Two black-haired girls she guessed were Val's twins and a couple of boys, all grade-school age, were sprawled on the floor, playing a board game, all of them chattering non-stop. In a rocker in the corner of the room Val sat contentedly watching the children.

Happiness for her friends' fulfilled lives waged war with anger and frustration with Rafe, with their ill-fated past, with their hopeless present, with their non-existent future. *What have I missed because I can't stop loving you, Rafe?*

"Jule, is that you?" Val, her glossy black curls still framing a sweet, rosy-cheeked face, greeted her with a wide grin and open arms. "Oh, my gosh, you're so thin and beautiful. Not that you ever weren't, but you're even more gorgeous now. Of course you see what having three babies has done for me," she said, indicating her full figure.

"I don't see Paul complaining," Maya put in. "You know your man likes curves."

"Mama!" Joey cried when he caught sight of his mother, excitement overtaking the little boy's intense focus on his blocks. "Look!"

Maya walked over and knelt to admire her son's creation while Val introduced Jule to her children and went about the business of catching up. "Are you back to stay? I hope so."

"That seems to be the question of the hour. I don't know yet."

"I shouldn't ask this I know, but you know me—I can't hold my tongue. Have you seen Rafe? He's still single, you know. Actually, I don't think he's ever been involved with anyone else but you for longer than maybe an hour or so."

"Val!" Maya chided. "Jule came tonight with Josh."

"It's okay," Jule soothed. "I know we're a hot topic. At least we were. And, for the record, Josh and I are just friends."

"Well, you'd be the first. I don't think Josh knows the meaning of the word when it comes to women. Does Rafe know Josh brought you?"

"Val, you're incorrigible."

Jule laughed as Val shrugged off Maya's rebuke. "Hey, I'm a married, stay-at-home mom with three kids. Not that I'm complaining. I love my life, well, most days that is," she said with a light sigh. "Is it too much to ask you to toss me a bone from single life in the outside world?"

"Wish I had one," Jule answered. "But there's nothing thrilling in my world. Just work and more work. And yes, Rafe knows Josh brought me tonight. Since my dad's been down, I've been working with some sick bison at the ranch so we can hardly avoid seeing each other."

"That must be hard for you. But then again, it's been such a long time and you both have your own lives and careers now." Val paused to reach down and hand her son a block that had skittered out of his reach. "Working with Rafe is probably just like being with an old friend, right?"

Jule bit back the temptation to reply with a sarcastic, *oh, yeah, right—if only.* Instead she pasted a smile on her face and tried to sound nonchalant. "Yes, right. That's exactly it."

Maya looked up from Joey to Jule, her brow lifted doubtfully, but she kept her thoughts to herself. "Val, do you mind staying with the kids a little longer? I want to show Jule the rest of the house before I put Joey to bed. My parents volunteered to babysit tonight but—"

"You know how I hate clocks." Azure Rainbow poked her head into the room, beaming at them all. "And we're here now."

A huge man hovered behind her. Jule would know Shem's burly scorpion-tattooed biceps and Azure's aging but pretty hippyish looks anywhere. Maya's parents had always been unconventional, to put it mildly. The opposite of her own traditional, conservative parents.

"I knew you would be," Maya said, coming to hug her parents. "Thanks you two. You remember Jule Santiago, right?"

Shem hefted himself over to Jule and wrapped her in a bear hug. "Why sure we do, honey."

"Your daddy once set a broken leg on a little wounded raccoon we adopted," Azure recalled, tapping her finger reflectively against her cheek as Shem moved to scoop up Joey and swing him high, much to the little boy's delight. "Of course we freed it as soon as it was well. We can only interrupt nature's flow when the universe opens a door to help one of its creatures for a time. Speaking of wounds, I do hope your heart has healed in all of these years. I remember how sad I was to hear about you and Rafe. Strange, though, I always thought destiny had brought you to each other. I've always trusted in destiny, you know. Take our Maya and Sawyer, now—"

"I hate to interrupt, Mom, but if I don't get back to my destined mate, he's going to be talking business all night with his brothers. And I do want to show Jule the rest of the house." Maya put her hand on Jule's arm and gave it a quick press, as if to warn her that if they didn't leave now they'd wind up hearing a discourse on destiny, heartbreak and/or the natural world according to Azure.

Jule smiled, glad to yield to Maya's coaxing. "It's great to see you again, Val, let's have lunch sometime when things slow down a little for me. It's good to see you both, Mr. and Mrs. Rainbow." As soon as she said it, she groaned inwardly, remembering they'd never gotten married.

Val smiled back and nodded. "It's a date."

"Sorry about that," Maya said as she led Jule back up the hallway. "Val's always said everything and anything that crossed her mind. And my mother, well, what can I say?"

"It's fine," Jule assured her. "I expected it. I mean, everyone knows—the gossip is too good to pass up."

"But you and Rafe are just old friends now, right?"

"Yes, of course." Maya raised a brow and Jule relented. "I suppose you aren't buying that."

"Maybe because I have a feeling you're not, either."

"Mind if we join you?" From behind them down the hall an unfamiliar voice interrupted their conversation.

Maya stopped and turned to greet the newcomers. "Hi, welcome!" She motioned two couples forward. "Sure, the more the merrier."

Jule recognized Catarina Ortiz, Val's sister-in-law, and Rico Esteban from her school days, though she hadn't known they were recently married. The other couple Maya introduced as Lia and Tonio.

"Lia is Joey's pediatrician," Maya explained. "She got us both through a pretty rough start. Joey was premature and born during a car accident. Long story for another day. Tonio's a firefighter at the same station as Rico and Sawyer."

When the group had exchanged greetings and Maya started to lead them through a sitting-area breezeway, Tonio asked her about the problem with Rafe's bison. "Sounds like it's serious. Sawyer says you're out at the ranch with Rafe nearly every day."

It was an innocent enough comment, but Jule read all sorts of meaning into it. *The boys down at the station must have some pretty interesting views on Rafe and me and what went wrong.* "It is serious, but we're hoping for a breakthrough soon."

They know everything. Jule could see it in the curious looks, hear it in the thinly masked comments and questions. Everyone was nice and they were too polite to out and out ask her about Rafe, but she couldn't shake an uncomfortable sense that discussing her and Rafe's past and how it was affecting them now was the highlight of the party.

She scarcely listened as she followed Maya through the rest of the house until they wound up back in the living room. The festivity, laughter and chatter filling the air only intensified Jule's feeling of isolation. She'd been gone so long she didn't share the sense of community and friendship between the others. Even growing up in town, she'd been so focused on her relationship with Rafe that she'd not made much room in her life for other friendships. In her own way, she realized, she'd isolated herself nearly as much as Rafe had.

Thanking Maya for the tour, she made the excuse of going to find Josh, intending to ask him for a ride back into town. She spotted him across the room, talking to an attractive older woman. As she neared him, a thin man, wearing glasses and carrying a little girl who looked to be about a year old on his hip, came up behind the woman and wrapped his arm around her possessively.

Josh caught Jule's eye and then her hand as she neared. "This is Dr. Gonzales, her husband Miguel and little Maria. Maya works with her at the clinic and if you ever need a miracle worker, I can vouch for her. With all of the aches and pains I've collected ridin' broncs and bulls, I don't know what I would have done without her and Maya's weed potions. And Miguel here keeps Dad out of trouble with Uncle Sam."

"Call me Sancia," the elegantly dressed woman said as she extended a warm hand. Her husband followed her lead.

"I've heard about yours and Maya's natural-healing techniques," Jule said after a few minutes. "Maybe we can talk sometime. I'd like to find out if some of them might work on animals."

"Anytime. That would be a fascinating experiment."

"Maybe I should let you work a miracle on my back," Jule added. "Working with those bison hasn't done it any good."

"My stubborn brother's the one who needs to get checked," Josh said. "Rafe's been hefting one load or another since he was old enough to walk. He'll never admit it, but his left shoulder's about useless some days."

"Maybe one of you will have a chance tonight to coax him to come see me." Sancia looked past Jule to the front of the room. "He just walked in."

Jule slowly turned in disbelief. It couldn't be. He wouldn't—

"Well, I'll be damned," Josh said with a short laugh. "Hell just froze over."

There was a long, extended moment when Jule stood tongue-tied and locked in place while around her she sensed, rather than heard or saw, the whispers and glances about her and Rafe.

It was Josh who shattered it by calling out over the crowd, "Rafe, we're over here. Come join the party."

Jule tried not to stare as Rafe responded and strode toward

them. Around her, people went back to their conversations, a few saying hellos to Rafe as he moved silently through them. His long hair was neatly pulled back in a sleek ponytail, bound by a single strap of leather. Tall and broad-shouldered, he wore snug-fitting jeans, his black cowboy boots and a tailored midnight-blue shirt that hugged the expanse of his chest and set off his black hair, dark skin and eyes perfectly. Watching him, Jule felt herself melting inside. He was nothing short of magnificent.

But he hadn't looked at her once. In fact, he seemed to be doing his best to avoid looking at her. When he neared he said a brief, curt hello to the group, giving her no more than a perfunctory nod.

Maya came up to him, glancing at Jule and smiling at him. "We're so glad you came. Can I get you a drink?"

"Beer, thanks."

"Coming up."

In her wake, several other people, including Sawyer and Cort, came up to them and Jule could practically touch Rafe's unease. Out riding the wide expanses around the ranch or in the corrals or barns, he was at home. Here, he looked as if slow torture might be a better alternative. She was calculating the odds of him bolting in the next ten minutes when things took a turn for the worse.

She caught sight of a distinguished elderly couple making what could only be called a deliberate entrance into the party. Jule hadn't seen them since she was a teenager, but she knew they had to be the Morentes, Sawyer and Cort's aristocratic grandparents.

"This'll be good," Cort muttered.

Sawyer turned to Maya, who'd just returned with Rafe's drink. "What are they doing here?"

"I sent them an invitation." She lowered her voice. "But, honestly, I didn't think they'd come."

Jule noticed Rafe's jaw go rigid and he narrowed his eyes at the couple.

"Think I'll have a look around the place," he said to Sawyer. Then, for the first time that night he looked directly at Jule.

She answered what she hoped was his unspoken question. "Maya showed me the house earlier. I can give you a tour."

"That's a good idea," Maya said. "I'm afraid I'll be occupied for a while."

"I want to see the place, too," Josh put in. But when Rafe shot him a dark stare, he backed off. "Later, that is. The party's just getting going. And I—hey, who's that in the corner, the one in red?"

Cort glanced at the woman Josh indicated and then prodded Josh in the shoulder, encouraging him in that direction. "Trina Hernandez. Do me a favor, go practice being charming before she decides to attach herself to me."

With a grin and a mock salute, Josh headed off at the same time Nova sidled up to Cort. "Need rescuing?"

He gave her a cocky smile. "You volunteering?"

"You have to ask?"

"Thanks for sticking around," Sawyer grumbled.

"Your wife invited them," Cort said, and left with Nova.

Jule touched Rafe's hand, encouraging him to go, too, as Cort and Sawyer's grandparents started making their way toward Maya and Sawyer.

They'd just turned to go when Mr. Morente held up his silver-tipped walking stick and called out to Jule, "Just a moment. Aren't you Julene Santiago? We know your parents well."

Jule grasped Rafe's hand and said softly, "This will only take a minute." Greeting the Morentes she fixed on a polite smile. "Yes, I remember meeting you when I was a little girl. It's nice to see you both again."

"And you," Santiano Morente said, ignoring Rafe as though he didn't exist. "We hear you've done very well for yourself. Your parents must be very proud of all you've accomplished."

Jule wanted to say that being her parents' child she didn't

have any choice but to succeed, but held her tongue. "My father is happy I was able to help him out after his accident."

Consuela Morente took her husband's arm. "Yes, do tell him he is in our prayers, please."

Santiano smiled at Jule. "You're going back to Albuquerque when your father recovers, I assume." His expression changed suddenly and he leveled a cold gaze on Rafe. "There's nothing in this town for a woman with your potential."

With that Rafe abruptly turned on his heel and strode off in the direction of the doors.

Jule's heart caught. "I—I was just going to give Rafe a tour of the house. So if you can please excuse me, I'm sure Maya and Sawyer are anxious to talk with you." That was an outright lie, given what she knew of Sawyer and Cort's strained relationship with their grandparents. But she wanted so desperately to have some time alone with Rafe. "I'll tell my parents I saw you," she said over her shoulder as she hurried after him.

Instead of heading to the bedroom wing, Rafe veered off through a set of huge, intricately carved French doors. As she came up behind him, he stopped, silently holding the door for Jule. She followed him out to an expansive patio crisscrossed with walkways and lined with flowers and plants. It was dark, but the moon was silver-bright against the velvet black of the sky. A cool fall breeze brought a nip to the air and when she shivered, hugging her arms, Rafe gravitated toward a blazing chimenea that sat in the center of a low adobe wall and round bench.

They sat down side by side, Jule warming her hands. Piñon-scented smoke flowed from the chimney of the outdoor firepot.

"You're shivering," Rafe said after a long silence.

"I didn't bring a sweater. I've forgotten how early the nights get cold up here."

Another silence stretched between them and then Rafe let go a long breath, as if he'd come to some decision but was far from happy with it. "Move over here. I can't have you getting sick, too."

Caring less about how many curious eyes might be watching them from inside, Jule slid closer to him. He reached his arm around her shoulders and pulled her to his chest. "You're freezing," he murmured, rubbing his hand up and down her arm. She shivered but not from the cold. "Do you want to go back inside?"

"So everyone can stare at us? Thanks, but no. I've had enough for one night. Besides, I'm feeling much warmer already."

"Yeah." He stared over her head at the fire. "I couldn't take any more of the Morentes and about half the other people in the room."

"But you came tonight. Why? You hate this kind of thing."

He didn't answer right away. She could almost hear him weighing what he thought he should say against telling her the truth. "I wanted to see the place," he said at last. "Sawyer's been messing around with it for over a year."

"You could have come over here anytime," she pressed him.

"What do you want from me?" Rafe backed away a little until he could look directly into her eyes. "Do you want me to say I came for you?"

Yes. "No, of course not." *Did you?* "It's just—odd that you came. You have to admit that."

"Maybe I needed a break. It's been a while."

"Too long, from what I hear."

He shifted to look away from her again. "Maybe."

The quiet this time felt heavy, almost oppressive. Jule wanted to change it, but there seemed nothing left to say. She nearly suggested they leave, so at least she wouldn't be stuck waiting on Josh or trying to find another way home, when Rafe's touch became a slow, tender stroking up and down her arm.

She closed her eyes, savoring sensation and every sweet nuance of feeling the nearness of him gave. Leaning against his chest brought back bittersweet memories of them lying together, laughing and talking like best friends, about everything and nothing.

"I wish we could talk like we did when we were kids," she said suddenly breaking the stillness. "When nothing else mattered."

"We're not kids anymore," he responded gruffly. "And everything else matters. Just ask your friends, the Morentes."

"They're my parents' friends, not mine."

"They're your class, not mine."

She straightened out of his hold. "That's not true. I'm not like them and you know it."

"But you belong with people like them. I don't. We come from different worlds. Always did, always will."

She hated the resignation in his voice, hated even more that he believed any of that mattered. "I don't believe that, I never have. Our pasts, our families, don't have to come between us. They only do because you won't let it go."

"I won't let it go because it's still the same," Rafe said. In the firelight, she saw the hardness in his face, could feel it in his body. "She was right in there. There's nothing here for you. Nothing."

"Nothing—and no one, right?"

"You know it's true."

"No, I don't. And you don't have the right to decide that for me." Anger flared up in her. "For your information, there's a good chance I'm here to stay. And you want to know why? Because you're here. And for some stupid reason I can't leave you in the past even though God knows you belong there. So you're just going to have to find a way to deal with that, Rafe Garrett."

Getting to her feet, she walked away and left him there, sitting alone with the fire. Yet as she neared the house, she glanced back to where he still sat, alone, outdoors with the pine trees overhead and the coyotes wailing in the distance, near the smoke of what could be an ancestral fire. He might be miserable inside somewhere, yet he was in his element. Maybe he did belong alone. Alone with the earth and animals and his beloved ranch. Maybe they were enough for him.

Maybe she only imagined him being lonely because she felt so horribly alone without him.

Chapter Six

Jule sat back on her heels, wiping at her forehead with the back of her hand. Outside the barn, the morning air was crisp and cool, with a breath of winter to come. But inside, working with the calves in the close confines of the stalls, she'd quickly shed her fleece-lined jacket in favor of shirtsleeves.

On one knee beside her, Rafe gently stroked the head and neck of the calf she'd been tending, murmuring to it every now and then. She smiled to herself as the calf nuzzled his palm, looking at him with its liquid dark eyes as if comforted by his touch and the low rumble of his voice. She appreciated him being here, particularly since she knew the bison were only a small fraction of the workload he shouldered and that he'd be paying for the hours he'd spent helping her by putting in a day that would last long past dark. Rafe had a calming effect on the animals; they instinctively seemed to trust him and that made her work much easier.

"This one is making progress, at least," she said. "Maybe we're finally getting somewhere with this new treatment."

"Maybe," Rafe admitted grudgingly. He caught the questioning lift of her brow and softened his tone. "Sorry. I'm just frustrated this is taking so long. I'd expected to have this figured out before now."

"I understand. I'm frustrated, too. But we've only been trying this new antibiotic a few weeks. And at least we're making some progress. I think we'll be able to get this under control before winter sets in."

"Can I have that in writing?"

Jule shook her head, smiling. Getting to her feet, she put her hands to her lower back, stretching protesting muscles. She felt as though she'd been in that half-crouching, half-kneeling position for days instead of hours. Tired, thirsty, stiff and smelling like bison, she thought longingly of a hot shower and a large lunch. Neither of which she was going to get soon, not with a full schedule of appointments waiting for her this afternoon at her father's clinic.

"You okay?" On his feet, Rafe was looking at her with a slight frown.

"Just getting old. And indulging my fantasies of food and a nap." She laughed at his doubtful expression. "I know, I need better fantasies." With a sigh, she began gathering up her gear.

Rafe followed her, watching as she stowed her stuff in her truck. When she turned to him, intending to tell him she'd be back tomorrow morning, he stopped her by speaking up first.

"How about lunch?" The question caught her off guard and her surprise must have shown because he hurried out with the rest of it. "You've been here all morning. I thought you might want a break before you head back."

Jule wanted to say yes, particularly since Rafe, standing stiffly, his eyes shifting everywhere but her direction, looked as if he expected her to refuse. But she wasn't really up to another meal at the ranch house with Jed, Del and Josh making things between Rafe and her more difficult than they already were.

"I figured we could go back to my house," Rafe said, a bitter humor twisting up the corner of his mouth as if he'd read her thoughts. "The last thing I want to do is see more of Jed than I have to. It won't be anything fancy. But I can rustle up something."

"You act as if I'm used to five-star restaurants and a live-in cook. You always did have this princess image of me, although considering the number of times you've seen me covered in dirt and manure, I've no idea where it comes from," Jule said with a laugh. He flushed and Jule smiled. "I hate to tarnish my golden glow, but it's none of the above and never will be. Most of the time my meals consist of whatever I can throw together in five minutes or less. I'll take anything you've got if you promise it includes a large glass of something cold."

Rafe visibly relaxed a little. "I can manage that."

Neither of them said anything during the ten-minute walk back to Rafe's house. The silence gave Jule time to think that she would rather not have had. She hadn't been to the house since the night she'd left him. She had mixed emotions about returning now. Things had been less strained between them since the party; at least they'd been able to work together without the tense silences and stilted conversation. They were far from comfortable with each other, though, even farther away from the intimacy they'd once had, when they could say anything, share everything, and not worry about being judged or rejected. But she wasn't about to let slip this chance to spend time with Rafe alone—without his family or his bison as a distraction—especially since he'd made the offer.

Standing in the doorway of the small adobe-and-pine house, though, she nearly changed her mind. Except for showing signs of neglect, the house was just as she remembered, a reflection of Rafe: built from the elements, spare and unfussy, smelling like earth and wind and faintly of smoke from a recent fire. It was far removed from the sprawling ranch house Rafe always refused to call home and from the sounds of civilization, giving it the feeling of being hidden away. A sanctuary, Jule had always thought it, safe from the intrusions of the outside world. Except for that last night.

She could sense the same awkwardness in Rafe as she felt in herself, but she was determined to ignore it.

"Have a seat," he said, indicating the couch, "I'll see what I can find in the kitchen."

"I'll help," Jule said. She waved off his protest and started to the kitchen ahead of him. "I've been bent over for too long. I need to move. If I sit down, you won't get me off that couch until tomorrow."

She was surprised to find his kitchen relatively well stocked; it told her Rafe spent more time eating alone than up at the ranch house with his family. But then Rafe had always been alone, save for her. It struck her that the past thirteen years must have isolated him more than ever. Yet he'd invited her here, let her in. And maybe that spoke of how alone he'd been more than anything else.

Her doubts about accepting his invitation slipped away. Whether he would ever admit it or not, he needed someone in his life who cared and no one had ever cared more than her.

They worked in companionable silence as Jule helped him put together sandwiches and reheat some leftover soup until she noticed Rafe had stopped working and was standing there, his job only half done, looking at her.

"What?" she asked, disconcerted by his nearness and the intent expression in his eyes.

"You were smiling," he said simply, as if that explained everything.

"I do that occasionally."

"This is the first time since you've been back that I've actually seen you look happy."

"I was thinking of the first time we tried cooking together," she admitted. She overlooked the comment about her being happy, not wanting to confess this was the first time she'd actually *felt* happy since she'd come home. Giving the soup another stir, she smiled again over the memory. "Do you remember? We tried to make tamales from scratch."

"And ended up with something that looked like dog food," Rafe said. "Didn't taste much better either. That turned out to be a helluva mess. I swear I've never gotten it all off the walls."

"It took me an hour to get it all out of my hair," Jule said laughing. "Although I thought you looked awfully cute covered in masa harina."

He gave a huff of laughter and Jule caught a spark in his eyes that she hadn't seen since they were kids. "I'm pretty sure that was your fault."

"Oh, no, it was your idea to begin with. I warned you then that if it didn't involve a microwave we were in trouble."

"That was the problem. I always believed you could do anything. I didn't listen to the warning." He stopped near her, plates in hand, and actually smiled, that slow, sexy smile she'd hadn't seen for so long, the one that never failed to make her heart clench and the room seem much warmer. "You did do a pretty good job with the scrambled eggs and toast we ended up with for dinner."

Jule rolled her eyes in mock affront at his gentle teasing. Inside she was singing.

It had been so long since they'd been together like this. And the part of Jule who was still that girl who believed love would conquer all felt a small ember of hope spark and flare to life.

For the first time in nearly as long as he could remember, Rafe felt almost relaxed. He didn't recognize the feeling at first; it gradually crept up on him as, over lunch, he and Jule recalled shared childhood memories. It grew stronger as he watched her smile and laugh, her dark eyes bright with it.

She'd always been able to do that to him. Jule, from the first time he'd laid eyes on her, had accepted him for what he was. She never expected him to be anything more or less, to prove himself worthy of her friendship or her love.

Rafe realized how much he'd missed it.

"This house has hardly changed," she said, glancing around

the large great room that doubled as a living and dining room. "Did you ever make any changes after your parents died?"

Rafe shook his head. "No, I guess…" He fumbled for the right words. "It always seemed like a sanctuary, the way it was. I used to come here a lot, even before I moved out. I never felt right in Jed's house."

"I can't imagine you anywhere else," Jule said softly. "I never could." She leaned her chin on her palm and stared off into space for a few moments, seemingly lost in the past. A few strands of hair had escaped her loose braid, brushing dark streaks against her face and throat. Rafe fought a sudden urge to put his hands there instead, there and everywhere else he'd dreamed of touching her since that one night.

She let her breath out in a small sigh. "I wish I'd known your parents."

"Me, too," Rafe said, grateful for the distraction. "All my memories are more like pictures and feelings." He found himself leaning back in his chair, telling her things he hadn't said out loud in forever. "I never could imagine my father anywhere else, either. My clearest memories of him are the times he'd take me riding or walking around the ranch. He'd always tell me this was where I was going to stay forever. He said it was the one thing I could always count on belonging to me. It's about the only thing I remember him telling me."

Jule was studying him intently and Rafe started to feel self-conscious about opening up to her like this. He felt like that kid he used to be, and maybe still in part was, always throwing up angry walls to keep people from getting too close, afraid they'd see him for what he was. But he couldn't hold the feeling for long. Jule wouldn't let him back away. She never had.

"I've always wondered about that," she said thoughtfully. "Why was your father so insistent you had a claim on this land? I know he and Jed started the ranch together but everyone always assumed Jed ended up the sole owner because of the money his first wife put into it."

Rafe shrugged it off. It was a sore spot with him, one that never healed. "Maybe it was just a feeling. Or maybe there was some agreement between them when Jed married Theresa."

Jule said nothing and Rafe knew it was for his sake. She'd never forgiven Jed for his treatment of Rafe nor Theresa Morente for abandoning him. "It must be frustrating for you, with Jed trying to find the son he's suddenly decided to acknowledge and wanting to divide everything five ways. Especially when it seems like you're the only one who cares about this place."

"Yeah, well, there's not a whole helluva lot I can do about it." He took a swallow of iced tea, trying to tamp down the anger surging up inside him. He looked away from her, not wanting her to see it in his face although he suspected she knew it all anyway. "All these years, I've worked to be the one who inherits this place. I stupidly stuck with the idea that if I worked hard enough, someday it would happen. I should've known better." He finally found the courage to look into her eyes and say what he should have said thirteen years ago. "All I ever wanted was to be able to offer you something. Something that mattered. I wanted to be the person you needed."

"Rafe—"

He shook his head sharply and looked away, not wanting to hear her deny what they both knew was the truth. "As it stands, my share won't amount to much."

"Your other brothers don't seem all that interested in what Jed wants to give them," she said tentatively, as if afraid to press too hard on the subject. "What does it matter what Jed decides to do if they're willing to sell or give their shares to you after he's gone?"

"There's no way I could afford to buy them out. And I don't want any favors," he said gruffly. "Besides, it would be just like Jed to tie things up legally so I'll never be able to own more than a fraction of this place."

Needing to move, Rafe abruptly got to his feet and began clearing the table of the empty dishes. He wasn't surprised when Jule followed him into the kitchen. She'd never been one to let him run away from uncomfortable feelings and in that respect, he didn't think she'd changed.

She surprised him, though, by leaning back against the counter and asking, "Have you ever had any contact with your parents' relatives? I would have thought that you have some family out there. Their tribal land isn't far from here."

"I never tried to find out," Rafe said as he dumped the dirty dishes into the sink. "I figured if I had any relatives out there, they didn't give a damn about finding me after my parents died. No one came looking for me and no one contested the adoption."

"Aren't you curious, though?"

"No," he said bluntly. "I haven't had much luck with family so far. I'd rather not go looking for more trouble than I've already got."

"Maybe, but—" She stopped as if something had suddenly occurred to her and then her face lit with excitement. "If I remember correctly, the Pinwa have an established buffalo herd. They've had it for several years now."

Not sure where she was going with this, Rafe wiped his hands on a dish towel with a shrug. "Maybe. I never looked into it."

"I'm sure they do. It might be worth our while to visit, take a look at their herd. Maybe they could offer us some ideas on helping the calves." His skepticism must have shown on his face because Jule stepped up and put a cajoling hand on his arm. "You might find you have family you actually like, or you'll maybe learn a little more about your parents," she said softly. "And at the very least, we could learn something worthwhile about how to better manage your herd."

Rafe nearly told her no. He didn't want to dig into his past and he doubted the tribe his parents had been born into would welcome him with open arms, ready and willing to offer him help with his bison problem. Although he had nothing substantial to base it on, he'd always had the impression that his parents had not been on the best of terms with whatever relations they'd left behind. Maybe it was because his father had left to partner with Jed Garrett, and maybe there was more to it, but Rafe wasn't all that interested in unearthing more family secrets. He had enough of those to contend with, what with Jed's search for his long-lost son.

It was the *we* that tipped the balance. How had his fight to establish a bison herd suddenly become theirs?

Except for one time—the last time she'd been here, in his house—he'd never been able to say no to Jule. She was looking at him with a mixture of hope and encouragement and he didn't have the heart—or the backbone—to push her away this time. Inwardly calling himself a damned fool for getting more tangled up with her than he already had, he gave in. "I suppose it might be worth a couple of hours' time."

Her smile lit up her face and Rafe promptly forgot his irritation and doubts, his only thought that it'd be worth a thousand surrenders if it meant she kept smiling at him like that.

"Good, how about this weekend?"

"Afraid I'll change my mind?"

"Yes," she said flatly and then laughed at his grimace. "So?"

"Fine, this weekend. Although you know this is going to be a waste of time, on both counts."

"That's one of the things I love about you, Rafe," Jule said lightly, briefly touching his face. "Your cheerful optimism."

Before he could think of a retort, she turned to the sink and began running water to wash the dishes. He picked up a towel to start drying them, smiling to himself.

Jule didn't have a reason to stay after they'd finished eating and clearing away the dishes, but she found herself lingering, wandering around the house, rediscovering once familiar things. She was smiling at the mess of papers and odds and ends on his desk when she spotted the sketchbooks stacked haphazardly on a corner. Picking one up, Jule began leafing through it, pausing over each of the finely detailed charcoal and pencil sketches that depicted a variety of native animals and plants, along with several different images of bison. She'd forgotten how talented Rafe was at drawing. How many times had she sat with him under the cottonwoods outside this house or at some particular spot they'd discovered while out riding, watching as he sketched something that had caught his fancy?

Rafe, coming back into the great room from the kitchen where he'd been getting her another glass of iced tea frowned as he saw what she was looking at. "I never could understand your fascination with that stuff." He brought her glass to her, setting it down on the desk at the same time he started to take the sketchbook from her. "There's nothing too exciting in there."

"I didn't know you still did this."

"Sometimes I get bored. I should find a better place for those."

Jule, flipping over pages, nearly let him take the book from her until she revealed a sketch that made her catch her breath. The head and shoulders sketch was a drawing of her, captured in fine, loving detail. In the past, Rafe had often done sketches of her, ignoring her laughing protests by saying he liked his sketches better than photos because a camera could never do her justice. This sketch, though, was recent, a portrait of a woman with a gentle smile and shadows in her eyes instead of a laughing girl.

She ran her finger lightly over the delicate lines and shapes, seeing herself through Rafe's eyes, seeing clearly the image of beauty and grace he saw every time he looked at her. She realized that was always how Rafe saw her, as something so perfect that he would never be good enough to call her his own.

The image blurred and she blinked back tears, moved by the emotion revealed in his drawing and determined not to let him see her cry.

Rafe's hand, arrested in the act of taking the book, moved to cover hers. The tremor in his light touch shuddered through her and suddenly, all of the feelings and memories she'd been holding back all morning rushed at her. Memories of laughter and loving, of making love with Rafe in this house, and the ripping pain that followed afterward when he sent her away.

Jule dropped the sketchbook back on the desk, overwhelmed by the war of emotions and long-denied desires. She could see in his eyes that Rafe felt it, too, and they stood staring at each other, the air between them vibrating with need and longing.

Rafe started to say something, stopped, cleared his throat. Jule could see he was trying to find the right words, or maybe any words. "I'd better get back to work," he settled on at last.

Disappointment hit her and Jule lowered her eyes. "Yes. Of course." She moved to get her jacket. Rafe stayed, not moving from his spot by the desk, only his eyes following her as she shrugged into her coat and slowly fastened the buttons.

"Josh is busy practicing for his next rodeo. He's no help to me right now," he said. "I've got more than the bison to deal with, especially with Jed laid up."

He was talking fast and hard, a sure sign he was unsettled. Jule tried to mask her own unsettling feeling by matching him in practicality. "I need to get going anyway. Between this and keeping up with the rest of Dad's practice, I'm having trouble fitting in sleeping and eating."

Rafe walked her back to her truck but before she climbed inside, Jule gave into impulse. Stretching up, she kissed him on the cheek, letting her hand linger there in a brief caress. "Thanks for lunch."

"You're welcome," he said gruffly.

She left him standing there, this time watching her as she drove away.

Chapter Seven

Shifting uncomfortably on the examining table, Jule couldn't hold back a sharp exclamation as the doctor probed an especially tender point on her lower back.

Sancia Gonzales left off her examination with a sympathetic smile. "Sorry about that. I don't think you've seriously injured anything, but those spasms can be painful."

"Painful, and very inconvenient right now." That was an understatement. With the amount of work she had to keep up, the last thing she needed right now was to be laid up with back problems. It wasn't the first time; when she was in college, a drunk driver had rear-ended her and she'd had back trouble ever since. Recently, the heavy workload at the clinic and the hours spent with Rafe's bison had left her stiffer and sorer than usual. But since yesterday, after an awkward wrench sideways to avoid being bitten by a particularly nasty-tempered pony, she'd been plagued by painful muscle spasms.

On her mother's recommendation, she'd reluctantly ended

up at Dr. Gonzales's wellness clinic, not really wanting to spend the time, but desperate for relief. She'd remembered Sancia Gonzales from the housewarming party and been favorably impressed, especially after learning Dr. Gonzales favored alternative medical treatments.

"The best thing you could do is get off your feet and rest for three or four days," Dr. Gonzales told her. She eyed Jule shrewdly. "But I'm guessing that isn't going to happen. I could prescribe painkillers and muscle relaxers. That would probably give you some relief—"

Jule shook her head. "I can't function with those things."

"I don't like them much myself," Dr. Gonzales said. "Why don't you try some heat and massage therapy? If you wait for a minute, I think Maya may be able to fit you in this morning. Trust me, it'll help."

Fifteen minutes later, Jule found herself in a gently lit room that smelled faintly of lavender and some other bittersweet herb she couldn't place, with Maya's hands firmly kneading the muscles in her back.

"I know it hurts, but it'll get better," Maya promised. "Just try to relax."

"Easy for you to say," Jule muttered, her voice muffled as she pressed her face into arm, trying to stop herself from gritting her teeth. "Those painkillers are sounding pretty good right now."

Maya laughed. "That's what Sawyer always tells me for the first ten minutes or so."

After about ten minutes that felt like the better part of an hour, Jule was just about ready to forgo the natural treatment in favor of good old-fashioned drugs when the pain and tension started to lessen.

"Better?" Maya asked as she worked her way up a few inches.

"Oh, yes, much better, thanks." Maya worked for half an hour until Jule felt warm and boneless and disinclined ever to move off the table. When she finally stopped, Jule made a little sound of protest. "Just five more minutes?"

She could hear rather than see Maya's smile. "Sorry, but that's enough for today. You need to take it easy, though, and come back in a day or two for another treatment."

"I'll come back every day if it means feeling like this." Reluctantly pushing herself up to a sitting position, she tentatively stretched her back and sighed at the relief from the pain. "Words cannot express my gratitude."

"No words necessary. How about a cup of tea? I've got about fifteen minutes before my next appointment and I could use a break."

Jule agreed and Maya left her to dress, coming back a few minutes later to lead her to a back room of the clinic and settle her on a comfortable chair with a cup of fragrant tea.

"I know you're still spending a lot of time at the ranch," Maya said, after asking after Jule's parents and her father's ongoing recovery. "How's that going?"

Jule recognized the subtle meaning behind the other woman's question. "You mean with Rafe? It's okay," she said, shaking her head when Maya looked apologetic and started to deny the query. "Things are—okay. We're going together this weekend to the Pinwa reservation. The tribe has an established buffalo herd and we're hoping to learn more about managing Rafe's herd. And maybe something about his parents' family."

Maya looked doubtful. "Do you think that's a good idea?"

"Rafe finding out more about his birth family? Why not?"

"It's just—maybe it would be better to leave it alone. Rafe's parents apparently cut themselves off from any family they might have had. Whatever the reason, it must have been something serious because it's unusual that no one from the Pinwa ever contested Rafe's adoption. It seems like Rafe has enough trouble with the family he's got now without digging into the past."

Maya's words, echoing Rafe's own feelings about searching out remnants of his birth family, gave Jule pause. Maybe this wasn't the best idea after all....

"You know, both Sawyer and Cort would like to try to make

things better between them and Rafe," Maya said. "Ever since Jed decided to find Cruz and divide up the ranch, the two of them have gotten closer to Josh but they haven't gotten anywhere with Rafe. Rafe seems determined to shut everyone out."

Even you? Jule heard Maya's unspoken question and normally would have shied away from sharing her personal worries with someone she had only started to get to know. But her concern for Rafe and Maya's sympathetic manner overrode her natural reticence.

"I'm worried about him," she said simply. "He's become even more of a loner than I remember. He's isolated himself so much I sometimes wonder if he'll ever be able to open up to anyone again." *Even me,* she mentally added, but didn't voice her fear aloud. She looked down at the cup in her lap, running her fingertips around the rim. "We used to be so close. We could tell each other anything and we never had to be afraid what the other would say or think. But now—" *Now, I wonder if I'm just fooling myself, believing it could ever be that way again.*

Maya touched her hand, her eyes soft with empathy. "I don't know. Rafe is so angry with everyone. Especially Sawyer."

"I think he feels like Sawyer and Cort left him behind."

"And Sawyer was always resentful because Rafe was the one Jed chose to keep with him instead of his own sons," Maya said with a rueful smile. "I never understood why they chose to blame each other. They were both kids and the real fault with this whole mess lies with Jed and Theresa. I never thought I could hate anyone but when I think of everything he's done, I come very close with Jed Garrett."

"He messed up so many lives," Jule agreed. "And he's still doing it."

"I'd like to see Sawyer and Rafe patch things up, though."

Jule agreed. "You're right. Rafe needs family, people who care about him. If he could accept that, it might change his attitude about a lot of things."

The thoughtful look Maya gave Jule made Jule feel a flush of warmth and glance away. "If nothing else, I'd love to see you again. When it's not so painful for you," Maya added with a smile.

"Well, I'm definitely coming back for another massage." She thanked Maya and left the clinic feeling better, not only physically, but in spirit.

Maybe Maya was right about changing Rafe's view of his brothers. Maybe if she could help Rafe toward reconciliation with his brothers, he would be more open to considering their relationship and where it might go.

Because, no matter how many times she told herself what a bad idea it was, no matter whether it really was a bad idea or not, she knew that from the moment she'd set foot back in Luna Hermosa, everything in her had been hoping and trying for a chance to make things right between Rafe and her.

There wasn't any point in pretending or wishing she didn't love him. She'd never stopped.

Instead, she'd been waiting and praying for the day when she could convince him it was meant to be.

The voices, interspersed with laughter, should have warned him to turn around and go back the way he came. But Rafe, back from a long ride to look over the bison herd and check on the cattle pastured at the far end of the ranch property, couldn't find the will to avoid the horse barn right now. He'd been up since before dawn and he still had hours of work ahead of him. All he wanted right now was to stow the saddle and bridle he was lugging and take a few minutes' break before getting back to it.

At least he wasn't likely to run into Jed, he thought, as he started inside the barn. Jed, even with a bottle of whiskey in him, never sounded that good-tempered.

He half expected Josh. He was brought up short for a moment when he saw Josh and Sawyer coming back into the barn from the other direction. Still bantering back and forth about something to do with the horses, they didn't see him at first, standing there in the shadows.

"Just so you aren't trying to pawn some wild thing off on me," Sawyer was telling Josh. "My boys aren't going to be ready for the rodeo circuit for a few years yet."

Josh laughed. "Considering one of 'em's about four months from making an appearance and the other's still working on running, I'm surprised you're worried about what they'll be ridin' in a few years. But hey, you want to spend your money, it's okay by me." Josh started to add something when he noticed Rafe and grinned. "You don't trust me, here's the man who can vouch for me."

The air suddenly vibrated with tension as Rafe's eyes met Sawyer's and for a moment, they stood silently eyeing each other.

"I'm looking to buy a couple of horses from your stock," Sawyer said finally. "Something smaller and gentler than what I've got for when my boys are old enough to learn how to ride."

Josh leaned against one of the stalls, arms crossed casually over his chest. "I thought those two three-year-olds, the paints. They're young now, but with good training, in a couple of years, they'd do just fine."

"Should," Rafe said shortly. He moved to put away the saddle he'd forgotten he was holding. "Josh knows horses."

"Wow, that was almost a compliment," Josh said, flashing a knowing wink and smile Sawyer's way. He straightened and started moving off toward the door. "You want to wait here, I'll go and get the paperwork and we can get this taken care of."

Without waiting for Sawyer's agreement, he turned and left Rafe and Sawyer alone.

There was an awkward silence as they both stood there, shifting around and looking everywhere but at each other. Sawyer at last broke it. "How's the work with the bison going? Has Jule been able to help with the problems you've been having?"

Rafe figured Sawyer wasn't that interested but needed to fill the silence. "It's going. It's better since Jule came back."

"And Jule?"

"What about her?"

Sawyer shrugged. "Nothing. I just figured it might be hard spending so much time together, considering how close you two were and everything that happened."

"That was a long time ago."

"Yeah, but some things don't change, do they?"

"No they don't," Rafe said harshly. "So back off." He could feel the anger building up inside, threatening to burst out. He didn't need to be reminded of the past, of feelings he'd rather forget, memories he'd managed to shove away in the dark corners of his mind.

"Or what? You're going to start another shouting match and then stomp off before we can finish it?"

"It's been finished for a long time. I don't know why you've decided now to pretend like you give a damn."

"I do give a damn, but most of the time I sure as hell don't know why," Sawyer ground out. His hands flexed at his sides and Rafe could tell he was having the same struggle to control his temper. "What I do know is I'm tired of pretending that we aren't family. Like it or not, we've both got Jed Garrett for a father, even if it's only in name. Maybe it's time we dealt with it once and for all."

"I stopped thinking about you as *family* when you walked out of here and your mother left me with Jed."

"We were kids. What was I supposed to do?"

"It didn't stop you from standing up for Cort." It wasn't what he intended to say; the words had just fallen out and with them memories of how Sawyer had protected his younger brother from an abusive Jed, taking the brunt of Jed's anger both physically and emotionally. Sawyer had never done the same for Rafe, although Jed and Theresa had largely ignored the boy they'd adopted. He'd never forgiven Theresa for leaving him with Jed, never forgiven either Jed or Theresa for treating him like he didn't matter, never forgiven Sawyer for seemingly giving up on him when Theresa had taken Sawyer and Cort and left Rancho Pintada for good.

They'd left Rafe more alone than he'd ever been—except for Jule. But he'd never admit that to Sawyer.

His one small admission, though, seemed to have dampened Sawyer's anger. "Cort's younger, he needed someone to look after him because our mother sure as hell never did. And we didn't have a choice about leaving. Jed settled for his share of our mother's money, kicked us out and kept you." Taking a long breath, he looked hard at Rafe then said quietly, "I resented you for being the one Jed chose. Even though he was a son of a bitch and still is, I never understood how he could completely abandon his two sons without a backward glance."

"Yeah, well it worked out pretty well for you, didn't it? Being raised on the Morente estate, being heir to all that money. You ended up with something." And got the chance to be something. All he'd ended up with was an unbreakable link to this land, the land he'd channeled all his passion into so one day he'd be the one worthy of inheriting Rancho Pintada. Now it looked as though Jed had killed that dream, too.

"Cort and I don't want anything to do with Jed's plan of splitting this place up between the five of us," Sawyer said, as if divining Rafe's thoughts. "You're the only one of us who cares about this place."

Rafe glared at him. "I don't need charity."

"Why not knock the chip off your shoulder for five minutes and actually listen," Sawyer said, scowling in frustration. "Did you ever stop to think that Cort and I have no interest in having to be responsible for any part of this ranch, even in name? It represents nothing but bad memories to us."

"That part's the same for me. But unlike you two, I wasn't born with a silver spoon in my mouth."

"Cort and I have made our own choices. You can, too."

Rafe gave a huff of disbelief. "Is that the best you got?" He heard himself, deliberately trying to antagonize Sawyer enough so that he'd leave. After all these years, Rafe found it hard even to think about putting aside all the resentment and bitterness that had kept him company for so long. Those feelings had kept him strong, or so he believed, and losing them meant he'd be vulnerable in ways he didn't want to think about. "Past or no past, this ranch *is* my choice."

"It was tough for us all when Jed and Theresa were together," Sawyer said quietly. "But I can remember when we didn't care about what they said or what they tried to do. For a while at least we were friends who'd become brothers."

"Like you said, that was a long time ago." The words, though, lacked his earlier heat. Rafe remembered, too, and for the first time in as long as he could recall, traitorous thoughts began to intrude, tempting him to believe that he could, even after all this time, begin to make amends with both Sawyer and Cort.

"Maybe it's time we started treating each other a little more like brothers instead of enemies," Sawyer said. "Like it or not, we are related."

Rafe couldn't bring himself to admit it aloud that maybe Sawyer had a point. He guessed Maya, the peacemaker, had had a lot to do with Sawyer's recent change in attitude. For the first time ever, secretly he was sorely tempted to think about the possibility of having brothers he could talk to and who might even lend a hand now and then.

With the bison situation, and with Jule being back driving him to the brink of madness, and maybe because he'd been alone for so long, dealing with everything life threw at him without anyone else to offer a hand to lift him up, he found himself actually listening to Sawyer's suggestion. He tried to think of some comeback, something that put a voice to his conflicting feelings.

Before he could frame any kind of reply, Jule walked up to them and time stopped.

She knew from the instant she saw them together that she'd interrupted something.

She'd come to do a bison check but fervently wished now she could back out of the barn and pretend she'd never been there. Sawyer's last few words, ...*we are related,* were the only part of the conversation she'd overheard. Some strong emotions she couldn't define hung heavily in the air and Jule felt uncomfortable for intruding on whatever was going on between them, albeit unknowingly.

"I'm sorry, I—" she started to say, but got no further as a voice behind her interrupted with a cheeky, "Well, I'm not. You're the best thing I've seen all day."

Jule turned to see Josh coming up behind her, grinning broadly. She inwardly groaned, wondering if the situation could get any worse.

Oblivious to the tension in the air, Josh handed a sheaf of papers to Sawyer before turning back to Jule. "I'd ask what brings you out here, but I figure it's gotta be Rafe's bison again. You're getting as bad as he is about those overgrown cows."

"I came to do another check. I should get to it," Jule murmured, ignoring Josh's teasing.

"I need to get going," Sawyer said although he hesitated, glancing at Rafe.

"Yeah, well, some other time," Rafe muttered. He turned to Jule. "Need some help with those calves?"

"Sure, thanks." She said her goodbyes to Sawyer and Josh and then started into one of the stalls as the two of them walked out together.

Rafe kept a brooding silence as she worked and finally, Jule couldn't stand it any longer. "I was finally able to contact someone with the Pinwa," she said as she finished with the last calf. "We've got permission to visit and talk to someone there about the buffalo."

"Yeah, fine," he said, not looking at her. He followed her out of the stall, apparently lost in thought. Jule wondered if he'd even heard her or had just given her the first answer that had come to him.

I'm pathetic, she thought, mentally kicking herself for not being able to exercise any self-control when it came to him.

Even as the thought came, Jule found herself reaching out to him, putting a gentle hand on his arm. "I'm sorry for interrupting you and Sawyer earlier. It seemed important."

Rafe shrugged off her apology. "It doesn't matter."

His walls were back, reinforced and higher than before. Obviously whatever it was did matter, and Jule suspected the two of them had been talking about something to do with their past and current animosity for each other.

"It does matter. Whatever it was is bothering you." He did look at her then, with a glower that warned Jule to back off. Her concern for him wouldn't let her do that. "I'm worried about you. I just want to help."

"You can't. And I don't want to talk about this right now."

"You don't ever want to talk about it, Rafe. Not anymore. But you need to."

"You don't know what I need," he snapped back. "So drop it."

Jule decided that might have been the best advice she'd gotten since she'd come back home. She'd thought they'd been making progress, but it seemed like every time, she was the only one reaching out, the only one trying to make things right. Was it really worth sacrificing her pride and her heart to keep pursuing a dream that very likely would never be fulfilled?

"Maybe I should drop it because it seems all you do is push me away," Jule flung back, getting angry with his determination to ignore every feeling that didn't have to do with bitterness or resentment. "You push everyone away and one day, if you keep doing it, eventually everyone is going to take you at your word and you're going to be left with no one and nothing."

"What do you want from me, Jule?" he ground out.

"Too much, obviously."

"I don't know what you want to hear, but I can't give it to you. I need—" He shook his head, turning away from her to shove his hands through his hair in a frustrated gesture, before swinging back to her. "I need to think—about things."

Part of Jule recognized that whatever had happened between Sawyer and him had put Rafe on the defensive and that she was probably pushing him too hard so soon after what had likely been an emotional confrontation. But the part of her that was fed up with giving and never receiving anything in return was stronger. "It's hard to have a relationship when only one of us is trying."

"I wasn't aware I had any *relationships*, with you or anyone else. So far, relationships have only caused me trouble. I stopped trying a long time ago."

"Except with your mistress." He looked startled and she gestured around them. "This place. Your only *relationship* is with *her*. There's not much else you seem to care about. But it's not going to be enough, it never has been, no matter how hard you try to make it enough."

He stiffened, his hands balling into fists, and anger flared hotly in his eyes. He kept it leashed, but Jule's own anger faltered a little. "I can't talk about this with you right now." Every word sounded forced out between clenched teeth.

"I know," Jule said, so quietly she doubted he could hear her. Her fury deserted her, leaving her feeling tired and miserable. "You never can."

Chapter Eight

Rafe's old pickup truck rattled up the steep, winding road leading to the secluded cliffs where the remainder of his parents' small tribe lived. He glanced again in the rearview to make certain the horse trailer he was pulling was staying stable on the bumpy road and then spared a quick sideways glance at Jule.

They'd scarcely spoken since they started the drive. Tension from the day before hung between them as heavily as the dust from the rocky mountain incline. They'd only been away from Rancho Pintada for an hour or so, but already, for at least a dozen reasons, he wished he hadn't let her talk him into making this trip.

He told himself he couldn't afford to be away from the ranch right now. It was only a day—they planned to drive back down late tonight—but being miles from the ranch, away from where he could control things, made him uneasy.

And then there was the prospect of facing his parents' family and former friends, knowing how they must feel about the way his mother and father had left the tribe to live in Luna Hermosa on Jed Garrett's ranch. He hadn't been back since he was a small boy to the secret valley where the small remainder of his family's tribe still lived. He hadn't been invited back. And he had no assurance whatsoever that he would be welcome when he showed up this afternoon.

But the real reason, if he were honest with himself—which at the moment was the last thing he wanted to be—was that he would be with Jule through the evening. Catching teasing hints of her sage-and-sunflower scent as it drifted from where she sat in the passenger's seat was already trying his senses and his reason. He'd been dealing with her being back in town as well as he had so far only because most of the time they'd spent together had been in the company of the bison. The fact that her time at the ranch would always come to an end within a few hours allowed him the luxury of keeping his emotions in check. When she was gone, and the pain and frustration revisited him with a vengeance, at least she was none the wiser.

He resolved to make this a quick trip, even if it irritated her to be rushed and to have to drive back down the mountain at night. He knew this would put a serious crimp in her plans, plans that didn't center only on learning about the Pinwa's bison herd, but also on forcing him into a position where he had to confront the ghosts of his parents' and his own past.

But that was her agenda, not his. He'd been alienated from the Pinwa almost from birth. It was too late to try to recapture a part of his past, his heritage. That had been lost when his parents sacrificed their roots and loyalties to their tribe to choose a course they thought would provide their son a more secure future than he would have had hidden away in a tiny village in the Sangre de Cristo Mountains.

As though she could read his thoughts, Jule suddenly spoke up. "Do you know how many of the Pinwa are left?" She shrugged at the questioning lift of his brow. "You've had a faraway look in your eye since we left. And you've scarcely done more than grunt once in a while at the jolts in the road. It makes sense you'd be thinking about your parents and the tribe."

"Yeah."

"So, do you know how many are left?"

"Only a couple of hundred, from what I gather."

"That's sad. They were once the largest pueblo in northern New Mexico, weren't they?"

Rafe didn't know whether to be amused or annoyed by her determination to make him talk about this. "That's what I've heard."

"What happened?"

"Don't know. I only know my parents were convinced there wasn't any future there. I haven't given it much thought."

Jule turned from him and gazed out her window. "I know."

"You know, but you don't want to accept that I'm okay with it. And don't think this little trip is going to fix anything. It's not going to answer all of those questions or solve the mystery of my lost heritage or make me want to return to my roots or whatever it is you've dreamed up." He knew he sounded gruff, but he wanted to get his point across before they reached the pueblo. He didn't want Jule meddling in his unresolved family problems any more than she already was.

She didn't answer and he didn't pursue it any more. As they reached the high country, the dirt-and-rock road turned from dry and dusty to damp clay. Jule rolled down her window and took a deep breath of air that smelled like rain on New Mexico clay, a fresh and earthy smell unique to the high country. "It looks like it's going to be a perfect fall evening," she said. "I love this time of year."

"Me, too."

Flicking a glance his way, she smiled a little before returning to her own thoughts. This time, the quiet between them felt lighter, as if they were sharing something deep and mutual in the silence just as they had so many times in the past. Rafe could easily conjure up the picture of them, resting on a fallen log by the creek that ran across a corner of the ranch, as closely side by side as two people could sit, staring into the gurgling water, saying next to nothing, yet perfectly content in their quiet communion. He found himself glancing over to her now to find her looking at him, her face even more beautiful with maturity, her soft eyes and hint of a smile even more perceptive with time and experience.

She knew him too well. Not talking didn't stop her from easily reading his moods and emotions. When they were children, the knowledge had comforted him, made him feel special, loved. Now it made him uncomfortable, vulnerable and downright irritated.

Abruptly he broke their eye contact and jerked his neck around to check the trailer again. "This is the last downhill to the valley. We'll be there in a few minutes."

"Good. This ride has done a number on my back. I'm ready to walk around."

When Rafe saw the first flat-roofed adobe buildings of his pueblo rise above the evergreen shrubbery and patches of yellow field grass that dotted the desert landscape, his stomach clenched. For a long, hard minute he considered turning the truck around.

Jule pointed out the window. "Oh, look, I see the bell tower on the mission over there. I wonder if they still ring it? I read somewhere that it's over two hundred years old."

"I'm sure someone will give you a tour," Rafe muttered, rounding the last bend that led to the narrow pueblo road. As he drove through the cluster of earthen homes and buildings, a few people walked outside to watch; children ran up alongside the truck. He pulled to a stop at the center of the pueblo near the historic mission where his parents had told him they'd been married.

As he and Jule got out of the truck, three men came up to

greet them. At first it was appraising, not warm. Rafe felt awkward, but refused to show it. "I'm Rafe Garrett and this is Jule Santiago. We came about my bison herd. I think you're expecting us."

A sturdy, dark-skinned man of about sixty with eyes and cheekbones that could have mirrored Rafe's nodded. "Welcome, nephew." He laid a strong hand on Rafe's shoulder. "I'm Pay Nantone. Your mother, Halona, was my sister. And these are my sons. We've waited many years for this."

Opposing reactions struck Rafe at the same time, gratifying and angry. After all this time, this was family by blood and they accepted him as their own without question. But if they'd been waiting, why didn't anyone come looking for him after his parents died?

His inability to come up with a reply that covered both those feelings prompted Jule to take a step forward. "Thank you for letting us come," she said, extending a hand. "This is a great privilege."

The elder of the sons nodded toward a long wooden picnic table set under an expansive old umbrella of a tree. "Our mother has food and drinks for you. She's waiting."

"Thanks," Rafe said, finding his voice. This was so far from what he'd expected he felt as if someone had pushed him off solid ground onto a crumbling, precarious ledge. "I need to tend to my horses first."

"I'll do that," the younger-looking of the two sons offered. "Mother won't be happy if she has to hold her meal any longer. You go on ahead."

Rafe and Jule followed the men to the table where immediately a handsome woman and a teenaged girl began to bring trays of food out from an adobe home.

"This is my wife, Mina, and my granddaughter, Tansy, your niece," Rafe's uncle said, introducing them to Jule and him.

The girl offered a shy smile while her huge black eyes searched his face. "You're so tall," she said finally, eliciting a laugh from everyone. Embarrassed, she practically dropped the plate of corn tortillas she was carrying and scurried back through the low, darkened doorway to her house.

Rafe and Jule enjoyed a small feast of corn, chili and bean dishes, and delicious, freshly baked kiva-oven bread, talking somewhat formally but politely all the while with the family. Rafe was glad no one asked personal questions or brought up his parents, instead focusing on the purpose of their visit, answering his and Jule's concerns about the tribe's bison herd. It made things easier, at least for now.

Later would be another story. When they'd finished, Pay saddled up with Rafe and Jule to head out to where the herd was grazing. Catching Jule's sidelong glances at him when she thought he wasn't looking, Rafe had no doubt the lack of family talk was frustrating her and she was waiting for him to start the conversation.

You'll be waiting a long time, he thought at her. Talking about bison was one thing, easy and comfortable.

Going hunting in the past was another, hard and unsettling, and not something he planned to do if he could find a way around it.

They spent the rest of the afternoon inspecting the herd and talking with Pay and another man Rafe's uncle called the pueblo's bison expert. Jule learned a great deal, piecing together clues that may have led to the cause of the epidemic in Rafe's herd. Of course, the isolation factor way up here in the secluded valley helped to protect the pueblo's herd. Down on Rancho Pintada, the herd would naturally be exposed to more possibilities for disease.

As they rode far out over the grassy range, the landscape changed. Here the foothills land lay in the shadows of blue spruce trees and rocky peaks. Jule watched Rafe interacting with men he should be as close to as brothers, yet had only met earlier today. Pay still hadn't mentioned one word about Rafe's parents. His only talk of family had been to share a detail here and there about his own sons and their families. When Rafe didn't respond with questions or even an appearance of interest, instead of growing impatient, his uncle wisely changed the subject. Apparently, Rafe's stubborn stoicism irritated her more than it did Rafe's uncle. She was getting so frustrated with Rafe, she had to resist asking about his parents herself.

"It will be dark soon, and cold, we need to ride back," Pay was saying. "We'll have a fire and a good supper back at the pueblo."

Jule looked out over the valley to where the golden blaze in the sky had begun to dip toward the horizon, spreading glistening salmon-colored streaks out in all directions across the blue sky like the fans of a thousand yucca plants.

"It's so beautiful here," she murmured, breathing in the crisp, cooling evening air. "I love the high country."

"If we don't get back before dark, you may not like it so much," the bison guide said. "That thin jacket of yours won't cut the fall chill up here."

With that, the group kicked their horses into a fast gallop, Rafe pulling out ahead of Jule in what she recognized as a direct challenge. Just as she had as a little girl riding bareback and barefoot next to him, she took the bait. She and Rafe shot out full speed ahead of the others, Jule immediately taking the lead.

Her hair fell loose from the clip at her nape and she shoved it over her shoulders, while turning back to look at Rafe. "I always beat you, you know."

He prodded his horse into a faster gait, almost catching up to her. "That was then."

"I don't think things have changed that much, no matter what you might believe." Darting out into a solid lead, she laughed out loud. *I'll show you,* she said to herself, then urged her horse, "Come on baby, let's make it crystal-clear to him how much things *haven't* changed."

Jule held her front running position all the way back to the pueblo. Only in the last several yards did the pounding of hooves at her back cause her to turn. In the end, Rafe overtook her by several paces. When he pulled up to a halt, he waited, breathing hard, the barest hint of satisfaction glinting in his dark eyes.

Jule eased back on the reins, stopping next to him. Her breath came in short gasps. "Okay, you've improved," she said, trying not to pant. She'd forgotten how demanding a hard ride could be.

He smiled slightly. "Maybe some things do change."

The others rode up moments later, both men smiling. "From the way you ride together, I'd say you two must have done it many times," Pay said.

Jule and Rafe exchanged a glance. Jule couldn't resist a smile and to her delight, Rafe smiled back.

"You could say that," he answered for them both.

"The trough and barn are over here. We'll get the horses settled then wash for dinner." Pay turned and looked directly at Rafe. His expression changed to something solemn, searching. "There are several people who want to meet you tonight."

"I'd planned on driving back this evening..." Rafe began, then stopped when Pay put a hand on his shoulder.

"They've waited a long time, Rafe. Is it so much to ask?"

Yes, say yes, Jule thought so hard at Rafe she was sure both men could hear her. *Please, give them a chance. Give yourself a chance.*

Rafe said nothing for so long Jule was nearly ready to kick him just to jolt him into a response.

"Yeah, fine," he said at last. "We'll stay for dinner."

He sounded so gruff Jule added a hasty, "Thank you."

"Good." Pay pointed to a small, square, earthen home situated behind his house beneath the big weeping tree and picnic table. "You can wash up there. The door is open. Come to my home when you're ready." With that he and the other man took the reins from Jule and Rafe and led the horses away.

Rafe turned on his heel and headed for the house at a pace that had Jule struggling to keep up with him. She interpreted the hard set of his shoulders and the jerking tension in his stride as anger at being cornered into something he didn't want to do. It was the same defensive hostility he'd worn at the party and in every other situation that put him in close proximity to people he was determined to keep at a distance.

Any conversation that touched on his family would earn her either stony silence or an angry, "stay out of my business," so Jule decided to stick to the bison.

"Your uncle's friend knows so much about bison. I learned a lot today, didn't you?" she ventured, mentally bracing herself because in this mood, even the bison might not be a safe topic with Rafe.

"They've been raising them for years. They ought to have learned something. But all of it's useless if it doesn't save my herd."

Jule sighed. He was right, but part of her had been hoping for something more. Part of her sneered at her ridiculous optimism. What had she expected? That some bond with his parents' family would spark a sense of belonging, of innate self-esteem, of hope, to come to life in him?

It was too late for that. Jed Garrett had no doubt effectively destroyed in Rafe any ability to bond with anyone or anything but the land of Rancho Pintada long ago.

She wanted to cry for him, for everything he'd lost and never had. Or maybe the tears were for her, for everything she'd had with him and lost.

At the entrance to the modest guesthouse, Rafe had to bend down to pass through the low, rustic wood-hewn doorway. Dusk had set in and they searched for a light switch. Failing to find one, Jule spied one oil lamp with matches at the side then several others set around the single room. She and Rafe went about lighting the lamps, illuminating the heavy logs in the Vega-lined ceilings, the whitewashed walls and brick floors. Two single beds covered with bright red, blue and green blankets flanked the walls on either side of the room. A small carved table, two chairs, a few painted pots and a beautiful woven rug completed the simple decor.

In the corner of the room, a colorfully tiled sink with several towels laid out beside it beckoned.

Still ducking his head slightly, Rafe quickly unbuttoned his shirt and threw it on the bed. Jule sat back on the other bed and pulled off her boots. As though he'd forgotten she was there, he headed for the sink and turned on the water. "You mind?" he asked with a backward glance at her.

"Go ahead. I'm enjoying sitting for a minute." Actually she was enjoying the sight of his bare, bronzed chest and muscular back a lot more. He'd grown so strong; everywhere she looked she saw hard muscle and sinew, from his arms, shoulders, chest and back down to the trim lines of his waist above his jeans. As he washed, each muscle flexed or rippled in the soft, hazy lantern glow. The years may have been hard on his heart and soul, but they'd been good for his physique. A little weight on his once lanky body suited him well.

An image flashed into her head: her locking the door, shutting out the rest of the world, and keeping him to herself for the night. Heat suffused her body and she felt it rise in her face. Surely, if he looked at her, he could see every desire as clearly as if she'd spoken them?

He didn't look. Finishing up, he grabbed a towel and rubbed his face and upper body dry, seeming oblivious. "Your turn."

For what? She stepped over to the sink, trying hard not to stare obviously. "I'm jealous," she said, plucking at her shirt. "I could use a bath."

"Don't let me stop you," he said over his shoulder.

Oh, really? Here she was practically drooling open-mouthed over him and he dismissed her as easily as another guy in a locker room. *We'll just see about that. Can I still at least tempt you, Rafe Garrett?*

Jule decided not to make it this easy for him. Maybe he didn't want her. And maybe his stubborn, senseless insistence that he wasn't good enough for her gave him the willpower to ignore his own desires.

Either way, he'd pricked her pride with his seeming indifference, and she couldn't let it go. She wasn't exactly schooled in the role of seductress, but then again, she didn't think Rafe was as immune to her as he kept trying to get her to believe.

With a light laugh, she tossed her head down to shake out her long, heavy hair then flung it back to run her fingers through it, sweeping it up into a careless knot. "You're right. Being shy is silly."

"What?" Rafe looked up from shaking out his shirt and accidentally let it slip from his fingers to the floor.

With painstaking slowness, Jule unbuttoned her own shirt, pulling it from the low-cut waist on her jeans. Fortunately—or maybe it had been wishful thinking—she'd worn a pretty pink push-up bra with a touch of lace rather than her usual cotton sports bra that showed no cleavage and reduced her down a size.

"I mean, we've seen each other with far less than this on, haven't we?" she nonchalantly threw out the question.

She glanced sideways at him. Seeing she had his attention, she reached her palms around behind the small of her back and did a partial standing back bend. "Oh, I wish I had Maya's magic touch right now. I haven't ridden that way in so long I've forgotten how hard it is on my back. Everything's so tight." She gave him her best innocent expression. "Would you mind playing masseur for a minute?"

Rafe just stared.

"It would really help," she coaxed. Stepping over to the sink, she held the edges and bent at the waist, her legs slightly splayed. "It's worst right where my jeans hit. Please?"

"Uh, Jule, I—"

"Don't tell me you can't do this. I know how good you are with your hands."

"We can't keep them waiting." His voice sounded husky and disconcerted.

"Five minutes, that's all I ask."

When she heard him suck in an unsteady breath and then move toward her, she smiled to herself.

For a moment, he hesitated, hovering behind her, close enough she could feel his heat. Then his thighs brushed her hers from behind and she bit her lower lip to repress a moan of pleasure as his large hands, warm and calloused, settled onto her skin, pressing with just the right amount of force versus gentleness.

"How's this?"

"Great. Fine. *Tortuous.* A little lower, please." She hoped he was suffering. But as his thumbs dipped just below the waist-line of her jeans to press at the points of her hips, she knew he couldn't be in half the agony she was. He'd turned her little game back on her and if she didn't stop this now, he was going to win without even trying.

"Um, that's perfect. Much better. Thanks. I'll just wash up now."

Straightening, she expected him to drop his hands and move back. Instead he stayed, unyielding to her silent request for a respite from the torment of having him touch her.

She felt the rise and fall of his chest against her bared back and the light, rhythmic touch sent shivers over her skin that had nothing to do with the chill of the evening. As if he had an eternity, he ran his hands up her back to her shoulders in a sensual caress that had Jule gripping the edge of the sink to keep from pushing herself into his arms.

Hooking his finger under the edge of one of her bra straps, he slid it off her shoulder and then kissed the place he'd bared. "Jule," he breathed her name, the sound aching with longing and need.

She leaned back into him, wanting him so much, so hard, it hurt. His hands tightened and he rested his forehead in the curve between her shoulder and neck. The scent and feel of him, the warm rasp of his breathing on her skin, wrapped her tightly and they stayed like that for several moments, the time stretched thin until it became too fragile to hold.

Jule couldn't bear it any longer, to be so close to him and

yet still so far apart. "I'd better finish up or we'll be late," she whispered.

"Yeah. Right."

Rafe abruptly let her go and strode over to retrieve his shirt. She hated the cold that replaced his warmth and hated even more his quick retreat from openly needy to closed and aloof.

Her little experiment might have worked but the results were unexpectedly bittersweet.

Inside Rafe's uncle's small home, Pay's family and some new faces were seated in a great room that dominated the living area. Pay introduced Jule and Rafe to the group before they all moved to seats at tables that had been pushed together and covered with cloths to make one long, brightly appointed dining table.

Jule spent most of dinner listening to the others. Her thoughts hadn't left her moments alone with Rafe in the little house out back; threads of conversation wove their way through the pictures that replayed in her mind and more than once she found herself missing something that was said.

"We hope you'll come to visit again now that we've finally met," Pay was saying. "We could learn much from each other."

Rafe ladled himself a third bowl of hot red chili and hominy. "I don't get away much. But I'll try to come back."

His promise surprised Jule; earlier, he'd seemed dead set on not getting any more involved with his parents' tribe than he had to. But she could see it pleased Pay.

"Your father wanted you to find security and fulfillment in that ranch. He gave up a great deal to try to provide that for you."

"I know," Rafe said gravely. "I just wish he'd found a way to do it without involving Jed Garrett."

"We've little now; Anoki had even less then. Before you were born, our cattle herd was in serious jeopardy. Anoki wasn't a farmer, he was a rancher. It would have killed his spirit to do anything else. So he and Halona made the choice to leave."

"Anoki chose to leave. Halona followed."

An elderly woman, her face deeply lined with decades of laughter and tears, spoke up from the shadows of a corner seat. Earlier, Pay had introduced her as his mother, Rafe's grandmother. Beyond a nod of acknowledgment, she'd said nothing. Yet Jule noticed how she'd watched Rafe, perhaps trying to see something of her daughter in Halona's son.

She leaned forward slightly, her gaze fixed on Rafe. "Anoki always wanted more, he never would have been happy staying here. Halona should never have gone. But she was young and maybe a little foolish."

"Anoki was an honorable man and Halona loved him," Pay said, a note of gentle reproach in his voice. "His only mistake was to partner with a man who wasn't so honorable."

"Jed is planning to divide the ranch between his five sons," Jule spoke up. Rafe shot her a scowl but she ignored him. If Rafe had a chance of proving his half claim to Rancho Pintada, he needed the help of his parents' family, the people who knew Anoki and Halona best and who might have shared their confidences about Anoki's claim on the ranch.

Rafe's uncle and a few of the other men who had been listening exchanged glances. "That wouldn't be a fair division, Rafe," Pay said. "You need to realize that."

Mina came up behind Pay before Rafe could answer and tapped her husband firmly on the shoulder. "Enough about business already. If all you do is talk business, Rafe and Jule won't want to come back. It's time for the moon-and-fire hour." She moved to Rafe and Jule and lightly touched each of them on the shoulder. "Come outside. It's a full moon tonight. Tonight we'll celebrate your coming back to us."

The entire party of about twenty guests moved outside, leaving the dishes and food for the teenaged children to clean up. A firepit had been lit, filling the air with the rich scents of piñon and a heady incense Jule didn't recognize at first. People gathered around the fire, sitting on blankets, some smoking, others talking quietly.

After a while, a woman began singing, a soft, almost haunting melody, the low hypnotic words sounding foreign and familiar—foreign to the ears, familiar to the soul.

The men invited Rafe to sit on one side of the fire with them while Jule was welcomed with the women. Overhead, an ivory moon hung low and weighty as though to give birth to the harvest. The leader of the group poured a thick liquid into a gourd cup, sipped and passed it to the next person. When it came to Rafe, Jule watched him sip hesitantly, wince slightly, then pass it along. Jule did the same, not sure whether she liked whatever it was, but certain it had an almost instant effect on her.

Minutes—hours?—passed almost like a dream for Jule. Between being tired from the day's riding and the potency of whatever celebratory drink was being handed around, she began to feel a curious detachment, as if she stood apart and watched herself in the midst of all these people, smiling and nodding, all the time knowing it wasn't really her.

Looking across, she saw Rafe watching her over the dimming firelight. Their eyes met and suddenly no one else existed. Desire seemed to dance between them in swirls of scented smoke and taunting leaps, teasing darts in the flames. The incense, sandalwood, Jule now remembered, permeated the air. Mesmerized by the hunger in Rafe's eyes, every bone in her body melted like warm honey, the sensation making her light-headed.

Rafe must have been feeling the same way because he got up and moved to her side. "I'm not up to driving back. How about you?"

"Definitely not." Jule tried to stifle a yawn. "I feel like all I want to do is sleep for about three days straight."

Rafe helped her to her feet and almost as an afterthought curved his arm around her shoulders. "We'll get an early start tomorrow then."

Jule nodded and leaned into him. Inside the little house, the air was almost as cold as it was outside. Instead of releasing her to go to the bed on the opposite side of the room, Rafe led her to his bed. He helped her out of her jacket and boots then stripped off his own. Guiding her down on the bed, he tucked her under the warm blanket before heading to the kiva fireplace in the corner of the room to light the small logs already cut and set ready to flame. When he returned to the bed he climbed in beside her, shifting to his side to look intently into her eyes.

She couldn't identify his expression, couldn't decide if it bothered or pleased her. "Rafe—"

"No. Don't." Without another word, Rafe took her face in his hands and kissed her, long, slow and deep.

Never hesitating, she kissed him back. It was a kiss full of tenderness and pain. Of forgiveness and remembrance. Of passion and friendship.

But hope? Could she hope that it could be all that and more?

Tonight she could only wonder, for an overwhelming sleepiness soon swept them both from that moment to separate dreams of moments gone by and moments yet to come.

Chapter Nine

The storm came quickly, sweeping over the land with a roar, flinging rain and wind at the house, rattling the windows and beating against the roof. Rafe stood watching lightning split the sky, giving him brief glimpses of shape and substance in the midnight darkness. The house was dark but he didn't pretend it was because he intended to sleep. He hadn't even tried.

He'd known agreeing to go with Jule to the Pinwa land was a mistake he shouldn't have made. For the last three days, he'd been paying the price.

Instead of answers about his past, he'd come back with more questions—unsettling questions about his true claim on Rancho Pintada. Why had Jed always insisted it would be worthless to look into his parents' background because no one among the Pinwa had wanted him? Why had Jed ever adopted him in the first place?

Those unknowns had revived a long-suppressed yearning in him to learn the truth, to finally understand his birth father and why Anoki had been adamant that Rafe belonged on Rancho Pintada instead of with the Pinwa. Why his mother had agreed even though it seemed she was conflicted. She hadn't wanted to leave the Pinwa, yet she had never given her son a chance to form any bonds with his Pinwa relatives. Some things didn't add up, raising questions in his mind. He had an uneasy feeling that if he found them, he wouldn't like the answers. That's why, until now, until Jule opened the door to his past by insisting they go to visit the Pinwa, he'd kept that door under lock and key.

Jule had started all of this digging up of his roots for him and Rafe didn't know whether to be grateful or resentful. Not knowing, at least, was familiar; he didn't have to worry about what was going to hit him from behind.

Nonetheless, those problems hadn't been consuming his thoughts for the past three days since they'd returned from their visit to the Pinwa. That honor belonged to Jule.

Fifteen-hour days, cold showers and attempts to focus on every other thing but her hadn't exorcised her from his head—or his body. Memories of her seemed to have seeped into his skin so that every touch, every sight or sound or scent reminded him of her.

It had been hell, being so close, wanting to touch her so badly that he swore he'd break without it. By the end of their night there, he'd been ready to give up a lifetime for one more day as Jule's lover.

She'd been avoiding him since then and he wondered if she felt the same. There was a time when he would have known. But that was a million yesterdays ago. And even if she did, what was he supposed to do about it?

He knew what he wanted to do.

He couldn't. Because if he ever let her that close again he wouldn't be able to let her go.

And being with her was impossible.

* * *

Jule tried sleeping. Again. Every night since she and Rafe had returned from their trip to the Pinwa reservation, she went through the same litany before climbing into bed: she needed the rest, without it she couldn't handle the heavy workload of clinic, patients and helping her mother. She was an adult with a strong will of her own; dreams shouldn't keep her awake at night.

All useless words and the last nonsense. Her dreams of Rafe had been haunting her nightly for years. Their trip together hadn't helped; if anything, it had made the dreams more tormenting.

For the last three days, she'd avoided the ranch—or more accurately, avoided Rafe.

Catalina had noticed but, apart from speculative looks, had wisely held her tongue. Jule was thankful for that much. In her present mood, she had no doubt she would have said something otherwise in reply that she would have later regretted.

She'd finally made up her mind she'd go back to the ranch in the afternoon, after she'd finished at the clinic. If nothing else, she'd agreed to take over her father's work, and that responsibility included Rafe's bison. It didn't make the thought of facing him again any easier nor did it make sleep come at all. She managed to doze off and on for a few hours until at one point, shortly after midnight, a loud clap of thunder jolted her upright. Storms didn't usually bother her, but, already edgy and tired, she couldn't go back to sleep and lie in bed for over an hour listening to the cacophony of wind, rain and thunder.

Finally, at about five, she gave up any pretense of trying to rest and got up, showered, dressed and went to make herself coffee. Fumbling for the light switch as she went, she took two steps inside the kitchen and nearly slipped on a puddle of cold water.

"What…" A fat droplet landed on her cheek and Jule looked up. A spreading wet stain marred the ceiling and water slowly dripped onto the floor.

The rain had slowed to a gentle patter so Jule pulled on her jacket and went outside to have a look. Sunrise barely edged the horizon and the cloud cover thickened what little light there was, making it impossible for her to see the location of the damage.

She gave up and went back in to do something about the mess in the kitchen and found her mother already there, mopping up the floor around the pan she'd put down to catch the drips.

"Here, let me finish that." She took the mop from her mother and started trying to contain the puddle that had spread over more than half of the kitchen floor. "I didn't wake you, did I?"

"No, the storm did that. I didn't know you were up until I saw the light on." Catalina gingerly edged around the water to start the coffeemaker.

"The storm woke me, too," Jule said, only half-truthfully. "I tried to get a look at the roof but I couldn't see anything. I don't think anything fell on it. The wind must have damaged part of it. There's not much we can do until it stops raining."

"I've been after your father to get that taken care of for years," Catalina said, with an exasperated shake of her head. "He's so busy but he wouldn't pay anyone to fix it. He kept saying he could do a better job himself and for less money. You know how he—" The strident ring of the phone interrupted her. She frowned as she hurried to pick it up.

As her mother answered, Jule paused in her mopping to check on the progress of the coffee, and was greedily inhaling the smell in anticipation of a much-needed infusion of caffeine when Catalina said, "Yes, we're leaving right away. Thank you."

Hanging up, she turned to Jule with a stricken look. "It's your father. He's had another fall."

Over an hour later, Jule stood next to her mother as Catalina held her husband's hand. Abran slept on, oblivious, but Jule knew without asking her mother would stay glued to his side until he woke again.

The doctor told them Abran had developed an infection.

Feverish and disoriented, he'd tried to get out of bed on his own and had fallen. The fall this time hadn't been as bad, only a few new bruises, but they were keeping Abran in the hospital long enough to get the infection under control and to make certain his hip was still healing well.

"Are you sure you'll be okay here on your own?" Jule asked quietly.

Catalina nodded, not taking her eyes off her husband. "You go ahead and go. Your father would want you to take care of things."

He'd expect it, Jule thought. She rubbed at her forehead, trying to ease the tension. Just as the full slate of clients and their animals expected her at the clinic. And Felix Ramos expected her at his ranch as soon as she could get away from the clinic. He'd called an hour after she and her mother had arrived at the hospital, agitated and wanting her there to deal with several of his sheep that had turned up sick. Jule also felt increasingly guilty about avoiding Rafe when she knew he needed her help with the bison, though she had no clue how she was going to fit in a visit to Rancho Pintada on top of everything else. Her plan to go this afternoon started to look tentative at best.

"I'm worried about the house," Catalina spoke into Jule's thoughts. "Something needs to be done about the roof." She glanced up at Jule in anticipation of her daughter's assurance it would be taken care of. "Do you think you could find time to have someone take a look at it? I need to be here with your father."

Jule put on a reassuring smile. "Don't worry, Mom. I'll take care of it."

She left her mother with a promise to return later in the afternoon and the weighty sensation of carrying everyone's problems on her shoulders today.

It didn't get better. The minute she walked in the door of the clinic, she was besieged, first by Lucia, her father's receptionist, who followed Jule as she went to stow her coat and bag, barely stopping for breath as she rattled off a list of problems that had come up, and then from a seemingly endless line of pet owners, all with various concerns that needed her immediate attention.

Underlying it all was the nagging knowledge she needed to get to the Ramos ranch and somehow to fit in a bison check.

Shortly before eleven, Jule flung herself into the chair behind her father's desk for a five-minute break and was seriously considering escaping out the window when the phone buzzed. It took all her willpower to answer without a sigh of exasperation.

"Jule?"

She nearly dropped the receiver. "Rafe?" She recovered enough at the surprise of hearing his voice to ask, "Is something wrong?"

"No. Not really." He paused and Jule could almost hear him carefully picking his words. "You haven't been here for a couple of days. I needed to check with you about the dosage for those newest calves and—"

"I can't do this right now," Jule snapped, unconsciously throwing his own favorite phrase back at him. "I'll try to get out there this evening, but whatever it is, it's going to have to wait until then."

"I didn't—"

"I'm doing the best I can, but right now everyone wants something and I can't do it all."

He didn't say anything for a moment, and Jule figured her uncharacteristic outburst had probably caught him off guard. "What's wrong?" he asked at last.

Anger, irrational and unguarded, flared up in her. "Why do you care? You haven't been too worried about how I feel about anything since I got back. Why does it matter now?" He started to answer but she didn't give him a chance. "You want to know what's wrong? Really? Well, let's see." Jule heard herself ranting, and despite the fact part of her was appalled at her lack of self-control, once she started, she couldn't stop. "My father fell again, so he'll be in the hospital longer and he and my mother expect me to become him, and that includes taking care of my father's business, taking care of my mother and finding someone to fix the damned roof. I've been bitten twice this morning and Mrs. Sanchez is accusing me of trying to kill her parrot. And then Felix Ramos is calling me every ten minutes because he's sure if I don't get out there pronto, all his sheep are going to fall over dead. Oh, and then there's you and your bison, which apparently can't get along without me for more than a day. Other than that, my life is wonderful!"

With her last defiant outburst, her anger abruptly deserted her, leaving her drained and a little embarrassed at having vented all her frustration on Rafe. Her frustration with him stopped her from apologizing. But since he probably figured she'd turned loco, she thought she should at least make an attempt to explain. "Look, this is just a bad time and I—"

She didn't get any further. Lucia poked her head in the door and with a rueful grimace announced, "Mrs. Sanchez is back."

Jule groaned, dropping her head into her hand.

"How about we try this again later?" Rafe's voice rumbled into her ear.

"Fine," Jule told him. "I have to go. I'll try and get by this evening. No promises."

She hung up before he could say anything else, wishing the world would just go away and leave her alone.

An hour later, Jule was getting ready to drag herself out to the Ramos ranch and check on the sheep when her mother called.

"He's mostly sleeping," Catalina said in answer to Jule's query about Abran. "Do you think you could come by earlier? I'm sure he'd like to see you and I could use the company."

"I'm sorry, Mom, but I can't. I can ask Lucia to come and pick you up if you want to go home, but I can't get away right now."

"No, no, I don't want to leave your father alone. I'll just stay until you can get here."

Jule sighed inwardly. One more thing to feel guilty over, she thought, as she hung up the phone and started to gather up her things. There wasn't much she could do, though, and so she tried to put it aside on her ever-growing mental pile of things to cope with later.

The office door opened again and expecting Lucia with yet another problem, Jule looked up in resignation.

Rafe was standing there.

Stunned, Jule just stared.

He shifted, not quite meeting her eyes. But there was a determined set to his mouth and shoulders. "I thought you could use a hand with Ramos's sheep."

Jule opened her mouth but her brain couldn't think of a single thing to say. It was so unlike Rafe, or at least the man he'd become, that she wondered if too many sleepless nights had left her delusional.

He seemed to think her hesitation meant she was trying to find a way to say no, so he hurried out with the rest of it. "Look, it sounded to me like you've got more than you can handle today." Stepping up to her, he took her hand in his. "Let me help."

Tears burned her eyes. Not trusting her voice, Jule nodded and Rafe's expression softened. His hand tightened around hers and she could see the relief in his eyes, as if her answer had been important to him. "Please," she whispered.

It was all the encouragement he needed. Rafe gathered her into his arms and held her for long moments, letting her lean on his strength.

It felt so good, like a sanctuary from everything bad and frustrating, she never wanted to leave. It had been so long since she had leaned on anyone, physically or emotionally, that her body and soul felt starved. She closed her eyes, savoring every nuance of the feel of his arms holding her, the sound of his heart against ear, the scent of wind and earth and him.

It couldn't last forever, or even ten minutes, though and Jule finally pulled back. "Rafe, I—"

"Don't," he said, silencing her with his fingertips against her lips. "You don't have to tell me anything." She could only nod and his mouth briefly quirked into a ghost of a smile. "Come on, I'll drive you out to the Ramos farm. You can catch a cat nap on the way."

She answered him with a smile.

Several hours later, after he'd helped Jule finish with the last of the sheep, Rafe leaned against his truck, watching her as she gave Felix Ramos some last-minute instructions and a promise she'd be back in a couple of days. The time he'd spent here with her was time he couldn't really afford to lose, considering everything waiting for him back at the ranch. But he hadn't been thinking about the ranch or his problems.

Instead, he'd been savoring a deep sense of satisfaction because Jule needed him.

He'd never seen her so vulnerable. In the past, he'd truly believed she could do anything, deal with any problem, that her strength was boundless. All those years, she'd loved him, but she'd never seemed to need him. She'd been the one who'd held them together, who'd fought for them. She'd been right that night they'd argued; all along, it had been her who'd been reaching out all these weeks, trying to mend what had been broken between them, while he'd given up on believing it could ever happen.

This morning, though, when he'd heard the stress and frustration in her voice, something in him cracked: the walls he'd put up to defend his heart against caring for her. He hadn't stopped to think. He'd just gone to her.

He straightened as she walked back to the truck, her hands bracing her lower back. "You've done all you can."

She shrugged, shaking her head. "Maybe. Right now nothing feels like enough."

"Trust me. It is. Come on, I'll take you back."

"I need to get to the hospital and—damn. I forgot about the house." Jule rubbed at her forehead, tightly closing her eyes for a moment. "I've got to find someone to take a look at the roof or Mom's going to have a fit. Any ideas?"

"Yeah," Rafe told her, taking her hand and leading her to climb into the passenger seat. "Let's grab some lunch and then I'll take a look at it before you call your mom. Maybe afterward you'll be able to give her some better news." When she only nodded in agreement, Rafe eyed her warily. "That was too easy."

"Remind me to protest later," she said, laying her head back against the seat. "Right now, I'm more than willing to let you take over for a while."

Stopping to pick up sandwiches on the way, Rafe drove her back to her parents' house and, after a quick meal, found a ladder and climbed up to the roof to survey the damage, first outside then in. "It's not too bad," he said, as he finished looking over the kitchen ceiling. "With a few supplies, I can fix this in a couple of hours."

"Rafe, I don't think—"

"Are you gonna argue with me or let me take care of it and spare yourself one of your mom's fits?"

Her mouth twitched in a smile. "I don't think I could handle an argument and a fit right now. But you've already done enough today. I can—"

"Go get your mom, check on your dad, and let me take care of this. Besides, she may have that fit anyway when she finds me here," he said with a wry smile. "So don't be so sure I'm doing you any favors."

"You are, believe me."

"And where have you been spending half your time the last few weeks?"

"That's part of my job. This is…" Fumbling for words, she gave up. "I want to do something in return."

"Then go get your mom and let me get those supplies and get to work. I'll take you back to your truck on my way."

Taking her to the clinic so she could retrieve her truck, Rafe pulled out behind her as she headed to the hospital feeling almost light-hearted. It was an emotional high, more intense because he couldn't remember the last time he'd felt anything like it.

And he didn't stop to think how dangerously addictive it could be.

Chapter Ten

Jule nearly took the coward's way out. She almost convinced herself it would be better not to tell her parents about Rafe being there, helping with the house repairs, until right before she and her mother pulled into the driveway. No matter when she told them, they'd argue and question her judgment in accepting Rafe's help, and, tired, with hours left to go in the day, she really wasn't up to defending her decisions.

But when she walked into the hospital room, she found her father awake and strong enough to barrage her with questions about the clinic and the Ramos's sheep and how she'd dealt with the more difficult of his patients.

Catalina sat next to him, her hand on his, trying unsuccessfully to distract him from his concerns about his practice. "You're going to have the doctor back in here making Jule and me leave," she gently admonished.

"I've been telling Mrs. Sanchez there's nothing wrong with that damned parrot of hers nearly every week for years now," Abran went on, ignoring her. "I hope you told her, Jule, that—"

"Abran! Jule can take care of whatever it is." Catalina turned to her daughter. "Did you find someone to look at the roof?"

Thinking Mrs. Sanchez's parrot would be a better topic, Jule nodded. "Don't worry about it. It should be fixed this afternoon."

Catalina beamed at her in pleased approval, but Abran eyed her with suspicious frown. "Who did you find to fix it? I hope you didn't call that Muñoz fellow. He wanted to charge me a ridiculous amount for something I could have taken care of in a few hours."

"No." *Better get it over with.* "Rafe volunteered to fix it. He's over there, taking care of it now."

For several seconds, both her parents just looked at her as if they expected her to say "Gotcha!" and take it back.

"You asked *Rafe* to take care of it? Rafe Garrett?" her father asked with a tone that suggested Jule had crossed a forbidden line. "Is there some reason why you couldn't have called someone qualified to take care of it? What were you thinking?"

"Rafe volunteered," Jule repeated. "And I was thinking that the roof needed repairing. Don't—" she said, holding up a hand when both her parents started to protest. "Please, Rafe's been great today. He showed up at the clinic and helped me deal with the sheep and he offered to help with the house. He's been there for me when no one else has. I couldn't have taken care of everything without him."

"I thought your leaving had finished these discussions about Rafe Garrett," Abran grumbled. "Apparently there are some things you still haven't outgrown because you continue to insist on defending him at every opportunity. And now this."

Tired of denying it, Jule said simply, "You're right, I haven't outgrown Rafe and I'm not likely to. But we're not going to argue it out right now." Going over to her father, she bent and kissed his cheek. "You're tired and Mom needs to get home. We'll be back tomorrow."

"You shouldn't have told your father about Rafe," Catalina said as soon as they'd left the room and started back to the parking lot. "You know how he feels about him. He hates the idea that you might be starting something with Rafe again."

"I can't fix that," Jule said. "I'm sorry if I upset you or Dad, but you would have told him anyway. And then he would have been more upset because he would have thought I was hiding it from him."

Catalina gave her a stricken look but didn't reply.

Jule sighed. "I'm doing the best I can, Mom."

When they got to the house, Rafe was still at work on the roof. Giving him the barest of glances, Catalina went straight inside, but Jule waited for Rafe to climb down.

Despite the chill in the air, he'd stripped off his jacket. Dampened by sweat, his shirt clung to him, and she found herself watching the play of muscle under the fabric as he backed down the ladder and strode over to her.

"It wasn't that bad," he told her, wiping a forearm over his brow. "An hour or so and I'll be done. Then I'll see what I can do about the inside. How's your dad?"

"Irritated at the world, but doing better," Jule said. She waved at the nearly completed repairs. "This will be fixed a lot faster than he will. Thanks to you."

Rafe shrugged off her gratitude. "Your mother's upset with this. Although probably nothing like your father."

She gave a short, sharp shake of her head. "It doesn't matter. They'll get over it."

"Not before they both give you a large measure of grief," he said, eyeing her knowingly.

"I told you, it doesn't matter. You're here and that's all that matters to me." She touched his forearm and felt the quick flex of muscle, as if he'd suddenly caught his breath. "You don't know how much it matters."

"It's no big deal," he said gruffly.

Jule smiled. "So you keep telling me. I'd better get inside.

I've got to finish cleaning up. If you need anything, let me know."

Contrary to Rafe's prediction, Catalina said very little over the next hour as Jule helped her finish cleaning up the mess in the kitchen. Knowing her mother was upset over the confrontation between Jule and Abran, Jule didn't press her to talk about it, deciding nothing she could say would sway her mother's feelings about Rafe being there.

She began to consider the idea of dinner when the door rattled with a sharp knock and she hurried to let Rafe in.

"That's done," he said, stepping inside the doorway. He glanced behind her as if he half expected her mother to be waiting and ready to show him the way back out again.

Jule couldn't help laughing. "Don't worry. She's not the type to throw things. The worst you can expect is a few reproachful looks."

"I'm not worried for me," Rafe said quietly. He searched her face and whatever he saw there made him frown. "I'm worried about you."

"I've had more than my share of reproachful looks. I think I'll survive. Come on, I'll show you the ceiling."

He followed her into the kitchen and Catalina looked up from pouring herself a cup of coffee when he shouldered his way through the narrow doorway. Rafe nodded to her and Catalina acknowledged it with a dip of her chin before turning to Jule.

"I have some letters to catch up on," she said, grabbing up her cup. "Let me know if there's something I can do."

After Catalina had gone, Jule dropped into a chair. Pushing her hands into her hair, she sighed.

"Well—" Rafe shrugged when she looked up. He shifted from one foot to the other, then muttered, "Could've been worse, I guess."

His reply struck Jule as absurdly funny, and she started to laugh, a substitute for crying that eased some of the tension tautening her neck and shoulders. "It could've been better, too, but my belief in miracles doesn't extend quite that far."

"The only miracle so far is she hasn't kicked me out. I'd better take a look at this before she changes her mind."

Surveying the ceiling, he got to work. Jule stayed, mostly watching him, enjoying the bunch and stretch of hard muscle under his shirt and jeans, the strength and efficiency in the way he moved, the intensity of his expression as he focused on solving the problem as quickly as possible. Occasionally, he asked her to hand him something; otherwise he said little.

Jule was content with the quiet between them. It was undemanding. Rafe had always been good in letting his silences and his actions speak instead of his words, and tonight she found that comforting, soothing the rough patches on her nerves left by the demands of the day.

He was just finishing when Catalina came back into the kitchen to return her coffee cup and paused to look over Rafe's handiwork. "You've done a good job," she said, grudging approval in her voice.

Rafe, starting to clean up, glanced her way. "It needs paint but it'll have to sit for a day first."

"I'm sure Jule can take care of that," Catalina said. She drew herself up, her hands pressed together. "Thank you for all the work you've done. I know it's been a great help to Jule." The words sounded forced and Jule knew her mother would rather Rafe left quickly but was too polite to come out and say it.

Rafe had obviously gotten the message. His expression shuttered in a way she recognized too well. Even so, he made an effort—for her sake, she was sure—to answer with an equal measure of stilted politeness. "I need to be going. I've got a lot of work to catch up on. I'm sure Josh hasn't gotten started on any of it."

"Why don't you stay for dinner?" Jule asked. Her mother stiffened and shot her a disbelieving glance. Jule pretended she hadn't seen. "It's the least I can do after everything you've done for me today."

He hesitated, looking from her to Catalina and back again. "Thanks. But I should go."

Jule walked with him back to his truck, upset with her mother and wishing she could find a way to keep Rafe here just a little while longer. Of all the days since she'd been back, this one had meant the most and she didn't want it to end.

"We could go get dinner out, before you go home," she suggested.

Shaking his head, he gently told her, "It's been a long day. You need to get some rest. And I don't want to make things worse for you with your mother."

Tears welled up inside her again, caused not just by the stresses of the day. She'd so rarely seen him like this lately, understanding and supportive. What could she say to make him see how much it meant to her that he cared enough to be there to help her.

Instead of trying to put her feelings into words, she stepped close to him, laying her hands against his chest. "Thank you," she whispered. "For everything."

Stretching up, she kissed him.

For a terrifying moment, he didn't respond. Then with an abruptness that caught her off guard, he pulled her fully against him and kissed her back. His mouth moved against hers, softly, full of feeling so sweet and deep Jule wondered how she'd lived without it so long.

She leaned into him, sliding her hands around his neck, wanting more, everything. Everything she'd denied herself for so long because it never felt right with anyone else. Only Rafe.

Wanting, needing him, she teased her tongue over his lower lip, inviting him to deepen the caress and was rewarded when he abandoned his reserve, his hands and mouth hungry for her as if he too had been starved of this feeling for too long.

For minutes—hours, days, time seemed suspended, she

didn't know for how long—she dared to hope she'd finally broken down his shield against wanting her, loving her. But then, she felt him make an effort to rein in his feelings and very gently, as if he were afraid of shattering something too fragile to touch, eased away.

She braced herself for the cold that would invade her heart and body when he let her go. Instead, Rafe slowly traced a finger over her cheek and mouth before gathering her into his arms. He held her for a small eternity, wrapped closely against him, his face buried in her hair.

And the cold never came.

Rafe stood under the freezing spray of the shower and decided if there were any mercy left in the world, he'd die right here and put his body out of its misery.

Apart from the night with Jule that was etched on his soul, he couldn't remember the last time he'd been with a woman. Those brief sexual encounters over the years hadn't meant anything but temporary release. He'd never call it making love. Except with Jule.

Slamming the shower off, he leaned his forehead against the cold tile. It had taken all his willpower to pull away from Jule and leave her tonight.

Everything in him had wanted to crush her to him and make love to her, right there, on her parents' front lawn, and then keep her with him and make love to her again somewhere else, everywhere else, so completely that she'd never leave again and he'd never be able to let her go.

And then what?

Loving her wouldn't change anything any more than it had thirteen years ago. Things weren't different; they'd only gotten older and their problems more complicated. He still had nothing to offer her and she was still out of his reach.

After today, though, he'd given up trying to convince

himself he didn't care. He couldn't lie to himself any more. He loved her. He always had. He always would.

And he didn't have a clue what he was going to do about it.

Jule lay back in the bath thinking about Rafe while trying to let the warm, lavender-scented water soak away her worries and frustrations and ease the tension she felt crawling over her back, up into her shoulders and neck.

It might have worked if the tension had come from the stresses of the day. She knew it hadn't. It belonged to Rafe and that kiss she couldn't get out of her head.

It had felt so good to lean on him today, and suddenly the realization hit her that maybe that was the reason things had been so good between them.

Jule thought of all the times she'd been there for him, shared his problems and his pain, but she'd never let him return the favor.

She knew that in some ways he idolized her and lacked the confidence he could ever be what she deserved. Today, though, she'd let him help her and, without trying, had let him feel as though he could be important to her, as though she did need him.

All these years, unconsciously, she'd been doing with him the same thing she'd always done with her parents—trying to live up to their image of someone strong and unbreakable, someone who could do anything, handle any challenge, tackle any problem. Rafe had never expected or demanded that of her, but she'd done it just the same.

Rafe needed to be needed, and she needed to let herself lean on him once in a while, to admit that she couldn't always be that unshakeable, reliable person everyone turned to when they needed help.

Rafe, her parents, nearly everyone assumed she could never stumble or fall.

Except they were wrong. She could, and the next time she did she wanted Rafe there to catch her again.

Only she didn't know if it was fair to expect him to want that, too.

* * *

This is a bad idea. The thought kept rolling around in his head even as he punched in Jule's cell number. He felt like a teenage boy calling for a first date. That was closer to the truth than Rafe wanted to admit.

He and Jule had never officially dated. They'd been together since they were kids and, without saying anything to each other, had stayed together until she'd left Luna Hermosa. He'd never really asked her out because there'd never been a need, she'd always been there. And after she'd gone, he'd never dated anyone else. He'd hardly call a few one-night stands he'd rather forget dates.

Now he felt totally clueless. How could he make this sound casual instead of desperate?

When he heard her say hello, he nearly hung up.

"Calling me twice in two days," she gently teased when she recognized his voice. "That's got to be a record for you."

"Yeah, well. Sorry it's early. I've got to come into town to run a couple of errands. I wanted to—I mean, I thought maybe we could meet at the diner. For breakfast." Rafe wondered if slow torture would be less painful than getting those words out.

"I'd love to," she said and the warmth and pleasure in her voice soothed over the tension in him, making it okay again. "What time?"

"Eight, maybe?"

She readily agreed and Rafe hung up a few minutes later, feeling pretty satisfied with himself.

He felt a lot better when he walked up to the diner doors and found her waiting for him, a happy smile lighting her whole face.

"Don't start," Rafe warned when Nova came over to their booth with coffee, curiosity written so clearly on her face that she might as well have stamped it there in neon lights.

"What?" Nova asked, all innocence. She flashed a knowing look between Jule and him. "I just came to ask what you wanted. Apart from each other, that is," she added with a wink that earned her a dark glower from Rafe.

When Nova had left to give the cook their orders, Rafe looked at Jule, surprised to find her smiling. "What's so funny?"

"You." She started to laugh. "If looks could kill—"

"I'd have been stepping over Nova's dead body a long time ago," he muttered, trying to sound gruffly serious and failing in the face of Jule's laughter.

Her high spirits continued throughout the meal as they talked about the bison and her work at the clinic and Jule's growing conviction that her father might not be able to resume his practice.

"Which leaves you where?" Rafe couldn't help but ask, not sure what answer he wanted to hear. She'd told him at the party she was thinking of staying for him. But he was pretty sure she'd thrown that at him to get a reaction, not because she'd given it any serious thought.

"Oh, I haven't thought that far ahead," Jule said with a seemingly nonchalant shrug. "Of course, the reason Dad wanted me here in the first place was to groom me to take over for him. I can't say that I haven't thought about it, but I haven't made any decisions yet." She finished with a questioning glance at him.

Rafe hesitated then said, "You need to do what you want and not let your parents talk you into anything."

He really wanted to beg her to stay. He held back because he wasn't convinced her staying in Luna Hermosa was best for her; it sure as hell would make his life more difficult than it already was.

"The St. John's festival is next week."

Rafe blinked, blindsided by the sudden change of subject. "Uh, yeah. I knew that."

"Come with me."

"I—"

"Please," she asked. She briefly touched his hand. "I'd like to go but I don't want to go alone." A sly expression crept into her eyes. "My only other alternative is Josh. And I know how you felt about that the last time I accepted his invitation."

Rafe let that one go for another more pressing question. "Why do I get the feeling this is about you trying to organize another family reunion?"

"I have no idea whether or not any of your brothers will be there," Jule said but her telltale blush told him he'd been right. "Would it be so bad if they were?"

"It'd be better if they weren't."

"Rafe…"

He held up his hands in surrender. "Fine. You win. This time," he warned, since she couldn't hide the satisfaction in her expression. "And only because I want to talk to Sawyer anyway."

"Really?" Her brows raised in surprise. "Why?"

"Some questions about Jed and Theresa," he said, deliberately leaving out any details. Since their visit to the Pinwa land, he'd been nagged by feelings that he'd been handed a clue to his past, but he had no idea what it was or what to do with it yet. He didn't want to mention anything to Jule until he had something more concrete to go on than suspicions and half-formed theories.

Jule looked like she had more questions begging to be asked. Instead she nodded, apparently accepting his explanation for now, though Rafe had no doubt she'd tackle him about it later. "Then it's a date? For the festival?"

She smiled as she asked, and Rafe was lost. Had been since the day she'd walked back into his life despite his best efforts to fight it. "Yeah," he said slowly, "it's a date."

Chapter Eleven

By the time the morning of the festival to honor St. John, the patron saint of Luna Hermosa, rolled around, Jule had most of her limited wardrobe strewn about her room. Since college, she'd had little time to shop for clothes; it was a luxury her schedule wouldn't allow. But today, she wished she'd taken the time to find something special. Everything she owned looked drab, overworn or out of style.

A soft knock drew her from where she hovered over the pile of discarded clothes on her bed. She looked up to see her mother, a wide smile on her face. "Good morning," Catalina said. "You're certainly up early."

"Rafe is picking me up for the festival in half an hour. We wanted to get there early enough to help ready the streets for the parade. I haven't done this since I was in high school, you know."

"I know," Catalina said, making her way through the mess in Jule's room. "And from the look of this, most of those clothes are probably from high school as well, am I right?"

Jule plunked herself down atop the heap on her bed, sinking her chin into her hands. Not bothering to raise her eyes to her mother, she sighed. "Not quite, but close."

"That's why I bought this for you." Catalina produced a plastic-encased hanger. "Here, try it on. I think it is perfect for today."

"What's this?" Jule looked at the plastic bag and then at her mother.

Catalina smiled. "Why don't you open it and find out?"

"I just didn't expect—you do remember I'm going with Rafe, right?"

"I didn't get it for him. You've been such a big help to me and your father, I wanted to do something for you."

"Oh, Mom, you don't need to do anything, but thank you." Jule unzipped the plastic and found a soft, casual fall dress inside. The fabric was a lush autumn bronze; the dress a simple shift that tied at the waist and flared at the bottom. The gift was doubly pleasing because she knew her mother saw Jule's attending the festival with Rafe as one more step toward a potential reconciliation that Catalina couldn't approve of. "It's so elegant, just like you."

"Well, you are my daughter and this one had your name on it. Besides, it should go perfectly with those boots you're so fond of. Now hurry, try it on. You don't have much time before he gets here."

Catalina helped Jule into the new dress and, as her mother had predicted, it fitted like a glove. Jule spun around in it once, loving the way the long skirt flared out in the air. She threw her arms around her mother's neck. "How can I thank you?"

"By hurrying up so I don't have to answer the door for Rafe in my robe and slippers. Now sit down and I'll French-braid your hair like I did when you were a little girl. That look will suit this dress perfectly."

Obediently, Jule sat at her dressing table, applying a little mascara and blush as her mother painstakingly braided her long, stubborn mass of hair. She pulled her boots on and took a last glance in the mirror. "You are a miracle worker," she told her mother as she hugged her tightly.

Catalina returned the embrace then pulled back far enough to stroke Jule's cheek. "My daughter, I wish I were."

"I really do appreciate this, Mom," Jule said. She took her mother's hand in hers. "Especially since I know how you feel about Rafe and me."

"How I feel doesn't matter today." Pressing Jule's hand, Catalina smiled a little. "Today, I've decided that is exactly what you need."

By the time Rafe and Jule found a parking spot not too far from the action at the center of town the sun was beginning to melt away the morning chill. They'd begun walking toward town when Jule touched Rafe's arm to stop him. "Wait. I'm sorry, but I don't think I'll need this coat and I don't want to have to carry it all day. May I put it back in your truck?"

Rafe nodded. "If you're sure." He hadn't said or done much more than that since picking her up, leaving Jule to wonder if he was having second thoughts about accepting her invitation.

"Yes. I won't need it until evening."

As Rafe unlocked the door and she tossed her coat inside, he watched her, the slow appraisal making Jule warm. "You look good, Jule. In that dress, I'll have to guard you from the wolves."

Jule turned, surprised. "I didn't think you'd even noticed."

"I noticed. The dress is new and you used to braid your hair that way when we were kids."

"That's because you used to pull my braid."

Rafe reached around to tug at the end of her hair. "Like this?"

"Ouch! You haven't grown up one bit! I should pull your tail right back." She pulled her braid away from him and started walking again. "But I won't."

"I get it," he said, catching up in a few long strides. "You're too grown-up and sophisticated for that now. Or, more likely, you know I'd have you pinned before you got close."

Abruptly, Jule whirled and lunged for his hair. "Oh yeah?"

Without so much as a flinch, he caught her wrists and brought her up against his chest. Because it was where she wanted to be, Jule gave up the struggle easily and tilted her head to look into his eyes.

"That was even easier than when you were eight," he murmured huskily. "Not much of a fighter are you?"

"I pick my fights these days. Something you could do more of, by the way."

For the first time this morning, Rafe smiled, slow and easy. "And you don't stop until you win? Is that how it is?"

"Yes. Exactly."

His grip on her softened and he shifted his hands so they were covering hers. His eyes looked almost black, so dark they hid any expression, the only clue to his mood the soft, rough quality of his voice matching the rub of his thumb against her palm. "Would you fight for me?"

For a moment, she stared at him, dumbfounded that he could ask that question. She'd been fighting for him—for them— most of her life. "I can't believe you're asking me that."

"Why? Because you won't anymore?"

"Because that's the wrong question." Jule pulled herself free of his hold and started walking away, in the direction of the festival sounds and activity. "What you should be asking yourself is will *you* fight for *me?*"

A few volunteers were still working on cleaning and clearing the main street when Rafe and Jule reached town. Everything had to be perfect to show appreciation to the town's patron saint for another good year. Preparations for the annual autumn event had begun weeks and weeks ago with musicians and dancers practicing their roles and preparing costumes.

Her mother had been cooking for two weeks, freezing stacks and stacks of her delicious flour tortillas. Other cooks would have made red chili, posole, beans and rice, enough to feed a good portion of the town at the feast at the end of the day.

"Hurry, the parade is about to begin," an excited little boy running past them was calling out to the volunteers.

"Is there anything we can do?" Jule asked a woman brandishing a large push broom.

"No, we're about finished." She looked up from her task. "Why, Julene Santiago, it *is* you. Nova told me you were back. I haven't seen you since high-school graduation. I'm sure you don't remember me. I'm Nova's mother, Darcy."

Jule had only a vague memory of Darcy Vargas. There was little of Nova in the short, sturdy woman, her light-brown hair sticking out in tufts from under a faded red bandana. Nova, sassy and beautiful, left an impression; Darcy, plain and quiet, would be difficult to remember. Not wanting to pretend to remember, Jule settled for, "It's nice to see you again."

"And Rafe," Darcy said. "Haven't seen you in a good while either."

"Hi, Darcy." He laid a hand on the broom handle. "Can I do that for you?"

"Oh, no thanks. I'm done. We'd better catch up with the others. They've all left to join the parade."

The three of them began walking to where the parade would start. Townsfolk of all ages flanked them, excited voices filling the crisp morning air.

"I hear you've been handling your father's practice and helping Rafe with his bison. Quite a lot of responsibility for a young woman. But then you always were an ambitious girl. I wish some of your drive had rubbed off on Nova."

Jule felt a little awkward. "My parents really didn't give me a choice," she said, regretting it as soon as the words came out of her mouth. "I mean—"

Darcy patted Jule's arm. "It's okay, honey. I was way too easy on her. After her daddy ran away I just wanted her to have everything her heart desired, I guess to try to make up for not having her father. Anyhow, I wound up spoiling her rotten and ruining any ambition she might have had."

"Nova doesn't need ambition," Rafe put in. "She's the best waitress in town. And she's got most of the men in Luna Hermosa at her mercy."

Darcy laughed. "Well, that is something isn't it? But it isn't anything like being a veterinarian. I'm sure you're very proud of Julène. She's really made something of her life."

The implication being Rafe had not. Jule's smile hardened. "So has Rafe. He's taken over most of the responsibilities at Rancho Pintada. And he's taking the ranch in a whole new direction."

"So I hear. I sure hope that buffalo herd makes it. But with Julene here, no doubt your animals will be fine in no time."

Rafe's expression gave nothing away. "I'm counting on it."

To anyone who didn't know Rafe as intimately as she did, there were no outward signs Darcy's careless comments had affected him at all. But Jule recognized the tightness around his mouth and jaw and knew Darcy had unwittingly hit him hard where it hurt most. This wasn't how she wanted the day to start, and she hoped they weren't going to run into any more old acquaintances who wanted to push her more tangible accomplishments and skills in Rafe's face.

Curling her hand around his forearm, she lightly squeezed. "I see some friends, we'd better say goodbye for now, Darcy. It was nice to talk with you again."

"You, too. Good luck to you both with those buffalo."

When they'd gotten safely out of hearing range, Rafe turned to Jule. "You're wasting your breath."

"What do you mean?"

"Trying to convince anyone around here that I'm good for Jed's ranch. They can't figure out why he bothered with me in the first place."

"I don't know that. You've been nothing but hardworking and dedicated to that ranch ever since you were a boy." The thought sparked Jule's secret jealousy. "Too dedicated some-times, if you ask me."

"I didn't ask you. You've always resented the time I put in there."

"I don't resent it and that's not fair." It was a lie, not a very good one. She did resent it, deeply and irrationally. "I'd just like to see you get some recognition for it."

"It's not going to happen with Jed," he flung a hand out toward the gathering crowd, "or from them."

Though he hadn't intended it, Rafe's gesture caught the eye of Val Ortiz. Jule saw her grab her husband, Paul's, arm and start in their direction. "Looks like you've brought us company for the walk to church, whether you wanted it or not."

"Not."

"It's too late now. The whole family is coming this way."

The family moved in beside Jule and Rafe in the procession of people lined up to follow the priest, who carried a statue of St. John, other clergy, a couple of dozen male dancers, the same number of female dancers and a band of strolling musi-cians.

"Good morning," Val said, her smile bright. Her eyes darted between Jule and Rafe. Jule could almost hear her questions. "Mind if we walk with you? We were supposed to meet Rico and Cat, but we got here late." She glanced down to Johnnie in his stroller, happily chattering at his sisters and any passersby who paid him attention. "Somebody is being potty-trained and wouldn't finish his task, if you know what I mean."

Completely clueless, Jule smiled anyway. "Not really, but I'll take your word for it."

"Good to see you, Rafe," Paul was saying. "I think this is the first time we've seen you at one of these parties."

"Yeah. Probably."

Two-word conversations were Rafe's specialty and Jule accepted with an inward sigh she was going to be trying to fill the gap all day. "Your girls look adorable today. I love their dresses," she told Val as she admired the beautiful traditional red, purple and pink-layered skirts they wore.

"I barely finished hemming those last night. Now that they're back in school and Johnnie has started day care, my schedule is out of control."

Again, Jule had no idea what it must be like to juggle a family, house and husband. But the contented smile on Val's face told her that however challenging it was, it suited her well.

"Val is amazing," Paul said. "I don't know how she manages it all." He bent to kiss his wife on the forehead. "We don't deserve you, you know?"

Val beamed. "I know. Just don't you forget it."

Jule ventured a glance at Rafe and caught him watching her again. The appraising look in his eyes made her uncomfortable. It was as if he could read her thoughts and knew her feelings better than she did.

Though she couldn't define it, she wanted some part of what Val and Paul had. Not necessarily the traditional family unit, but at least the tenderness, closeness and love they so obviously shared. Like Maya and Sawyer and so many other couples she knew, Paul and Val made it seem so natural, so easy to be in love. Why did it have to be so complicated and difficult for Rafe and her?

Rafe offered her no answers. Instead, his impassive expression and the hard set of his jaw reminded her he couldn't—or wouldn't—ever be able simply to love her.

As the procession moved toward the old adobe church where they would ask for a blessing for the saint, Val chattered with Jule, and Paul managed to get a few words of conversation out of Rafe about the ranch and Rafe's brothers.

Paul picked up one twin and nudged Rafe to pick up the other so the girls could see the activities above the crowd. Rafe looked taken aback at the casual request but after a moment's hesitation, complied. He picked up the little girl easily, but held her awkwardly, as if he were afraid of doing it the wrong way.

The sight of Rafe with a child in his arms distracted Jule from the spectacle in front of them. He looked uneasy with a role he'd never played before, but the girl simply held to his shoulder and laughed, her happy smile a sharp contrast to Rafe's near scowl.

As they walked down Main Street they all watched the excitement around them unfold. Male dancers, dressed in black pants and red shirts, led their partners, women wearing bright-red skirts with layers of blues, greens and pinks underneath, through a series of traditional steps all the way to the church. The dancers shook gourd rattles in one hand and played a three-pronged instrument with the other. Strolling guitarists set the music and pace for the dancers as they wove in and out through the procession.

"Papa! Look! The *toro* and the *auvelo!*"

Jule turned toward a little boy's voice. Close by she saw Sancia Gonzales, her husband Miguel and their three children. The youngest boy sat atop his father's shoulders, bouncing excitedly and pointing to where a man dressed as a *toro,* or bull, darted toward the *avuelo,* or witch doctor. The two carried out an elaborate and entertaining skit, skillfully creating the appearance of a bullfight with a magical witch doctor who would manage to suppress and tame the bull by the time the crowd reached the old adobe church at the end of the road.

Gradually, as people entered the church, they fell silent. Rafe set Paul's daughter down and she grabbed her sister's hand. Jule smiled, watching as the two little girls tried to squeeze their way to the front of the church for a bird's-eye view of the blessing of the saint.

Jule slid into a pew, Rafe following her. They knelt side by side as mass began. Jule's thoughts drifted to what it would be like to have a wedding in the beautifully simple old Mission church. These were the rough-hewn pine pews her family, and most families in town, had sat in since she was a little girl. She'd certainly been to enough weddings here while growing up.

Once, when she was ten and Rafe twelve, she'd even attended her own.

Stealing away from the ranch, they'd ridden a single horse into town. They'd sneaked into the church and gone through the motions of their own make-believe wedding, using rubber bands for wedding rings. But not until now with Rafe so close his arm and thigh brushed hers, had she let herself imagine their real wedding taking place here.

She opened her eyes and found him watching her. For a moment, she glimpsed the emotion layered in his dark gaze, tenderness, regret, longing and something akin to grief, as if he mourned everything lost in the past.

"I remember," he whispered huskily.

"I married you that day wearing dirty overalls."

"You were a beautiful bride. A little young maybe. But beautiful."

Laughter and tears tussled for control. "Only you would say that."

"Because it's true." He gently brushed his fingers over her cheek. "You're still the most beautiful girl I've ever laid eyes on."

Their exchange had attracted the attention of several of the people sitting near to them. Noticing the sidelong glances they were getting, Jule took Rafe's hand, lacing her fingers with his. "If we don't behave, Father Biega is going to kick us out of church again, just like he did that day."

Rafe smiled a little and appeared to focus on the service. But he didn't remove his hand.

When the blessing was complete and everyone had taken communion, Jule watched as the saint was handed over to the head of the household whose honor it was to house him for the coming year. The ritual had been the same as far back as she could recall.

"I remember the year my father had the saint," she said to Rafe as they rose from the pew to return to the procession. "Our house was like Grand Central Station. My mother loved playing hostess to all the visitors who came to ask for blessings. But my dad was counting the days until it was over."

"I wouldn't know much about that. The only time I've been in this church is that day we were here."

"Really? I would have thought Theresa—"

"Theresa took her own sons. She didn't bother with me. Jed isn't Catholic, so he didn't bother either. I was the outsider then and still am."

"It was nice when we were children, and neither of us knew that or cared," Jule said quietly.

"I've always known it. But the day I was with you in this church, I didn't care."

People were pouring out of the church on either side of them now, but Jule didn't want to leave yet. Suddenly, filled with old memories and feelings, she wasn't done with the subject. She grabbed Rafe's hand, pulled him out of the line and over to a darkened corner near a red-velvet draped confessional booth.

"What?" he asked. "I thought were supposed to head over to St. John's new home for some big dinner."

"In a few minutes. I'm not done with this."

"I am."

"Don't walk out on me this time."

His back to her, Rafe stopped, paused then turned. "This isn't the time or the place."

"Tell me then, when will it be the right time or the right place?"

"What's the matter with you? Why are you pushing this now?"

"What's the matter with *me*? The matter with me is I can't stop loving you!"

If she'd expected her outburst to erase all the heartache and the wasted years and have him pulling her into his arms and confessing in return that he'd never stopped loving her, she was doomed to disappointment. Instead, Rafe's scowl deepened and she could see the effort he was making to control his temper in the convulsive flexing of his hands.

Around them, friends and acquaintances darted glances at them and whispers to each other. They could have been alone for all either of them noticed.

"Why can't you say it?" Jule took a step toward him, angry and desolate and afraid all at once. "Why? All these years and I just want to hear you say you love me."

A tear slid down her cheek and it did what none of her words had been able to. With a muffled curse, Rafe jerked her into his arms and held her, sobbing, against his chest.

He held her like that for what seemed like hours, gently stroking her hair, her back, while the church emptied of people and she cried for them both.

When finally she'd spent the strongest of her emotions, Jule pulled back a few inches and saw the splotch of mixed mascara and tears she'd left on his shirt. "I'm sorry," she mumbled. "I think I've ruined your shirt."

"You know me. I couldn't care less."

"I do know you, Rafe. That's the point. I know you better than anyone."

"Maybe." He drew in a long breath then let her go, stepping back a pace to look her in the eye. "That doesn't mean I'm good for you. Don't—" he said when she started to interrupt. "Look around. You have all this, your family, your friends, your career. Where would I fit in? Like I said, I'm the outsider. Always have been, always will be. If I took you into my world, you'd lose all this. We'd both end up miserable. You'd end up resenting me and I'd end up hating myself for taking you away from this just so I could have you. What would that make me? How could you call that loving you?"

She started to deny him, but he shook his head, a quick, sharp gesture. "You want me to say the words? I can't. I won't. It'll only make things worse because we both know it doesn't change anything."

Jule wanted to rail at him, cry and scream, fight, until he

stopped believing any of that was true. But she was too tired, too drained to know what to say. Did he love her? He'd essentially admitted he did. But so much he wasn't willing to ruin her life by being with her? How could she fight that?

"Rafe…" Stopping, she could only look at him helplessly.

"Come on," he said gently. Taking her hand, he led her out of the church.

They walked up the main street, now silent and empty in the waning light. All that was left of the festive parade were some bright streamers, a few balloons, confetti and candy wrappers. To Jule's eyes, all of the bright colors looked blurry, dull and shadowed now.

She had no idea where Rafe was taking them until he guided her down a couple of side streets to an adobe home set back off the road. Outside, along the driveway and rooftop, candles set in sand inside brown paper bags, *luminarios,* had been set up to announce the festivities and the saint's new home.

"They're probably serving dinner," he said.

"I'm not hungry."

"You need to eat."

He wasn't about to take no for an answer, though this was the last place Jule wanted to be right now. She didn't have time to protest as he prodded her through the door. The moment they were inside, Maya spotted them and came over to say hello. Her welcoming smile faded to concern when she took a closer look at Jule's face.

"Is everything all right?"

"Fine," Rafe said shortly. "Jule's just tired."

Tired, yes, Jule thought as, making a quick retreat to the bathroom, she looked at her tear-streaked face in the mirror. *Tired of pretending. Tired of fighting for something that probably should have died a long time ago. Tired of being alone.*

She was still feeling almost numb from their confrontation

in the church, but she pulled herself together and buried her hurt. Gathering her courage to be social again, she reentered the crowded living area where Maya was waiting.

"There's room at the table close to us," she said, leading Jule into another room where several long tables had been set up.

Rafe looked up when she sat down next to him, but neither of them said anything. There didn't seem to be anything left to say between them. After about ten minutes, Rafe muttered an excuse, leaving Jule alone with Maya.

People came and went freely, sitting long enough to eat, but not lingering at the tables because so many people needed to take turns sharing in the first meal at the saint's new home. Dinner over, people moved out to the brick patio strewn with paper lanterns to listen to Spanish music, dance and continue celebrating into the wee hours.

Jule didn't want to stay past dinner, though. The day already felt too long.

"Here, have some chili and beans. It will warm you up," Maya was saying.

Sawyer walked up then, Joey on his hip. "Here, this will help, too," he said, handing Jule her coat.

"What? Where's Rafe? I left this in his truck."

"I know. He dropped it off and asked me to tell you goodnight and to give you a ride home. He said he has an early morning, so he couldn't stay but he didn't want to ruin your evening."

Jule let her spoon fall to her bowl. "It's a little too late for that," she said taking the coat from Sawyer.

Maya laid a hand atop Jule's. "Want to tell us about it?"

"There's nothing to say." Jule shoved aside her bowl. "It's—it should have been over a long time ago. All he can see is the past. He refuses to believe none of that matters to me."

Sawyer shook his head. "I wish my brother would get his head out of his—" Maya looked pointedly from Joey to him and he shrugged. "Sorry, it's true."

With an impatient, "Daddy!" Joey tugged at Sawyer's shirt

and stretched his hand out toward the table. Sawyer pinched a piece of tortilla and handed it to him.

"What did he say?" Maya asked Jule.

"What he's always said. That I don't need him and that it would ruin my life if we got together."

"He might be right there."

Maya raised a brow at her husband. "If you're not going to help, then can you please find someplace else to park yourself?"

"I don't know if anyone can help at this point," Sawyer said. "For whatever his reasons, Rafe's isolated himself from just about everything human. So he's probably right in thinking he's not going to be a help, Jule, career-wise or socially."

"Why is that all everyone thinks I care about? My professional career and my social status?"

Sawyer and Maya exchanged a glance. "Well, let me put it this way," Maya began. "People have judged me all my life by my parents' behavior. In my case that was a definite negative. With most people," she amended when Sawyer flashed her a wicked grin. "In your case, well, expectations are high, as I imagine they always have been from your parents. People want the best for you because they love you."

"But they don't know *who* is best for me." After the day she'd had with Rafe, Jule's frustration level was nearing its peak. "It's my heart, my life, only *I* know that."

Maya smiled at her and squeezed her hand. "I'm not the person you need to convince of that."

Jule thought a long, hard minute then turned to Sawyer. "Can you please—"

"Give you a ride home so you can get your car?" Handing over Joey to Maya, Sawyer pulled his keys out of his pocket. "I'm more than happy to contribute to the cause. But you've got your work cut out for you with Rafe. He's had too many years to perfect being angry at the world."

. Jule knew that. She had to try, though. One more time, she had to try.

Chapter Twelve

A minute ago the water was so hot it almost scalded his skin. Now Rafe was jerking back out of the shower to avoid a frigid spray.

"Damn," he cursed the old, erratic water heater he'd meant to replace about a year ago. "Perfect end to a perfect day," he muttered, climbing out of the shower and grabbing a towel. He rubbed his chest and arms dry then wrapped the towel around his waist and headed out to his kitchen to grab a beer. His house on the back end of the Garrett ranch needed attention badly. It was just one more thing he'd neglected because of his intense focus on the ranch and now his herd.

He'd hoped a hot shower would not only rid him of the dust from the parade and the smell of grass and dirt from the pasture where he'd retreated after leaving Jule in town. Instead, all it did was aggravate his already frustrated state of mind. He paced his small kitchen, chugging his beer. Finishing it in a few gulps he went to his bedroom and pulled on a fresh pair of jeans, a shirt and his boots. It was getting late, but he wasn't going to go to bed tonight without confronting Jed. He'd been thinking about it since he'd come back from the Pinwa reservation and tonight he was in the perfect mood to handle whatever Jed dished out.

When he'd picked Jule up this morning, he'd actually allowed himself a shred of hope that their day in town would be lighthearted, a respite from the intense emotional ups and downs her coming back had caused. *Fool,* he thought, realizing he should have gone with his gut instinct and avoided the whole thing. Being in town with Jule today only reminded him how well she fitted in with the people there, how well Jule would—and could—fit in anywhere. Her poise, her pedigree, her demeanor, her grace, her manners. Everything about her was all class. Without trying, she commanded respect. Without bragging, she was admired. Without him, she was fine.

With him—a disaster.

And yet, she said she wanted him. She'd told him she loved him. Why? He had nothing to offer her. Not unless he made his own way, made a name for himself apart from Jed Garrett, apart from his past, apart from his brothers. Unfortunately, he needed Jed and his brothers to give him a chance to make that name for himself—he needed them to sell him their shares of the ranch. Except, even if they would, he didn't have the money to buy them, nor did he have enough collateral to get a loan. It was the worst sort of catch-22.

He didn't want charity. He'd been working toward ownership all his life, paying for it with labor and whatever profit he could get from his own ventures—such as the bison herd. He needed something big that was his, something that could give him an identity, a place in this community, something that would earn him respect and give Jule and her parents pride in him. He needed to be the man she deserved.

And then maybe she would need him.

* * *

"I want to talk to you," Rafe said after Del reluctantly allowed him into Jed's bedroom.

"I told him you were exhausted, honey," Del said, padding over to fluff a pillow behind Jed's head. "But he kept insisting this just couldn't wait until morning."

Jed thrashed her hand away. "Stop fussin' over me, woman." He looked around her to where Rafe stood at the end of his bed. "What in the hell brings you here this time of night? It had better be good. I don't want to hear it tonight if you're gonna tell me something else is wrong with those damned bison of yours."

"It's not that. The calves Jule injected last week are improving. It looks like this vaccine is going to work."

"So—then what's so important you're keeping me up?"

Rafe glanced at Del, deciding whether or not to ask her to leave. He chose not to; she might have some information he needed. Besides, she'd hear it all from Jed anyway after he left.

"I went to visit the Pinwa."

"I heard. Don't know why you'd do that now and go and stir up trouble for yourself."

"They've had a buffalo herd for years. Jule and I thought they might have some advice and they did."

"Well, good for them. Do I need to hear this?"

"Yes, you sure as hell do."

"Rafe!" Del said. "Don't you talk to your daddy like that."

"Let the boy get it out of his system. Let me guess, your long-lost relatives filled your head with a bunch of bunk about me and your *other* daddy, right?"

Biting back his temper, Rafe said evenly, "No one said much about my father. Except that he was honest and honorable and tried to do right by his wife and son."

"Well, that ain't got nothin' to do with me," Jed told him. "Our business was strictly business. Till he left you an orphan."

"Business is what I want to talk about."

Jed squared his jaw and sat up a little. "This oughta to be good."

"My uncle and a few others seem to think it wouldn't be fair for you to divide the ranch up five ways." Rafe leaned over and placed his hands on the bed. "Why they would say that?"

Jed's eyes narrowed, but before he could say anything Del marched over to Rafe. "Jed adopted you and took care of you. He raised you as a son. How dare you ask him such a question? Why, especially, when here he is sick and in his last years and all he's doin' is tryin' to do right by all of you boys?"

"I didn't say he wasn't," Rafe said through gritted teeth.

"Well, then, what's the matter with you?" Del slapped her hands to her ample hips. "Are you going to get greedy now, just because you're still on the ranch and the others have made lives of their own? You know my Josh is going to be a rodeo star. He won't get stuck in this little town, on this ranch." She stopped cold, whirled back to Jed, her cheeks suddenly flushed. "Not that this place isn't the best place on earth for us, honey, but you know my Josh, he's a restless sort."

Jed snorted. "He's a spoiled sort."

Rafe held his ground. "I want to know the truth. I deserve that."

"You've gotten way more than you ever deserved. You—" A fit of wheezing and coughing interrupted him and it was a long minute before he could speak again. His voice came out harsh and raspy. "I could have sent you back up into those hills with the Pinwa where you'd probably've wound up picking corn and chilis the rest of your days. Instead I gave you a chance here, to make something of yourself. I gave you what your mama wanted you to have, a chance at a better life. And this is the thanks I get."

He supposed he ought to feel something, a shred of pity or sympathy, or even gratitude. But he couldn't remember ever feeling any softer emotions for Jed. Fear, resentment, anger, even hatred—Jed had earned all those from him over the years.

"The thanks you got was me working every day on this

ranch for the last twenty-five years. Without me, you wouldn't have turned the profit you have and you know it."

"And that's why you'll get your share of it when I'm gone. You can do whatever you want with it—as long as your brothers agree. Now, I'm done with this. Turn out the lights on your way out."

Del moved to take Rafe by the elbow and usher him out. He shook her off but he left, knowing he'd get nothing else out of Jed tonight.

Casting a reproachful glance at Rafe, Del said to Jed on her way out, "I'll bring you your milk and medicine in a few minutes. You just lie there and calm yourself right down."

"He's hiding something," Rafe muttered under his breath. "I know it."

"You ought to do a better job of keeping your thoughts to yourself," Del said as she pushed past him on her way to the kitchen. "I don't know what those folks of yours told you, but you've got it all twisted up if you think Jed hasn't done the best he could by you. He didn't have to honor your parents' wishes you know. He could have sent you away."

That part was true. At least as far as he knew. Jed had always told Rafe his parents had wanted him to grow up on the ranch and learn the business; he'd repeatedly insisted there was nothing for Rafe with the Pinwa and that no one with the tribe wanted to take him in.

The first half of it seemed to go along with what the Pinwa had told him. The rest Jed had obviously invented for his own reasons, since Pay and his family had gone out of their way to welcome him as one of their own.

Pay had also told him Rafe deserved more than a one-fifth share of the ranch. Rafe didn't see how it was possible if Jed had been the one to finance most of the business—even if it had been with Theresa Morente's money. The problem was no one seemed to know for sure what kind of deal Anoki and Jed had struck in the early days of Rancho Pintada. If, as his uncle had hinted, Anoki had been a full partner from the start, then Rafe did deserve a half share in the land.

If he did, then maybe, in addition to expanding the bison herd, Rafe could take over the primary business of raising cattle, something Jed had neglected for a long time in favor of Josh's passion for horses.

The mainstay of the ranch had been dwindling and would die from neglect if someone didn't pay it some attention. His brothers couldn't care less about any of it. Josh was supposed to be overseeing the cattle operation with Jed sick, but he only did the minimum, enough to fool Jed into thinking he was working and to appease his mother. And Rafe couldn't honestly see Sawyer or Cort ever wanting a hand in the business.

"Yeah, he could have sent me away," he said, finally answering Del. "But the one thing I learned from my father before he died was to trust my gut instincts. And right now, instinct's telling me it's not that simple. Jed knows something more. I plan to learn what it is, one way or another."

Del shook her red-nailed index finger at Rafe. "Don't you make threats to me. This is my home, too. And you'd do well not to forget that."

"I'm not making threats. All I want is the truth."

No light shone through the windows of Rafe's house as Jule approached his door. It was late and she probably shouldn't have come. Smoke rose in curls from the chimney and she could smell the piñon wood he used for fires. Maybe he was still awake.

Choosing to ignore the unwelcoming darkness, she knocked lightly on his door. After several minutes, when she was half thinking she ought to turn and leave, she heard the deadbolt turn and Rafe opened the door to her. He stood framed in darkness, bare-chested, his hair hanging loose and disheveled, wearing only a pair of black flannel boxers.

He stared at her, his expression questioning whether she were real.

"Rafe, I—"

"It's cold," he said abruptly, his voice low and graveled. "Come in."

"I'm sorry, I know it's late." She followed him inside, trying to ignore that he was scarcely dressed, the soft darkness of the room, the rapid pulse thrumming through her veins.

Rafe flicked on a lamp then went over to toss a few logs on the dying fire. Even in the near darkness, his movements were more animal than man, quick, agile, sharp yet graceful, and always with an all-seeing awareness of everything and everyone around him.

"Have a seat," he said, indicating his one living-room chair. He swept his jeans from the back of it then tugged them on. "So, you've got my attention. Why did you come?"

Jule bristled. She was glad he'd started off with his usual brusqueness; it did wonders to cool the heat watching his body stirred in her. She took the chair he'd indicated while he took up pacing in front of the fire. "I'd like an explanation, for one thing. You left me at the party without so much as a good-bye and sorry I'm dumping you."

"I didn't dump you. I told Sawyer to tell you—"

"Oh, yes, your leaving a message with your brother makes it so much better. Sometimes you can be a real jerk. You know that?"

"Yeah. So I've heard."

Jule sighed. This was not going well at all. She had to make the third time a charm. "No matter what we said to each other, I didn't deserve to be abandoned like a stray cat you picked up and decided you didn't want to take care of after all."

Rafe stopped his restless striding back and forth and turned to her, firelight forming an orange-and-yellow aura around him. The diffused light made him look even taller and wilder than usual, less civilized, more predatory. It was an image that might have been daunting. But for Jule, the illusion both mystified and attracted her. Rafe might be rude and inconsiderate at times, and he might be primal and aggressive at others, but he would never hurt her. At least not physically.

Hurting her heart was another story.

"I had to get out of there," he said finally.

"Because of what happened at the church?"

"That, and because I didn't belong there."

"You're the only one who believes that."

"No." He resumed his pacing, the tension radiating from him almost as palpable as a living thing in the room. "This is my world, here. I'm not comfortable in yours. I make everyone else uncomfortable being there. I would have ruined your dinner with the others, so I left."

"That's an excuse. If you don't want to be seen with me, why don't you just say it straight out?" She'd promised herself on the way over she would not get emotional or upset, but that resolve was rapidly slipping away. "The truth is you don't want reminders of our past. You know people are gossiping whenever they see us together and it bothers you."

"You're right. I don't want to be reminded." He whirled on her and in two strides stood looking down at her. "Why can't you understand? You're perfect. Too perfect. At least for me. That's what people are saying. That's what they've always said. Don't you see?"

"No, I don't see." Tears blurred her vision, threatened to choke her voice.

Kneeling in front of her, he started to reach out to her then stopped himself. "It's like I said before, what would I be if I didn't give a damn about the consequences of us being together? You say you're willing to pay the price. But how could you respect me if I didn't put you above what I want? I can't do that to you. Not and live with myself. When no one thinks I'm good for you, I have to listen."

After a long pause, Jule answered softly. "Maya and Sawyer do."

"Sawyer?" Rafe gave a short laugh, the sound harsh, discordant. "Yeah, right. My *brother*."

"He gave me a ride to my house tonight so that I could come see you. He could have discouraged me, but he didn't."

"Maya probably didn't give him a choice."

"Sawyer volunteered."

Rafe fell silent. Getting to his feet, he walked back to the fireplace and spread his arms and hands, leaning forward against a carved shelf beside it. He stared a long while into the fire. She could feel his thoughts, radiating, intense, hot as the fire's glow.

Unable to help herself, Jule got up and went to him. After a moment's hesitation, she touched her hand to his back. A shudder went through him and the muscle under her palm flinched.

"I can't change where I came from, who my parents are or what my reputation might be," she said softly. "But all of that doesn't make me need you any less. It doesn't make *you* any less. It just seems to make you not need—or want—me at all."

When he said nothing and didn't turn around, Jule let her hand slide away from him. Feeling stiff and hurting all over, she walked to the door. She grasped the knob and pulled the door open wide enough to feel a sharp rush of cold night air.

Then she felt the burning heat of his hand at her back, spinning her into his arms.

Rafe pulled her against his chest and kissed her with a passion that made her knees buckle. Scarcely giving her time to catch a breath, he kicked the door closed behind her and pulled her closer still, devouring her mouth with his until they both had to break free long enough to draw breath.

Running his hands with a tender fierceness over her back, he nuzzled his face in her neck, pausing to nibble and kiss her there. Jule moaned softly and arched back, opening herself to his exploration. Rafe found her mouth again, tasting, probing, demanding a response from her she was only too willing to give.

Jule realized how starved she'd been for the taste of him, the feel of his powerful hands at her back and waist. She'd wanted this for so long, dreamed of it, ached for it so many long, lonely nights. As he traced the curve of her lower back to cup her backside in his palms and pull her against him, she heard her own soft cry of pleasure, answered by a low, rough sound from deep in his throat.

She reached under his arms to grasp his shoulders and he lifted her easily. Wrapping her legs around his waist and locking her arms around his neck, she lost herself in their kiss as he carried her to lay her gently back on his bed. He lay down beside her, stroking her cheek, looking deeply into her eyes.

"Do you know how long I've pictured you here? How many nights I couldn't sleep, thinking about this?"

Jule smiled, tracing his mouth with her fingertip. "I think I might have some idea."

He bent to kiss her face, her throat, pushing down the shoulder of her dress with barely concealed impatience as his touch became hungry, urgent. Shoving his hand under the hem of her dress, he ran it along her thigh to the curve of her hip at the same time as he continued his hot open-mouthed kisses over her neck and throat.

"I can feel your heart," Rafe mouthed against the pulse below her ear. "It's like you've been running."

He nuzzled lower and she gasped softly. "I *have* been running—for thirteen years. Trying to get away from here, and trying to get back."

"So have I. My God, woman, so have I." Kissing her deeply, he moved his hand to the inside of her thigh, sliding upward just high enough to make her crazy with wanting him to touch her everywhere. "Remind me again why we've taken so long to get here."

The words cut through the sensory fog clouding her brain and Jule stiffened a little. "Are you sure you want me to do that now?"

"No," Rafe murmured, continuing his seduction of her body. "Forget it."

Her body was more than willing to forget it. But a dark, insistent voice in her head whispered it wasn't right.

"Rafe, wait." She caught his hand, stopping him from pushing her skirts any higher. "I can't do this."

"What?" He sounded disoriented.

"Yes, what? What are we doing?"

Breathing hard, he stared at her, looking as though she'd suddenly slapped him. "If you don't know—"

"I *don't* know. It feels like sex, not love. Maybe it's been too long or maybe it's what you've decided to settle for. As much as I want this, I also want a future, not just one more night. You've made it clear we can't have that. So, whatever this is, it's not enough." Struggling upright, she pushed herself away from him to sit on the edge of the bed.

"Damn it, Jule." Rafe rolled onto his back, pressing both palms against his eyes. After a moment, he dropped his hands and jerked off the bed to his feet. "I'm trying," he said, his back to her. "I know you don't believe that. But I'm trying to make it enough."

"I know," she said quietly. "But is it ever going to be?"

Chapter Thirteen

Jule decided she must be a glutton for punishment. That or she needed someone to give her a good shake and demand she explain why she kept coming back to Rancho Pintada and Rafe when any other any other sane woman would have run screaming in the opposite direction.

She told herself she was here, working with the bison, because she refused to let what had happened—or *not* happened—between her and Rafe get in the way of her responsibilities.

The problem was, she'd used that excuse so often even she didn't believe it any more.

Rafe, doing a fairly good job of hiding his surprise as she pulled her truck up next to the barn, eyed her skeptically when she told him she'd only come to check on the bison, but he said nothing, pitching in to help her without question.

The relative silence between them at first seemed like a blessing to Jule. But after nearly two hours of it, with the tension between them so looming and oppressive, she wanted to do something—anything—that would shake Rafe out of the shell he retreated into every time she got too close.

She almost regretted not staying last night, giving in to what they both wanted. It wouldn't have resolved anything. Deep down inside, she knew it would have made things worse. Except, today she might have been able to think more clearly. Instead, the anticipation, the wanting that had become an ever-present ache, made it difficult to think of anything else.

Finishing, she had started to pack up with the intention of making a quick retreat when she looked up and found Rafe watching her with an unsettling intensity.

"Jule…" he started, stopped. Cleared his throat and turned away, then back again. "Last night—"

"It was a mistake," she said shortly.

"Was it?"

"Yes, because I should have known better than to believe anything between us could be stronger than your damned obsession with this piece of land!"

"That's not the way it is and you know it."

"No, Rafe, I don't know it. A long time ago, maybe I did. Before everything went wrong. But not now." Her frustrated anger abruptly deserted her and Jule couldn't hold her voice firm. "Not now."

Not giving him time to reply, not wanting to hear him justify or apologize or deny, Jule spun quickly on her heel, at the same time bending to snatch up her gear. The quickness of the motion made it awkward and she jerked forward, nearly losing her balance. A sharp pain shot from her lower back into her hip.

Jule gasped and grabbed for the side of the stall. Instead of the hard wood she found herself clutching Rafe's arm as he stepped up behind her, bracing her with his body.

"What is it?" he asked, his voice sharp with concern.

"Nothing…I just—" She tried to straighten up and immediately regretted it when another spasm twisted her muscles and nerves. Gritting her teeth, she made herself lean on him for support as her only other alternative seemed to be collapsing at his feet in an undignified heap. "Give me a minute. It'll pass."

"Say that again without looking like someone just kicked you in the gut and maybe I'll believe it." Without asking, he scooped her into his arms and strode toward the barn door, ignoring her feeble attempts to squirm away.

"Put me down! I told you, I'm fine."

He never broke stride or slowed down. "Yeah, okay."

"Rafe, stop, I mean it. I just need to rest for a few minutes."

"Sure. You can rest." He glanced at her once as he continued his relentless pace away from the barn. "In my bed."

"I'm not going."

Rafe crossed his arms over his chest, looking down at Jule where she lay on his bed propped against several pillows, glaring up at him. "Not listening."

"Oh, there's a surprise. So, what? You're going to throw me over your shoulder and force me to go to the clinic?"

He didn't reply, figuring it was safer since that was pretty close to what he'd been thinking.

Her eyes narrowed dangerously. "You wouldn't dare."

"Wanna bet?"

"No, I want to strangle you."

"That threat would be a lot scarier if you could get up off the bed on your own."

Jule heaved a sigh and pressed a hand to her forehead. "Look—I'll be fine, really. It's nothing I haven't dealt with before. I'll go home, rest, and tomorrow I'll call Dr. Gonzales. I promise."

She was cajoling now, looking up at him with an expression that invited him to give in and let her have her way. *Not this time, Julene.* He handed her the phone. "Call her."

"I told you—"

"Call her now. Or I'm not letting you out of this bed."

He won the staring contest this time. He swore he could hear her teeth grinding as she snatched the phone from his hand and punched in the clinic number, muttering under her breath the whole time.

Rafe sat down next to her as she waited to talk to Dr. Gonzales. Her braid had loosened and without thinking, he brushed a stray strand back from her cheek, absently stroking his fingertips over her soft skin as he half listened to her telling Dr. Gonzales about her back. He hated seeing her in pain. Even though she'd insisted a dozen times over that it was an old problem that could be eased with a few therapy sessions, he couldn't help but worry that she was making light of it to stop him from making a fuss.

Seemingly of its own volition, his hand moved down the curve of her neck to her nape, lightly kneading the tense muscle there, the motion more caress than massage. She trembled and for a moment closed her eyes, leaning back into his palm, losing the thread of her conversation.

The voice at the other end recalled her and she flushed. "Um, that's not necessary. I'll be fine, really." She listened a moment, then, "Please, I don't want you to—I can drive myself. No, I can—Maya?" She stared at the phone and then up at Rafe in exasperation. "She hung up. This is all your fault."

"Probably. But at least tell me what I did."

"Maya's coming out here. She insisted. You've got everyone making a big fuss over nothing."

"It doesn't look like nothing to me. I'd rather take you to the clinic."

"Don't you ever give up?"

"Yeah," he said softly, his fingers playing with the hair at her nape, reacquainting himself with the texture and scent that had been burned into his memory so many years ago. "But not this time."

He saw the struggle in her eyes, the struggle to pretend his touch didn't affect her, to hide the longing and the desire to touch him in return. He should stop now, but she wasn't stopping him and touching her felt too good.

"You know, for someone who usually ignores his own injuries, you're quick to insist on carting me off to a doctor," she said. "I remember when you got this—" Reaching out she traced a line from just under his heart, across his ribs, following the path of an old scar hidden by his shirt. Her fingertips lingered on his chest, toying with a button, studying it as if she found it fascinating.

"Damn bull almost got lucky," he said gruffly, distracted by the slow slide of her fingers up and down the line of buttons.

"You were bleeding everywhere, and I was scared to death and trying to find someone to get you to a doctor. But all you were worried about was getting your hat out of the corral before it got trampled."

She smiled, almost to herself, and Rafe's breath hitched. "It was my favorite hat."

Slowly, she raised her eyes to his. "You could have gotten another. But I can't replace you."

"Did you try?" The words were out before he could think that he didn't want to hear the answer.

"I wanted to," she said. The slight edge to her voice could have been anger or echoes of past pain. "Sometimes I pretended I could hate you for pushing me out of your life. I thought that would make it easier. But I never found anyone to make me believe it." She paused then, so softly he almost missed the words, asked, "Did you?"

"Try? No. My longest relationship after you lasted two days." Admitting it to her stabbed him with shame and regret. He looked away from her, not wanting her to see it in his eyes, to give her another reason to think less of him.

Jule touched his face, drawing his gaze back to her. "It doesn't matter."

"Yeah, it does matter. I made myself not care, about anyone. I thought that would be easier. How can you look at me and know what I am and say that doesn't matter to you?"

"Because I know you," she said simply. "And what I see is so much different than what you believe."

He shook his head, not trusting it was, but wanting, with everything in him, for it to be true.

When Maya arrived half an hour after Jule's call, Rafe was surprised to see Sawyer with her.

"He thinks just because I'm pregnant I need a bodyguard," Maya said over her shoulder as she started for the bedroom to check on Jule.

"I don't want to be delivering another of our children along the side of the road," Sawyer told her, earning him rolled eyes and a half smile before Maya disappeared into the bedroom.

"How's Jule?" Sawyer asked when he and Rafe were alone.

"She says okay," Rafe told him. Too tense to sit himself, he gestured Sawyer to a chair.

But Sawyer stayed standing, leaning against the end of the couch to watch Rafe pace a few steps then stop to stare at the closed bedroom door. "Maya didn't seem to think it was anything too serious."

"It wouldn't have been anything at all if she hadn't been here to begin with. She didn't need to be out here today."

"So this is *your* fault?"

Rafe turned on him, ready with an angry retort, only to find Sawyer smiling knowingly at him.

"I hate to interrupt your wallow in guilt, but she wouldn't have been here if she didn't want to be," Sawyer said.

Maya came out before Rafe could form a comeback. "It's just another spasm. I'm going to stay for a bit and try and some massage and heat therapy. She should be okay after she's had some rest. Which I need you to convince her to get," she added, looking pointedly at Rafe.

"Don't count on me," Rafe grumbled as he went to check on Jule.

He found her pretty much as he'd left her, sitting half propped on the pillows and now looking distinctly disgruntled.

"I told you this was a lot of fuss over nothing," she said the minute he walked in the room. "I need to—"

"Rest. Look," he said, interrupting her next argument. "A couple of hours rest won't kill you. I'm going to finish up a few things. I'll be back to check on you later."

Not giving her time to marshal any more protests, he left, letting Maya slip past him on the way out.

"Need a hand?" Sawyer offered as Rafe snagged his jacket to start back towards the barns.

Rafe's first instinct was to refuse. He'd pushed away people for so long, it was second nature. But for some reason, it meant something to Jule that he at least try to put a few patches on his broken relationship with Sawyer and Cort. So he bit back the automatic "no" and instead came out with a gruff, "Yeah, okay. Thanks."

They worked together for more than an hour, finishing up with the bison and then moving on to other work, not talking much. The silence was, if not comfortable, at least not antagonistic, made easier by their focus on the jobs to be done.

Maya found them when they were halfway through loading hay bales into one of the barn lofts. "Jule's fine. She fell asleep, which is probably exactly what she needs right now," she said, coming over to slide under her husband's arm. "I need to get back. I've got one more appointment this afternoon before I pick up Joey."

"You go on without me," Sawyer told her. "I'm not on duty until eight so I'm gonna help Rafe finish up here. I'll catch a ride back in a couple of hours. That is if you think you can manage without your bodyguard for a while," he added with a grin.

Maya kissed him lightly before slipping out from his hold. "You know, you're lucky I love you because otherwise I'd never put up with all this hovering of yours."

After she'd gone, Rafe briefly considered going to check on

Jule to assure himself she was okay. He stopped himself, not wanting to wake her, and decided to wait until he and Sawyer had finished.

It was the easy way they'd worked together, silently agreeing to put aside their past differences at least for now, that prompted Rafe to bring up a subject he'd avoided even thinking about for most of his life until Jule came back and started him questioning his ties to Rancho Pintada.

"There's something I—" he began, when he and Sawyer were leaning against the corral fence, taking a break between jobs. Sawyer looked at him questioningly, waiting, as Rafe struggled to find the words. "I wanted to ask you, about Jed and Theresa. If you knew anything about my—the adoption. Why Jed wanted it. Because I know Theresa didn't."

"I'd like to say it was because he wanted to give you a home after his one-time partner died," Sawyer said. "But we both know Jed's always been too much of a bastard to be that altruistic. All I can think is there must have been something in it for him."

"Yeah, well I'm beginning to think I know what it was."

"The ranch?"

Rafe nodded. "Jed's always told me that my father helped him get the ranch started. But Jed said he was the one who put all the money into it and the only claim I had was that my father lived and worked here." He hesitated, reluctant to voice his suspicions out loud, not sure of Sawyer's reaction. "But if my father really was legally his partner—"

"Then by rights half the ranch is yours," Sawyer finished. "I've wondered about that, but my mother told me the same thing, that Jed owned the ranch because her money had paid for it. That's about the most she ever said. Most of the time she refused to talk about Jed, except to say he'd kept you but didn't want Cort and me."

"You got lucky."

"It didn't feel that way. For a long time." Staring out over the sprawling land, Sawyer was silent for a moment then said quietly, "It hurt. I hated him but he was my father. And I could never figure out what made you so special and me so unworthy, that you got to stay while I got kicked out. Maybe it didn't make sense and maybe it was stupid, but I resented you for being the one Jed wanted."

Rafe snorted disbelievingly at the idea of Sawyer, the one who'd succeeded at anything he'd ever tried, as being considered unworthy. "There's nothing special about me. Neither Theresa nor Jed *wanted* me. Jed just got another ranch hand for cheap."

"I guess," Sawyer said slowly. "Something about it doesn't sound right, though."

"If you know, I'd like to hear it."

"I don't know, about that anyway." He looked Rafe straight in the eye. "I do know you and I have wasted a lot of time at each other's throats over something we had no control over." When Rafe didn't answer right away, Sawyer added, "Cort spent a lot of years trying to get me to see that. It took me almost losing Maya and Joey to make me realize he was right. I'd convinced myself I could never be what they needed because of who my parents were and the mess they'd made of our lives when we were kids. But I was wrong. They screwed up, but it doesn't mean I have to repeat their mistakes. I'd like to think that one day you'd realize it too and we could put the past where it belongs."

After so many years of telling himself family didn't matter because no one he'd called family after his parents died had cared about him, it was hard to admit to himself that maybe he'd been wrong. Harder still to admit that to Sawyer. "I had my own share of resentments," Rafe finally settled on. "Maybe…maybe I let it get in the way of—a lot of things."

Sawyer gave a huff of laughter. "Maybe?"

"Yeah, maybe," Rafe said gruffly.

"I'll take that—for now." He smiled a little then asked, "So, what're we going to do about this situation with the ranch?"

Rafe's surprise must have shown on his face because Sawyer smiled and clapped him lightly on the shoulder. "Get used to it. I'm not letting this go and I know Cort won't want to either. And we'll have Josh behind us, even if it's only because he's got a fear of being saddled with actual responsibility."

Sawyer's willingness to help him and his acceptance of Rafe's ideas about the ranch broke something in Rafe—a part of the wall he'd built up around him to protect himself from caring. Jule coming back into his life had started the slow destruction of it and now it was in danger of crumbling altogether. "I don't know how I'm ever going to prove I've got a right to half a share in this place," Rafe admitted. "Jed's sure as hell not going to confess any time soon."

"No, but there's got to be another way. One that won't scratch your pride too much." Sawyer stared off at the ranch house in their view, silent for a few moments. "We'll figure it out," he said at last. He turned to Rafe. "Just don't let it be the most important thing in your life."

Sawyer's words echoed Jule's so much that Rafe could almost hear her speaking instead of his brother. "It has to be," he said, not expecting Sawyer to understand.

"Does it? Is it worth sacrificing what you could have with Jule?"

Rafe didn't have an answer.

When he got back to his house several hours later, he found Jule in the kitchen. She'd made herself coffee and was standing by the window, nursing her mug.

"Are you supposed to be up?" he asked. She didn't look like she was in pain, although she moved a little stiffly.

"It's not terminal," she said lightly. "I told you it would pass. Maya's a miracle worker." She glanced behind him. "Where's Sawyer?"

"Josh came back from his running around and was going back into town again. Sawyer caught a ride with him."

"I should get back, too."

They looked at each other and Rafe felt his conflict of feelings echoed in her. It was probably best, after last night, that she go. But after last night, he wanted more than ever for her to stay.

"I'll drive you," he offered. "You can pick your truck up later."

"That's not necessary." She fidgeted with the handle of the mug. "There's some left," she said, holding up the mug. "Do you want a cup?"

Rafe shook his head. "I could sit down. It's been a long day."

They moved by silent agreement into the living room, taking opposite ends of the couch.

"Did you and Sawyer get a chance to talk?" Jule asked once they were settled.

"Yeah, some." He hesitated to confide too much to her, knowing how she felt about the topic of the ranch. "He thinks I'm right about Jed lying about my claim on the ranch."

"You sound surprised."

"Maybe. I guess I'd gotten into the habit of thinking of Sawyer as the enemy."

"And now?"

Rafe gave a half shrug. He stretched his arms along the back of the couch, his fingertips brushing her shoulder. "We're better, I guess."

"How about us?" Jule asked softly. When he looked at her questioningly, she put down her mug and moved close enough to touch her hand to his chest. "Are we better?"

"Do you want us to be?"

"How can you ask me that?"

"I—after last night…" He let his arm drop lower so he could curl his hand over her shoulder, drawing slow patterns with his fingertips. He watched the movement to avoid looking at her, not wanting to see what was in her eyes. "I don't know what— how much—you want."

"I should be asking you that question," she murmured. Leaning into him, she traced her fingers over his face, his mouth.

It was an obvious invitation, an enticement for him to take things further, to convince her that their being together was right. He wanted to, so badly it hurt. He held back, though, not willing to push her into something she would regret later.

She seemed to take his hesitation for rejection and abruptly pulled away. "I should be going," she said, starting to get up.

Rafe stopped her by moving swiftly to drop on one knee in front of her, blocking her retreat. "No. Don't." He didn't stop to think about whether this was the right time or the right thing to say. He only wanted her to understand. He wanted to keep her from walking out of his life again. Maybe it was wrong and it would make everything worse. But right now he didn't care.

"I love you," he said huskily.

Jule stared at him, a stunned expression on her face. Tears welled in her eyes.

"I never stopped."

She laid her palm against his cheek and started to lean in to him, but he gently stopped her, taking her face between his hands. "But before anything else, I have to do this. I have to figure out if the ranch is mine."

Anger, frustration flashed in her eyes. "Why does it have to be more important than us?"

"It's not more important. But without it, there is no us."

"Why? Why does it matter so much?"

"Because this is all I have to offer you. I have to do this. For you. You deserve more than I can give you right now. Please." He would beg her right now if he believed it would sway her. "Try to understand."

For several terrifying moments she said nothing, moments in which Rafe figured she was thinking of a way to tell him she was leaving him for good. And he deserved that and more for the way he'd treated her. But part of him couldn't stop hoping against all odds that she would understand.

Finally she nodded and there was a new look of resolve in

her eyes. "I'm helping you figure this out so you can settle it, once and for all. This time you're not pushing me away."

He smiled a little, feeling almost light-headed with relief. "Would it work if I tried?"

"No. Not this time."

Rafe gave up the fight to keep his distance. He shifted to bury his hand in the hair at her nape, drawing her into a kiss, long and deep. He shouldn't have. But this was too desired, too good, and he didn't want to stop. He prayed she wouldn't turn him away this time. He needed this, one more time, he needed her. Right now, he'd give a lifetime just to have her one more day.

Leaning back, he caught her gaze with his and he could think of only one thing, one word to tell her everything.

"Stay."

Yes. The word trembled on her tongue, so close to having a voice.

"I meant what I said," Rafe said softly. "I love you."

"I know. I love you, too. More than you'll ever know."

"But—"

"But you're telling me that it doesn't matter what we feel unless you can settle this question of the ranch." Jule took his hand, needing to touch him, to hold onto the reality of him loving her. "How can I trust that things aren't going to end up the same as before? What if you can't prove your claim? What then?"

He glanced away and Jule knew the answer.

"I can't do it again," she said. "I can't love you and be your lover and then lose you again. I just can't. I'm not that strong."

She waited and when he said nothing, she gripped his hand more urgently, drawing his eyes back to hers. "I want to believe it can work. I've always loved you, I always will. There will never be anybody else. I want to believe it's the same for you."

"It is," he said fiercely. "You know that."

"All I know is that every time we get close, this piece of land and everything in the past comes between us."

He looked at her and Jule could see his struggle not to overwhelm her arguments with the force of passion. He wanted her. The truth of it burned in his eyes and communicated itself through the tension in his hands where he touched her. For a moment she thought desire would prove the stronger.

"Jule, I—" He stopped, shook his head. Letting her go, he got to his feet and paced a few steps away before turning back to her. "Will you stay a while? Just—be here?"

This time the word came easily. "Yes." She got up and went to him, putting her arms around his waist and laying her head against his heart. He responded immediately by wrapping her in his arms, gathering her closer, his cheek resting against her hair.

"Thank you," she whispered.

"For what?"

"For this. For understanding." Knowing he loved her, respected her feelings enough to hold back and bury his needs for her sake made her love him all the more.

Rafe shifted back enough to brush a kiss over her forehead, his mouth moving down over her cheek to her ear. "Being understanding is painful," he murmured.

Jule's laugh was smothered by his mouth on hers. He took advantage of her parted lips to kiss her deeply, taking his time to taste and explore, leaving her no doubt that he wanted much more. When she neared the point of forgetting every reason why they shouldn't do this, Rafe broke the kiss and stepped back.

Breathing hard, he ran his hands over his hair, linking his fingers briefly behind his head as he struggled to regain control. "That didn't help," he said finally, his mouth quirking up at the corner in a rueful smile.

"No," she agreed, feeling breathless herself.

"I think I'd better find something else to do. How about I grab a shower, then make you dinner?"

"That sounds relatively painless," she said, smiling back. "I can get dinner started while you're cleaning up."

"No, you rest." He started unbuttoning his shirt as he headed for the bedroom. "I mean it, Jule," he warned when she would have protested.

"Bossy," she muttered, but let him have his way for once.

Fifteen minutes later, he was back, in worn jeans and a denim shirt he hadn't bothered to tuck in, his hair loose and still damp from the shower. Jule followed him into the kitchen, perching on a high stool to watch him as he quickly put together a simple meal.

After they'd eaten and he'd cleared the dishes, Rafe lit a fire in the living-room fireplace and took her hand, leading her to sit next to him on the couch. Jule went willingly, didn't question what felt right. He put his arm around her and she curled into his side, her feet tucked up under her, pillowing her head on his chest. She felt his fingers untangling her braid until he'd freed her hair and then the gentle stroke of his hand over and through it.

The peaceful silence and the warmth of his body, the rhythmic caress of his hand, lulled Jule into a feeling of sleepy contentment. She let herself enjoy it, her eyes drifting closed, and for a while, dreamed that it would last forever.

Chapter Fourteen

An insistent ringing woke Rafe from a half doze about midnight. It took him a second to realize it was the phone. Jule stirred sleepily, but her eyes stayed closed as he gently untangled himself from her and got up to answer it.

"Rafe?" Maya's voice caught him off guard.

"What's wrong?" he asked, immediately thinking something had happened to Sawyer since he couldn't imagine any other reason Maya would be calling him at this hour.

"It's Cort. Sawyer and Rico took him into the emergency room a little while ago. Someone ran him down."

"Ran him—how is he?"

"From what Sawyer told me, it's bad," she said, and Rafe could hear a tremor in her voice that sent a spike of foreboding through him. She took a deep breath and even over the phone it sounded shaky. "Sawyer is there alone. Rico had to leave, and I can't find Josh. I don't want to call Jed. I've got Joey, I can't be there until I can find someone to stay with him.

Will you—would you go to the hospital? Maybe I don't have the right to ask. But Sawyer sounded… I don't want him to be alone if—if the worst happens."

Foreboding notched up a level closer to fear. Rafe didn't know Maya all that well, but she was obviously upset and the way she'd talked about the worst happening made him believe that *bad* didn't begin to cover Cort's condition. At the same time, he felt a pang of intense regret that he might have left things too late, at least with Cort. And a prick of shame that Maya could wonder if he cared.

"I'm leaving now, Maya—" He didn't know what to say that wouldn't sound like hollow assurance.

"It's okay. Just—thank you."

Jule was awake and on her feet when he hung up with Maya. "Is it Sawyer?" she asked.

"No. It's Cort," Rafe said as he hurriedly pulled on his boots and shoved his hands through his jacket pockets, searching for his truck keys. "Someone apparently ran him down. Maya said it's bad. I'm going to the hospital. Sawyer's there alone right now."

Jule already had her own boots on and was getting into her coat, obviously taking for granted she was coming with him. Rafe didn't question it. It felt natural to have her with him. He wanted her there, just like all the other times she'd been there for him when he needed her most.

They didn't talk much on the way, but she kept her hand on his thigh the whole trip, telling him she understood and shared his worry without saying a word.

Rafe made it to the hospital in record time. They found Sawyer in the E.R. waiting room. Sitting in a chair, his head in his hands, Sawyer didn't see them at first. Rafe, holding fast to Jule's hand, started inside, but Jule hung back.

"Go ahead," she said softly, giving his hand a squeeze then letting go. "I'm going to try to reach Josh again. I'll be there in a few minutes."

Rafe nodded, and when she'd walked away to try Josh's cell

NICOLE FOSTER   181

phone one more time, he walked into the waiting room.
Pushing back a feeling of awkwardness, he sat down next to
Sawyer.

Sawyer looked up and Rafe was struck hard by the expression of anguish on his face. "Rafe." His voice sounded rough,
as if it hurt to speak. "How—"

"Maya called."

"Yeah, I didn't know if you would…" Sawyer cleared his
throat, straightening up a little and shoving a hand through his
hair. He was still in uniform and for the first time, Rafe noticed
the smudges of blood on the white shirt. He inwardly winced,
figuring they belonged to Cort. "I guess she told you?"

"Only that someone ran Cort down. What happened?"

"Cort was getting close to breaking up a big drug lab just
outside of town." Sawyer spoke quickly, as if getting it over
with would make the ending easier to take. "Apparently one of
the guys involved decided to put an end to his investigation.
He caught up with Cort in town and hit him going about sixty-
five. Rico and I got the call. I didn't know it was Cort until we
got there." He stopped, swallowed hard. "The cops got the
guy. I wish I'd been there when they caught him."

Rafe nodded, understanding Sawyer's need to break the
man responsible in two. He felt more than a little of that
himself, seeing Sawyer like this and knowing without being
told that whatever condition Cort was in couldn't be good.
"How bad is it?"

"Broken shoulder, arm, collarbone, ribs. Concussion.
Probably some internal damage. What else, I don't know. Doc
kicked me out of the examining room after we got him in
there." Rubbing at his temple, he briefly closed his eyes. "His
blood pressure bottomed out on the way here. We almost lost
him. Damn, it's been over an hour!" Sawyer jerked to his feet,
striding over to the door to look in the direction of the examining rooms. "What the hell's going on in there?"

Rafe got up to go stand by him and after a moment's hesitation, put a hand on Sawyer's shoulder. There wasn't anything he could say. But he sensed Sawyer appreciated the contact, having someone there to share his worry.

They stood there like that, waiting, for several minutes until at last a doctor came striding out of one of the examining rooms, giving directions over his shoulder on his way to the waiting room.

After confirming Sawyer's assessment of Cort's injuries the doctor said, "He's bleeding internally. We'll have to wait for the X-ray and CT-scan results to know the full extent of the damage. In the meantime, we're trying to stabilize him so we can prep him for surgery."

"And?" Rafe asked, not liking the lack of reassurance in the doctor's voice.

A damning hesitation. Then, "We're doing everything we can." The standard response that meant everything might not be enough.

When the doctor left, Sawyer put his forearm against the doorjamb and leaned his forehead against it. Rafe felt a tremor go through his body and gripped his brother's shoulder more tightly.

For the first time in almost as long as he could remember, the word *family* meant more than just people he'd tried not to care about.

"I demand to see my grandson." Age hadn't diminished the imperious tone in Santiano Morente's voice. Jule turned to see Santiano shaking his silver-tipped cane at Cat Esteban while Consuela stood by, straight as a slender rod of steel, staring down the intimidated young nurse.

"I'm sorry Mr. and Mrs. Morente, but no one can see Cort right now." Cat glanced behind them as if in hopes that one of the nurses from emergency would come rescue her. She worked in pediatrics and had come down during her break to check on Cort after hearing from her husband what had happened. She'd immediately been cornered by the Morentes who, recognizing

Cat, wrongly assumed she would be able to gain them access to Cort. "If you'll just have a seat—"

"We will not." Santiano slammed his cane onto the gray tile floor. "Now you listen to me—"

Jule looked over to where Sawyer and Rafe stood on the other side of the E.R., absorbed in conversation. So many people were milling about—hospital personnel who knew Sawyer, officers from both the Rio Vista County Sheriff's Department where Cort worked and the city police station—that fortunately for them at least, neither of the brothers had heard or seen the Morentes yet. She hurried over to Cat and interrupted Santiano's tirade. "Hello, Mr. and Mrs. Morente. I'm so sorry we're meeting again under these circumstances."

"Julene, thank heavens," Consuela said, laying a hand atop Jule's arm. "Surely you can talk some sense into this young lady. We have to see Cort. That wife of Sawyer's—" Consuela's mouth pulled into a thin line of disapproval, making it obvious what she thought of Maya "—called us to tell us Cort was seriously injured. Although why Sawyer couldn't be bothered..." She pulled a lace handkerchief from her delicate handbag and touched it to her nose and eyes. "Those awful people Cort works around, those drug sellers, what have they done to our grandson?"

"Calm down, dear, hysterics won't help Cort," Santiano said, taking his wife's fragile, wrinkled hand in his and patting the back of it. "Julene, surely you can tell us something?"

"I'm sorry, I don't know much more than you do." She looked to Cat, eyes pleading. "No one does."

"Rico told me it was serious," Cat said. "But I'm sure you'll get a better report from the doctor soon."

"This is terrible," Consuela said, dabbing the tears from her eyes. "Why did he ever go into this horrid profession? He didn't have to do this, you know. He should have stayed in law school instead of throwing away his future because of that woman he was involved with. And we offered him and Sawyer control of all of our restaurants. But they wouldn't listen.

Stubborn, foolish boys, both of them. And now look what has happened to our baby Cort."

Cat and Jule exchanged a look. Picturing Cort Morente as anyone's helpless infant was a near-impossible leap of the imagination. But, nonetheless, Jule tried to understand how Consuela felt, knowing she was helpless to do anything for her youngest grandson. "I'm afraid all any of us can do right now is wait."

Jule caught Rafe's eye then, noticing he and Sawyer had stopped talking and were looking her way. Rafe's expression questioned whether she needed him and Jule answered with a nod and an inward sigh of relief as he and Sawyer made their way through the confusion in the waiting room.

"Sorry, I didn't know you were here," Sawyer said, the words directed at his grandparents, but he looked at Jule and Cat in silent apology. He bent to hug his grandmother, nodding in cool respect to his grandfather. "You two should go home and get some rest. They're going to take Cort into surgery soon. We won't know anything for hours."

Santiano eyed Rafe up and down. "What are you doing here? This is a family matter."

Jule moved to stand at Rafe's side. Why hadn't they asked her that? She was far less family than Rafe was.

Rafe stiffened, but before he could reply Sawyer stepped in front of him. "He is family. My family."

Consuela let out a little gasp and covered her mouth with her handkerchief.

Santiano squared his shoulders, assessing Sawyer, then Rafe. The lines in his brow drew together in a scowl and he focused hard on Sawyer. "So that's how it is now."

"That's how it is from now on." Sawyer looked to Rafe.

Rafe stepped up beside him. "I'm here with Sawyer until they kick us out. If that makes you uncomfortable, you might as well leave."

Cat stared wide-eyed at the exchange, but Jule could only

look at Rafe in wonderment. What a sad irony that it took Cort's crisis to bring these two brothers to the point of forgiveness. And yet, if Cort recovered... It was impossible and insane right now to measure whether it would be worth it all, but she couldn't help that the thought had crossed her mind.

Just when Jule thought the Morentes would leave and things would settle down, in walked Maya followed by Shem and Azure. Maya immediately hurried over to her husband and into his arms.

"Oh, my gosh, talk about the odd couples," Cat whispered to Jule as her eyes went from the Morentes to the Rainbows and back. "This is going to be one of those Twilight-Zone nights."

"Is there a coffee shop here?" Jule whispered back. "I'm suddenly very thirsty."

Cat darted a quick look at her watch. "I've got to get back to work. Good luck escaping." She smiled at Maya and reached out and briefly squeezed Sawyer's hand before slipping out of the waiting room.

Santiano's expression said he'd had enough. He took his wife's arm. "This I will not tolerate. It's obvious, Consuela, we're not needed." He shot a razor-eyed glare at Sawyer, barely acknowledging Maya with a glance. "Or wanted here."

Sawyer, holding his wife close, chose to ignore the jab. "I'll call you as soon as we know anything."

The Morentes marched past the Rainbows as though they did not exist.

But Azure tried to catch their attention. "We're sending all the positive power of the universe out to help your grandson."

"We think of Cort as one of the family," Shem echoed the attempt at civility. "We've got all our friends holding a vigil for him."

Jule inwardly winced at how coldly the Morentes treated Maya and her parents. She felt almost guilty that they'd gushed over her only minutes earlier.

The sudden warmth of Rafe's hand at her back distracted

her from the tensions of the moment. "You look tired. Let's go find a place to sit down. I think Sawyer and Maya can handle this for a few minutes."

"It's going to be a long night—" Sawyer's eyes went to the clock on the wall and he grimaced "—day. You don't need to hang around—"

"Yeah. I do," Rafe said, almost challenging Sawyer to disagree.

Sawyer nodded then, after a moment's hesitation, reached out and briefly rested a hand on Rafe's shoulder. "I'm glad you're here."

"We all are," Maya agreed, exchanging a smile with Jule. "But Rafe's right, you should find a place to sit and I'm going to send my husband in search of coffee. Here—" she said, handing him a bag. "You can change on the way. I'll entertain my parents for a while."

Jule knew Maya was trying to distract her husband, at least for a few minutes, from worrying about Cort. As Sawyer reluctantly left at Maya's urging, Rafe pulled Jule aside to a couple of empty chairs.

"I'm fine. You're the one who must be exhausted," Jule said when they sat down.

"No. Just worried about Cort. The doctor didn't sound too reassuring. Sawyer's afraid, although he hasn't said anything."

"He must have said something. Something has definitely changed between you two."

Rafe let out a wry laugh. "It's about time, wouldn't you say?"

"After twenty-five years? No comment."

"Thanks."

"I almost fainted when I heard Sawyer defend you to his grandfather."

"I thought *Consuela* would faint."

"What happened? What changed?" Jule asked him softly.

Rafe leaned forward, elbows resting on his knees, his hands balled loosely in front of him as he stared at the gray floor. "The possibility that he—that *we*—might lose Cort." His voice held the weight of worry. "I guess it hit us both hard. It was like all those years of resenting each other hadn't happened. Or maybe we saw how stupid we'd been to blame each other for what Jed and Theresa did."

Jule leaned over and began massaging the tense muscle at the back of his neck. "Hmm," she murmured in a soothing tone, not wanting to distract him from his thoughts and hoping he would open up even more. "You and Sawyer have been through a lot together."

"Yeah, my parents' deaths, divorces, Jed and all the crap he put us through. For a while, we were just trying to survive it. We don't need to share the same blood to be brothers."

Jule's heart caught in her throat. "After what you've been through, I'd say you *do* share the same blood, along with the sweat and tears."

Rafe lifted his head and took her hand from where she was still massaging his nape, turned it over and pressed a long, gentle kiss into her palm. "I'm glad *you're* here."

"Me, too," she murmured, savoring the tenderness of his touch. This felt right, them together, facing trouble as one, instead of fighting what was meant to be. New arrivals, though, distracted Jule from her brief savoring of the renewed closeness between her and Rafe. "Speaking of brothers, your youngest just strolled in."

Rafe followed her gaze to the E.R. entrance. "Looks like he either closed down last call or opened the morning saloon."

Jule noticed the much older man walking beside Josh, not at all the lady-killer sort Josh would be partying with, but rather a serious, straight-shouldered man with a stress-weathered face. "Who's that he's with?"

"Frank Rentaria, the sheriff. Cort's boss," Rafe said, waving them over.

"How is he?" Frank asked after shaking Rafe's hand and nodding a vague greeting to Jule. "Sorry it took me so long to get here, but I wanted to handle the interview with the guy who ran him down myself." The hard note in his voice spoke volumes.

Josh, slightly bleary-eyed, shifted his glance between Rafe and Frank and then settled on Jule as if he found her the most sympathetic of the bunch. "Is Cort gonna be okay?"

"We don't know. He's in pretty bad shape," Rafe said. "They were getting him ready for surgery. Frank, this is Jule Santiago, by the way."

"I know of your family. Nice to meet you."

Jule offered her hand. "You, too. Were you there when it happened?"

"No. I was at home. The Luna Hermosa dispatcher called me after it happened." He put a hand on Josh's shoulder. "I was on my way here and I passed the watering hole where this cowboy's truck was parked outside. I figured if he was in there he hadn't heard about his brother."

No wonder Josh hadn't answered his cell phone, Jule thought. He was probably too busy hitting on some pretty young thing in a place too noisy to hear yourself talk, let alone hear the phone.

Josh looked a little sheepish. "I followed Frank right here. Has anybody seen Cort?"

Rafe shook his head. "And no one's likely to for quite a while."

One of the deputies who had been waiting for news of Cort came up to them with cups of coffee and Josh quickly took a cup, swigging it down whiskey-style. He turned to Frank. "How's this going to affect his job?"

Frank shrugged. "Hard to say. Let's just hope there's no permanent damage and physical therapy can do the rest."

"Let's just hope he makes it through surgery," Rafe said.

The group fell silent, each lost in his or her thoughts.

Jule noticed out the front window of the E.R. that the sun had come up. "I'd better call my mother," she said to Rafe, "or she'll be sending out the police to look for me."

Rafe nodded and she stepped aside to make the call. "Good morning," she said when her mother answered on the first ring.

"Don't you tell me you spent the night with him, Julene Maria, just don't you tell me that!"

"I spent the night at the hospital, Mom."

"The hospital! Why didn't you call me sooner? What's happened? Is it your father? Has something happened to you?"

"No, it's not Dad or me. It's Cort Morente."

She heard her mother's sigh of relief. "Thank heavens. I mean, well I don't mean that. I'm only relieved it's not you or your father. What happened?"

Jule filled her mother in on the bare details then told her she planned to spend the day at Rafe's side, so she wouldn't be available at the clinic or to take her mother out to run errands.

Catalina fell silent, then with a new composure in her voice gave Jule the warning she was in no mood to hear. "You are getting far too involved in that man's personal life. That family is a mess. Some even say it's cursed. Why do you want to complicate your life by becoming involved with this?"

"Mom, I—"

"I'm not finished. It's not too late to distance yourself. Those bison are better. Your father is improving. You can leave soon and go back to Albuquerque, or, better yet, move to Arizona or Texas, away from that family and that man."

"And what about Dad and the business?" Jule asked, trying hard to tamp down her exasperation.

"We can hire the help we need for now. When your father retires, we can move to a nice retirement community near you."

Jule sighed. The last thing she needed right now was to get into a discussion of her future with her mother. Especially since, in her dreams, she envisioned her future here, in Luna Hermosa, with Rafe. "Mom, I don't want to get into any of this right now. I haven't slept or eaten. But I'm staying with Rafe all day or longer if he needs me. If there's some place you absolutely have to go to today, I'll find someone else to give you a ride."

Another long silence spanned the invisible line connecting

their voices. "I'm fine. Do what you have to do. I love you, Julene. I only want what's best for you. Remember that."

Her mother's last words lingered as Jule hung up. She knew her mother and father loved her. But her parents also wanted to run her life. Sooner or later, they'd have to accept that that wasn't possible. Not anymore.

When Jule returned to the group, Sawyer and Maya had joined Rafe, Josh and Frank, along with a newcomer Jule didn't recognize at first.

"I can't believe it. We were just playing basketball last night," the man was saying as Jule took her place by Rafe.

"Jule, I don't know if you remember Alex Trejos," Sawyer said. "He's a good friend and long-time basketball buddy of Cort's."

Jule and Alex exchanged greetings, and, as they did, Rafe, in an uncustomary show of affection, slipped his arm around her waist. Jule wondered, slightly pleased at the thought, whether Rafe could actually be jealous of Alex? She didn't see a wedding ring on Alex's finger and he was attractive enough, though in her estimation he didn't compare to Rafe or any one of his drop-dead-gorgeous brothers. He did give her a definite once-over when she walked up, but men just did that out of habit, didn't they?

Whatever the reason, she was enjoying Rafe's momentary display of possessiveness.

"He's been so preoccupied lately, more than usual," Alex was saying, "which is saying a lot. I knew he was working on something big, but he never said much about it."

"It didn't help that he was on his motorcycle," Josh put in. "Not much between him and that truck that hit him."

"If it hadn't been the bike," Rafe said, "it would have been that other excuse for transportation he uses, that Jeep he won't keep the top on."

Sawyer shook his head. "Cort's always been fearless."

As Jule listened to them, the ray of hope that had sparked to life earlier between Sawyer and Rafe grew with every exchange of caring and concern they were sharing over Cort. There was a bond between them, just as she'd suspected. And if only that bond could be nourished and grow, maybe one day their broken family would be whole. But Cort had to get through this and be a part of that family, or it would never be complete.

Time slipped by as family and friends milled restlessly around the waiting room. Finally, shortly before noon, an exhausted-looking surgeon emerged from behind double doors that led to the operating room. Everyone gathered close, falling silent.

"It was touch and go for a while, but we've stopped the bleeding and set the broken bones," the surgeon said. He pulled his surgical cap off and wiped his brow.

Rafe held tightly to Jule's hand, pressing hard. She squeezed back, glad he could find comfort in her touch.

"I'm not going to sugarcoat this," the surgeon went on. "His condition is still critical and there's a good chance he's going to need more surgery on that arm and shoulder. It'll take months for him to heal completely and longer in physical therapy."

"But he *is* going to recover," Sawyer said, the statement half question, half a demand for reassurance.

"He's not gonna have any permanent problems, right?" Josh added.

"I can't answer that yet," the doctor said. "It's too soon to know for sure. But Cort's young and strong, so he'd got the best chance possible of recovery."

Frank spoke up then. "Good enough to stay on the job?"

The doctor hesitated. "Like I said, it's too soon to know. But if I was making an educated guess—" He looked at Sawyer, Rafe and Josh in turn. "If I were a brother of his, over the next few months, I'd be dropping some strong hints about him finding another line of work."

"That'd be more likely to kill him than this," Rafe muttered.

"That's like asking me to give up riding rodeo." Josh, for the first time, looked upset. "I'd rather cut off my left foot."

Jule didn't know Cort as well as his brothers, but from her impressions and knowing how obsessed Josh was with chasing the next rodeo title, she guessed Rafe had hit close to the truth. "But as long as the three of you support him, don't you think he'll eventually adjust?"

The brothers exchanged doubtful looks. "Cort isn't exactly the flexible type when it involves his job," Sawyer said finally. "It's not really a job with him, it's more of a mission."

Jule didn't fully understand the comment. But she vaguely remembered her mother telling her the gossip around town when Cort had dropped out of law school and joined the sheriff's department after his fiancée was killed by an addict.

Rafe nodded. "Doesn't seem like he's ever gotten over that woman he lost years ago."

As soon as he'd said it, Jule saw realization dawn on his face. He'd accidentally described himself in front of everyone who knew the whole story about their past. Despite the worry over Cort, she had to smile at the irony of Rafe's slip.

The tension dropped a notch. Barely suppressed smiles popped up all around the circle. Josh laughed outright. "Look who's talking."

Perplexed, the surgeon asked, "Am I missing something?"

"Yeah, me, too," Frank added.

"Inside joke," Rafe said wryly. "Glad I could at least make everyone smile."

"Part of our convoluted family saga," Sawyer explained.

The surgeon frowned a little, then with a shake of his head went on to give a few more details about the surgery and recovery process. When he'd finished he added, "Cort's going to be in recovery for several hours before we move him into ICU, so you all might as well go freshen up and get something to eat."

After the doctor hurried off, Sawyer put a hand on Rafe's shoulder and another on Josh's. "I don't know about the rest of you but I'm starving. You're all invited to breakfast at the diner on me."

As the group broke up and everyone headed for the door Jule paused, reached up and kissed Rafe on the cheek.

He smiled. "What was that for?"

"Because I'm proud of you."

"Of me? Why?"

"For giving Sawyer a chance. For caring about Cort. With everything that's gone on in the past, I can only try to imagine how hard all of this is for you."

Rafe opened the door of the hospital onto the light of early afternoon. Clouds had begun to gather, dimming the sun, but compared to the close confines and weighted atmosphere of the waiting room, even the diffused light seemed brilliant. They paused a moment as their eyes adjusted and Jule took a long breath of the first crisp burst of fresh sage- and piñon-scented air.

Pulling her close, Rafe brushed a kiss atop her head. "It's been a long night. But today's been a long time coming. I guess it's about time we all started to look forward instead of back."

Chapter Fifteen

Rafe pulled his truck to a stop in front of his house, leaning his head back against the seat and closing his eyes for a moment. It was a mistake. Exhaustion washed over him in a wave and it took a serious effort on his part not to give in and fall asleep right there.

Jule hadn't made it as far as the house. Halfway home from the hospital, he'd made some attempt at conversation, gotten no response and glanced over to see her curled up sideways on the seat, sleeping. He almost hated to wake her but sleeping in his pickup truck, in the cold, wasn't going to do either of them any good.

Letting himself out, he walked over to the passenger side, unfastened her seatbelt and gently scooped her into his arms. The motion and the slam of the door as he kicked it shut roused her and she blinked sleepily around her before realizing he was carrying her into the house.

"Sorry, I didn't mean to fall asleep," she said, stifling a yawn.

"You're lucky I made it here," he said as he let them inside and made straight for the bedroom. "You were supposed to be keeping me awake."

A pale light filtered into the rest of the house but thick clouds from a quickening storm overcast the late-afternoon sky and with the shades drawn, the bedroom was spread with shadows. Setting her down on the bed, Rafe dragged back the quilt and sheets before turning back to Jule. He helped her out of her coat and then knelt down in front of her and pulled off her boots.

"What are you doing?" she asked.

"Putting you to bed." Tipping her back onto the pillow, he took off his own boots, slid in beside her and pulled the blankets up over them both.

Jule went still and he could almost hear her thinking, trying to sort out what he had in mind.

"Sleep," he answered her unspoken question. "I don't know about you, but the only thing I've got any energy left for is closing my eyes. I'm not letting you drive home until you've gotten some rest." When she didn't say anything, he added, "Jule, I swear I—"

"Will you hold me?"

Not waiting for his answer, she shifted to lie by his side, slipping her hand over his chest. Rafe reacted instinctively, putting his arms around her and pulling her close, her head pillowed on his shoulder.

If he hadn't been bone-deep tired and his resistance at low ebb from the emotional ups and downs of the day, being this close to her, in the bed where he'd first and last made love to her, would have been hell.

Instead, it was comfort and warmth, and the only thing he needed.

Jule woke to warm darkness and Rafe's arms around her. For a few moments, she thought she was dreaming again of desires beyond her reach. The slow steady sound of his breathing and the familiar scent and shape of the body cradling hers made it real and she remembered him putting her in his bed, promising only to hold her while they slept.

She wanted to switch on the light so she could see him, but didn't want to wake him. She couldn't resist touching, though. Propping herself up on her forearm, she lightly swanned her fingers over his cheek, the edge of his jaw, and his mouth, slightly parted in sleep, her caresses less sensual than reassuring. What had just happened to Cort reminded her of how quickly the unexpected could change everything.

The near tragedy had left her with a keen sense of all she and Rafe had lost in the past thirteen years. They'd wasted so much time on things that didn't matter when held up in contrast to their feelings for each other. They were still wasting time instead of seizing second chances.

Absorbed in her thoughts as she absently traced a line along his collar to the hollow of his throat, she didn't realize he'd woken until she heard the sudden quick intake of his breath and his hand covered hers, stopping her motion. She felt his body tense.

"I'm sorry," she murmured. "I didn't mean to wake you." She sensed him watching her and again resisted the temptation to flick on the lights. Not being able to read his expression made her feel vulnerable, uncertain of what to say or do next.

"You okay?" he asked.

"Yes. Fine, I—fine."

Suddenly she could sense every nuance of being pressed up against his side as if every nerve in her body was suddenly hypersensitive. Collapsing into bed with Rafe, dead on her feet and too tired to think, was one thing. Waking up with him, without the mental fuzziness of exhaustion, and knowing it would take little more than a glance and a touch to turn this into something other than an interlude of rest and comfort, was another.

"Not one of my better ideas," he muttered, more to himself than her. Pushing the covers off himself, Rafe slid out from under her and sat up. "Think I'll get the fire going again. You stay here and get some rest."

He started to get up and she didn't want him to leave.

"No, don't." She moved quickly, sitting up and putting her hand on his thigh at the same time to stop him. Leaning into him, she softly kissed him and whispered against his mouth the only thing she could think of to tell him everything she felt, everything she wanted.

"Stay."

Fighting every need, every desire, every instinct that screamed for him to take what she offered without questioning, Rafe hesitated. He put his hands on her shoulders, half caressing, half holding her far enough away that he could think.

"What's different?" he made himself ask. "What changed? You said you didn't want—"

"I've always wanted. And we've changed."

Maybe they had and he hadn't noticed. It had come so slowly, or all tonight—or it didn't matter because he no longer had the will or the strength to push her away again.

Slowly gathering her into his arms, threading a hand through the silken tangle of her hair, he searched her face, cursing the darkness for putting her in shadows.

As if her thoughts echoed his own, Jule reached around him and switched on the lamp. "I need to see you," she said softly. "It's been so long…"

Rafe looked into her eyes, stretching the moment of anticipation until it was thin and taut. Then he kissed her, long and deep, taking his time because he wanted it to last forever.

She nearly broke his resolve to be patient with one kiss. Opening herself to him, giving as equally as she took from him, she made him want everything, now, and he fought the urge to take her then and there, hard, fast and passionate. But that brought to mind the brief encounters that he'd used as a substitute for loving Jule in the years they'd been apart. Jule deserved the best of him.

Rafe hoped he could give it to her.

He was becoming increasingly worried about his ability to please her. Since Jule, there'd been no tenderness, no caring between him and the women he'd bedded. He'd forgotten, if he'd ever learned, the art of seduction or even gentleness.

He didn't know he'd withdrawn from her until she touched his face. "What's wrong?" The soft lamplight showed him the uncertainty in her eyes. "If this isn't what you want—"

"It's all I want. You know that." Rafe fumbled for the right words. "It's not you. It's me. I'm not...I haven't been the man you said you knew. I don't know—if I can be what you need."

"You've always been what I need," she said. Her eyes slid from his and she focused on a point in the center of his chest, her fingers rubbing at the edges of his shirt until finally, she looked back up. "I want to be what you need, too. But there's never been anyone but you. I know there've been others..."

Rafe swallowed hard against the sudden tightness in his throat. "I never made love to any of them. Only you."

Pulling her close to him again, he kissed her with all the tenderness he could find inside. "I love you," he whispered against her ear. "I love you, Jule. You're everything, the only thing I need."

The words sounded woefully inadequate to describe his feelings for her and so he gave up, pushing his doubts aside, letting his body tell her what he would never be able to say.

He bent to kiss her and she met him halfway, kissing him back with all the love and longing she'd kept locked inside her heart for so long. This was what she'd been waiting for since the day she'd come back to Luna Hermosa. For the past thirteen years.

All her life.

Not breaking their kiss, Rafe gently lowered her to lie

among the tangled bedclothes. He moved to one knee beside her and slowly, watching intently, he began to undress her. When he'd tossed aside the last of her clothes, he paused, just looking at her with an expression so near to humbled reverence, as if he couldn't quite believe she was real and knew he didn't deserve it if she was.

Tears blurred Jule's eyes. "I love you," she whispered.

Wonderment vying against uncertainty on his face made him seem vulnerable. "Why?"

Before she could answer, he kissed her, a soft sensual kiss meant to distract her from pursuing the question. When he pulled back, she'd forgotten why it was important or that there'd ever been a question.

He touched her then, lightly at first, his calloused fingers following the curve of her neck to her throat, skimming the valley between her breasts and lower, to the curve of her hip. The intimate caress fed the need in her to feel his hands—no, all of him—against her skin, to touch him in return.

Shifting upward, she knelt before him and began unbuttoning his shirt, murmuring, "My turn."

"Not yet. Jule stop," he groaned when she pressed herself closer, teasing, tempting him. "I need to get—while I can still think."

"I like the idea of you not being able to think." But she waited, impatiently, as he made a hasty search through the nightstand drawer to find what he wanted. When he turned back to her, Jule picked up where she'd left off.

Rafe smiled at her eagerness and turned her fingers clumsy by sliding his hands up her arms and over her breasts. The simple act of pushing a button through its slot became hugely complicated when he cupped her breasts in his large hands, fingering her nipples while his mouth found the sensitive area behind her ear.

Finally finished with the buttons, Jule splayed her fingers over his chest and leaned forward to press a kiss against the hollow of his throat. She both felt and heard the low noise he made, half growl, half groan. Yanking off his shirt, he pulled her against him so they were skin to skin and covered her mouth with his, kissing her hungrily, almost desperately, as if he wanted to make her part of him.

Tangling her hands in his hair, she pushed closer, made wanton by the feel of hard muscle, the ragged sound of his breathing, and his hands, stroking, touching her back, along her thighs, her hips. She started working free the button of his jeans but he gently pushed her hands aside to finish the job himself, standing away from her long enough to strip off the rest of his clothes before tumbling her back on the bed.

He followed her down, moving over her, touching her everywhere, not just with his hands, but his mouth, tongue, teeth, making her wild as he fed the need to have him inside her. Unable, unwilling to wait any longer, she wrapped her arms around his neck and her legs around his hips and all but begged him to finish what they'd started.

"Jule…" Rafe groaned against her mouth. "Wait. I—"

"Yes, now," she murmured between hot, hurried kisses. "It's right. You know it's right."

At the last word she angled her hips to fit against his and his resistance snapped.

Sliding an arm under her shoulders to gather her closer, he thrust into her and she arched up, taking him deeper. From somewhere, he refound his patience and began making love to her with an achingly slow, stroking rhythm, leading her closer to the edge until she was burning from the inside out, and finally she fell.

The feeling crashed over her, destroying the last of her defenses against completely and irrevocably loving him. When she felt him shudder inside her, burying his face in the curve between her shoulder and neck, she felt dampness on her face and realized she was crying.

Rafe nuzzled her throat, kissing her ear, her cheek and then abruptly pulling back to look at her with apprehension in his eyes when his mouth grazed her tears. "Did I hurt you?"

"No, it's just—" Taking a trembling breath, she smoothed her fingertips over his face, the features she loved. "I'd forgotten what it was like. That it could be so…"

There weren't any words. Rafe seemed to understand and didn't press her to explain, only brushed lingering kisses against her cheeks, her forehead. Rolling onto his back, he took her in his arms again, pulling the tangled bedclothes up over them and holding her as he had when they'd slept, saying nothing and everything with simply his touch.

Jule woke up alone, this time to sunlight edging around the shades, streaking the room with gold. She pushed herself up against the pillows, dragging a hand through her tangled hair. It might have all been a dream, making love with Rafe, except their clothes still lay scattered on the floor, and she could smell his scent, distinctively male and Rafe, on her skin and the rumpled bedclothes.

Not quite sure how to feel about finding herself alone after everything they'd shared the last two days, she was on the verge of getting up to find him when Rafe came into the bedroom carrying a tray. His only concession to dressing had been to pull on his jeans and with his hair loose and tousled and wearing nothing else but a slow intimate smile, he made her forget her brief unease and remember everything in vivid detail from the night before.

Setting the tray down on the bedside table, he bent and kissed her lingeringly. "Good morning," he murmured.

"Good morning." She tried not to feel self-conscious about being the one naked in bed. Those jeans definitely gave him the advantage. "What's all this?" she asked, nodding at the tray.

"I made you breakfast. Thought you might be hungry."

He grinned and she blushed. To hide her discomfort she scooted up a little higher on the pillows, pulling the bedcovers up under her arms.

"I hope we're sharing," she remarked as he put the tray on her lap and she looked at the mound of scrambled eggs and toast he'd piled there. The aroma made her stomach rumble and she realized how hungry she was. Suddenly, seeing the trouble he'd taken for her and how at ease he was with her for the first time in years, any uncomfortable feelings vanished. This was Rafe, her best friend and her lover again. She didn't have to hide or pretend with him. "I only see one fork here."

"Like you said, we're sharing." Climbing into bed beside her, he punched his pillow up behind him and snagged one of the coffee mugs off the tray.

"Have you heard anything about Cort this morning?" Jule asked after a few minutes.

"Yeah, I called earlier. He's still on the critical list, but they said he's holding his own. I'll run by this afternoon." Finishing off his coffee, he set the mug aside and forked up a bite of egg, feeding it to her. When she'd swallowed, he rubbed the pad of his thumb over her lips. "Sorry," he said, sounding anything but. "I forgot the napkins."

"Oh, that's too bad. I can be very messy." She drew a line using her fingertip through the butter on a piece of toast and then held up her finger. "See?"

Rafe leaned over and took her finger into his mouth, lightly sucking. "Good you've got me around then."

The low, husky timbre of his voice sent a shiver over her that turned into full-blown trembling when he gathered up a fistful of her hair to bring her closer and ran his tongue over her lower lip.

Jule managed to shift the tray off her lap and onto the bedside table despite the serious distraction of Rafe nuzzling his way along the line of her jaw to her ear. "I don't want to keep you from work," she said, the end of the sentence ending on a sharply indrawn breath as he pushed the bedclothes down and his hand found her breast.

"What?" he mumbled.

She leaned her head back, baring her throat to the hot, open-mouthed kisses he was trailing over her skin. "Work. The ranch."

"Later. I'm busy."

The most reply Jule could make at that moment was something resembling a satisfied "Mmm…" in response to Rafe kicking the covers completely away and working his mouth farther down her body.

Knowing he was totally focused on her made the pleasure all the more keen. For the first time, he'd put her ahead of the ranch, made their being together a priority. Maybe, like her, what had happened to Cort had made him realize this was more important than anything else; maybe it was just love.

"Yes," she agreed. "Much later."

"I really should get back." Jule yawned, stretched, shifting to a more comfortable position against Rafe's chest. "Lucia's going to quit if I don't at least check in at the clinic and I'm pretty sure my mom has decided by now that I've moved in with you."

They were lying together on the couch while they waited for Jule's clothes to finish drying. It had been nearly eleven when they'd finally gotten out of bed after a reluctant mutual agreement that they both had things that needed to get done today only to get sidetracked for another hour when they decided to shower together. Rafe then offered to do her laundry since Jule hadn't changed in nearly two days and refused to go back into town wearing only his shirt, no matter how good he insisted she looked in it.

Actually, Rafe thought she looked better out of it, but she was right about having to at least acknowledge real life. He had two days' worth of catching up to do and he didn't think Josh had bothered with any of it, unless his little brother had gotten a sudden fit of conscience over being in a bar, trying to decide between his pick of women, while the rest of them were worrying over Cort.

The problem was he was happy right now, happier than he

could ever remember being, and he figured the moment they walked out his door to rejoin the rest of the world that the bubble of contentment he'd been living in the past day would be shot to hell.

"Maybe you should," he said, almost to himself.

She leaned her head back against his shoulder to look up at him. "Maybe I should what?"

"Move in with me. Stay with me."

Jule started back, looking stunned. Rafe was pretty sure he looked about the same since the words had just fallen out of his mouth without any conscious thought on his part.

"I—" She twisted around so they were face to face. "Are you serious?"

"What would you say if I was?"

There was what seemed to Rafe like a painfully long pause and then she said slowly, "I don't know. It depends."

"On what?"

"On whether or not it's permanently. Or if it will only last as long as things go the way you want them to with the ranch."

"If I asked, it would be permanently."

"So are you asking?"

Was he? Rafe wanted to say yes. He wanted to have this, have her, every day, for the rest of his life. But it was hard to convince the part of him that had never believed he deserved her that no matter what happened with the ranch, loving her would be enough.

"I want to go back out to talk with the Pinwa, see if I can learn anything else," he said, avoiding answering her question.

Jule lowered her eyes, but not before he saw disappointment there. "If you can wait until the weekend, I'll go with you."

"I want you to." Gently, Rafe cupped her face with his hands so she looked at him again. "I know I don't have the right to ask. But just give me a little more time."

She nodded. "Just promise me it won't be another thirteen years."

"I promise," he vowed softly and kissed her. It started off a tender touch of his mouth against hers, but she leaned into him and he wrapped his arms around her and it quickly became all heat and urgent need.

"I love you, Jule," he told her, not able to say it enough as desire took over and they shut reality out for a little while longer.

Chapter Sixteen

"This is only our second time here, but somehow I feel so at home." Jule grabbed her backpack and climbed out of Rafe's truck. Rafe's relatives were already walking toward them.

Rafe picked up his own bag and followed her. "It's hard not to when they're all waiting to greet us with open arms."

"Something Jed's never done," Jule said under her breath. But Rafe heard her. "Jed doesn't do warm and fuzzy."

"That's the understatement of the century."

Not wanting to ruin the evening with angry thoughts about Jed Garrett, Jule focused instead on the small group of people coming toward them. Rafe's family looked so at peace, so satisfied in their way of life. Their obvious contentment radiated outward, somehow easing the worry and stress of recent days over her relationship with Rafe, Cort nearly being killed, and the bisons' illness. Sweeping in a slow breath of cold, refreshing evening air, she savored a moment to absorb the sheer beauty around her.

A low early-winter sun, moody and deep orange as it sank

behind the distant horizon, set a dramatic backdrop against the darkened green pines and sienna earth. Draped in heavy woven blankets in striped hues of red, blue, green and brown, Rafe's uncle and his family blended naturally with the earth, mountains, sky and trees. With slow deliberation they embraced both Jule and Rafe.

Maybe because of his recently renewed bond with Sawyer or their own newfound intimacy, Jule noticed this time Rafe more easily returned the gestures of family ties and affection. It was as if the events of the past few days had eased some long-held tension in him, leaving him more open and receptive to loving and being loved. She couldn't help feeling both grateful for the change in Rafe and hopeful it would keep them together, no matter what direction his search for the truth about his parents and the ranch took him.

"Welcome back," Rafe's uncle Pay said, hugging Rafe then reaching up and wrapping his blanket around his nephew's shoulders. "We were sorry to hear about your brother. Is there any change?"

Rafe shook his head. "We stopped by the hospital before we left. He's still critical. There's not much we can do but wait."

His wife Mina echoed Pay's gesture, draping her blanket around Jule. "He and you are in our thoughts," she said as Jule thanked her with a smile.

The elder of Pay's sons, Kimo, was with them. He shook both their hands. "You must be hungry. My wife and Tansy have prepared a meal for you."

"Thanks, starving actually," Rafe said. "We didn't have time for dinner before we left."

The group headed back to Pay's house, the last hues of primrose sunlight softly yielding to the white glow of the rising moon. Rafe swept his blanket around Jule, pulling her close to him. "We needed this."

"I know. I feel more relaxed already. What is it about this place?"

Rafe shrugged. "I'm learning along with you. But there's something here."

"Magic, maybe?"

"Maybe," he said, smiling slow and easy and Jule's breath caught at the remembrance and promise of passion in his eyes that belonged to her alone.

He ducked to enter the low-ceilinged adobe house. There in the open family area, a simple table was set. Tansy was scurrying about at her mother's command, placing plates and bowls of delicious, spicy-smelling foods in the center of the table. A blazing fire lit the kiva fireplace at the back of the kitchen and dining area, lending a generous warmth to the gathering.

Rafe's grandmother occupied the spot she'd been in last time they'd come there, close to the fireplace with a view of the whole room. Jule noticed she nodded his way as they came inside, her black eyes narrowed and contemplative. His grandmother seemed to be studying him again. But the intensity with which those all-seeing eyes of hers followed Rafe around the room was actually a little unnerving to Jule. She could certainly see from whom Rafe inherited his ebony eyes and that piercing gaze of his.

When everyone was seated, Pay said a few words to the family in his native tongue, then, as everyone began to pass the food and enjoy the meal, he turned to Rafe. "How is your herd?"

"Better, thanks. Your advice seems to be working. We switched antibiotics and started the regime your expert recommended."

"It's something I never learned in school," Jule said. "None of the other vets I contacted had ever heard of that treatment either, but I won't forget it. Thank you for sharing it with us."

"Rafe is family. All we have, from our ancestors to those of us who are left, we'll share with him."

Visibly moved, Rafe set his fork down. "I appreciate that, more than I can say. I wish—I'm sorry I didn't come sooner."

The happy chatter around the table fell to a low hum as everyone paused to listen to the exchange between Rafe and Pay.

Jule keenly felt Rafe's discomfort. He'd spent his life avoiding emotional ties to almost everyone and despite the progress he'd made repairing his relationship with Sawyer, he still instinctively began throwing up the walls when he came too close to confronting his feelings. But it seemed his estranged family wasn't going to let him get away with that any longer. For that she was grateful.

Pay poured an odd but pleasant-smelling drink into a cup then passed the pitcher. "You need to know the elders discussed coming to get you, after your parents died, and again when you became a man. But both times we decided against it."

"Why? Didn't my parents ever bring me to visit? Didn't they ever come back?"

"No, they didn't." A slight frown, compounded of regret and what might have been bitterness, passed over Pay's face. The gesture was so quick, Jule wondered if she'd imagined it.

"We'd hoped Anoki and Halona would return to us, at least to visit, after you were born. We never understood why they didn't." He glanced at Rafe's grandmother. She said nothing. Sitting there, alone in the shadows, her expression was unreadable. "Our mother, Lolanne, accepted their decision and asked us to as well. But for many of us, their choice was…hurtful." Pausing, Pay focused on the table in front of him before adding, "Halona was my sister, and I loved Anoki like a brother. It was hard to forgive them."

"Rafe, it was never because we didn't want you here with us," Mina said. "It was hard to accept that your parents had left us for good. We're a very small tribe now. We missed them, and we missed watching you grow up."

"You sure did that," Pay's younger son put in. "You're nearly a foot taller than most of us!"

Everyone laughed a little, easing the tension, and Jule reached under the table to lay her hand on Rafe's thigh.

He reached down and squeezed her hand. "Now that I've finally met all of you," he said, his voice low and full of angst, "I wonder if I would have been better off growing up here."

"That's difficult to know," Pay said slowly. "And still too soon to answer."

"What do you mean?"

When Pay didn't respond, Kimo tried. "What my father means is that you haven't found what we call your peaceful time. You're still struggling with your life's choices, your work, your mate," he said with an apologetic nod to Jule. "You can't know where you belong until you decide what it is you really want in your life. Or maybe don't want?"

"Believe me," Rafe said with a rueful grimace, "I'm trying. It's just—hard."

His admission surprised Jule. Apart from her, she'd never heard him admit his personal struggles to anyone. His pride and solitary, stubborn nature would never permit him to say something so private to Jed or his brothers, except maybe Sawyer and only very recently, since he and Sawyer begun, tentatively, to open up to each other. Her heart twisted for him; Rafe truly was trying to come to terms with his past, present and future and only she knew how difficult it was for him.

"We know you're searching," his uncle was saying. "We'll help you in any way we can."

"You already have. More than you realize."

When the conversation lulled, Tansy spoke up. In her quiet way, she seemed excited. Jule noticed her eyes sparkle as she asked Pay, "Can we go now? The moon is up."

"If everyone is finished, then, yes." He turned to Rafe and Jule. "Tonight we'd planned on a hike to the hot springs to bathe beneath the moon. It's an old tradition. The air is cold but the water is warm. It's a very pleasant way to end the day."

"That sounds wonderful," Jule said. "I haven't been to a hot springs since I was a little girl. Remember, Rafe? We rode over to the hot springs near Taos when we were kids."

A hint of a smile lifted the corner of Rafe's mouth. "How could I forget?"

"You two have known each other a long time," Mina said as Jule helped her begin to remove dishes to the kitchen.

"Since we were children. Then I left for college. I've only been back a few months." She hoped her short but thorough answer would stop any further questions she knew Rafe wouldn't want his relatives pursuing.

His relieved expression thanked her for not leaving the task of explaining their relationship to him.

"Are you here to stay?" Mina continued.

Yes hovered on the tip of her tongue, begging to be released. She didn't dare look at Rafe, afraid of what she might see in his face. "That's a hard question to answer right now. I have a lot to consider."

Mina wrapped an arm around Jule's shoulders and squeezed. "Then don't answer it yet. I'm sure the answer will come to you when the time is right."

Jule held up the lantern Mina had given her to illuminate her path. The trail to the hot springs meandered up and down a few rocky outcrops, gaining in incline as they hiked.

Soft, white light from the moon and countless stars helped to guide them through what would have been the pitch black of night. "What a perfect night," she said to Rafe as they continued to climb. "I'll bet the view from here in daylight is spectacular."

He stepped up behind her and patted her backside. "I like the view I have right now."

"Rafe!" Jule laughed and playfully slapped his hand away. "They'll hear you."

"Doubt it. They're twenty feet ahead of us."

Around the next switchback in the trail, Jule saw the rest of the group descending along a sharp decline. "The springs must be down there," she said pointing to a vague, black smudge in the landscape below. "I can smell the mineral water."

"After this hike, I'll be ready for a soak in it."

"Somebody's out of shape," she teased.

"Comes from not having you around to chase after. Although…" The dark rumble of his voice and the warmth of his breath suddenly caressed her ear. "I can think of a couple of other forms of exercise I like better."

"Riding? Tossing hay bales? Walking the fence line?"

"Careful, Julene. You'll have me thinking you've lost your imagination."

He kissed her ear and she laughed, taking his hand to walk the rest of the way down. They followed the trail's descent, the sound of rushing water greeting them at the bottom near a river. Rafe's uncle and cousins were already lighting a small fire at the river's edge. As Jule and Rafe neared the others who stood warming their hands near the burgeoning blaze, she inhaled the spicy, musky smoke of incense that had been added to the fire.

"There are several small pools over there," Pay explained, pointing and holding up his lantern to show Jule and Rafe where to go. "But be careful, it's rocky and the rocks are wet. Each pool is surrounded by rocks, so you'll have privacy."

Tansy started crawling up a group of rocks, agile as a little goat. "I was first to get here, so I get the biggest pool."

Her parents followed. "Wait for us," Mina said. "You're not going alone."

"Oh, Mom, I know my way with my eyes closed."

Pay followed his wife's lead. "We don't care. We're coming with you," he said as he and Mina left the others to try to keep up with their eager child.

"Stay here as late as you like, the guesthouse is open and waiting for you," Mina said before following her husband around another grouping of rocks. "You have your blankets and your lanterns. There is only one trail back, so you'll be fine if we leave before you do."

Rafe nodded. "Thanks. We'll see you in the morning, then."

Flushing at the implication in his words, Jule let Rafe take the lead and climbed after him in the direction of a pool his uncle had pointed toward. When they found it, hidden like a private rock-encased cove created just for them, Rafe pulled her close. "It's been too long since we went skinny-dipping in the hot springs, hasn't it?"

Jule laughed, remembering when they'd stolen away one summer day to do just that. "It's a good thing Jed and my father didn't catch us that day or they'd have separated us for good."

"We got away with a few things back then." Rafe slid his hands up under her shirt, gently rubbing the small of her back. Holding her beneath the moon's ethereal glow, he slid his hands up further along her spine.

"Hmm…and what do you think you're going to get away with right now?"

"A lot of things."

"Oh, yeah?"

"Yeah," he murmured, nuzzling her neck as he slowly moved his hands around to the front of her shirt and began pressing one button after another through each hole. "Beginning with this."

She shivered slightly, partly from the cold of night, partly from anticipation. Before slipping her shirt from her shoulders, Rafe reached down and pulled a blanket from the backpack they'd hastily stuffed. "Much better," she murmured when he wrapped it around her shoulders.

"Hold that and I'll help you out of those jeans."

"I get the feeling you're enjoying this," she said but stood still for him, stifling a prick of embarrassment at having Rafe undress her in the open, with his relatives nearby, by indulging in the pleasure of his hands stroking her body. He knelt before her, unsnapping her jeans and sliding them down her thighs, taking care to caress her hips, thighs, knees and calves all the way to her feet.

"Now the boots." He eased her backward to sit on a flattened rock, double-checking to make certain her blanket stayed wrapped around her legs. The care he took with her—patiently untying her hiking boots then pulling boots, socks and jeans off and setting them carefully on top of a rock so they wouldn't get wet—both pleased and humbled her. In this mood, he was so attentive and affectionate, it was hard to remember there was anything between them but love.

"Thank you," she said softly. "Now let me help you."

"I'm not finished yet." He began to trace a path back up her legs. "We're skinny-dipping, remember?"

The roughness of his fingertips along her skin excited her. "I remember."

Rafe leaned in to kiss her, a long, searching exploration. As he did, his hands found her panties, gently easing them from her legs. He paused to caress her thighs and belly before reaching behind her back to remove her bra and cup her breasts in his palms, then brushed his lips over each one. He took his time to taste and tease her and she gave herself to the primal need he roused in her with the simplest of touches.

Feeling a little light-headed from the barrage of sensations he was eliciting in her, she shifted back and took a long breath. "My turn," she said, her voice echoing slightly against the rock walls.

"No, it's too cold. You need to get into the warm water." With that, Rafe swept her, blanket and all, into his arms and moved over to the edge of the hot pool. Steam rose from the water into the night, kissing her face with warm moisture. He eased the blanket from her shoulders, tossing it back up onto a rock. "Climb in and I'll join you. I don't want you to catch a chill."

"But—"

"Don't argue with me, woman."

"I've never noticed until lately how bossy you've become," she grumbled in mock affront. But when the crisp air hit her bare skin, Jule decided this once she'd obey without question.

She slid into the sensuous, warm rolling waters of the pool and sighed. "Oh, this is beyond heaven."

Tempted to close her eyes, she couldn't when Rafe started undressing, his silhouette highlighted by moonglow. He pulled the leather strap from his hair and the locks fell to his shoulders, giving him that primitive, wild look that always made her knees weak. Even in near darkness she could make out the sinewed flexing of his biceps and thighs as he removed his shirt and jeans. The last time she'd seen him undress and jump into a hot spring, he was a scrawny, gangly boy. Despite the heat rising in her, the thought made her giggle.

Rafe paused from stripping away the rest of his clothes. "Am I that funny?"

"I was remembering what a cute naked boy you were that day we went skinny-dipping. What's funny is that I hardly noticed you were naked." That part was true. What she didn't add was that now she was thinking only of how he'd definitely become all man—and that *cute* was a far cry from any word she would use to describe him.

"Well, I noticed *you* were naked that day," he said as he lowered himself into the water beside her.

Jule shrugged, her slender shoulder brushing his muscular arm. "Boys will be boys."

"Maybe, but I sure didn't know what to do about it then."

"I'd say you've learned a thing or two."

Rafe maneuvered to sit behind her, leaning against the wall of the pool. "Think so?" He eased her between his thighs and put his hands beneath her back so she could relax and float out in front of him.

"You were just uncertain of yourself before." She lay back into his large hands, letting him support her as the warm water washed over her. Her long hair fanned out all around her in the water, forming a moonlit halo.

"Not sure I've made much progress in that regard," Rafe said, sliding down a little further into the pool. He wrapped his arms around her waist, moving her onto his lap beneath the water. "I'm still not where I want to be."

"You mean you haven't gotten to your 'peaceful time,' as your family calls it?"

"Something like that," he murmured against her neck. Pulling her closer to him, his legs drifted around hers and, letting the water pillow them all around, he rocked her in his arms. "Or maybe more like this."

They stayed that way, basking in the water and in each other. Except for the swish of the water and the occasional howl of a distant coyote or hoot of an owl, the night was silent. The aroma of the incense had drifted on the breeze into the rocky shelter of their little cove where it caught, swirling in the air around them, bringing desert and mountain scents together and blending hypnotically with the mineral aroma in the pool.

Feeling as though she was floating, inside and out, Jule turned over and wrapped her arms around Rafe's neck. She let her body, light and free, drift atop him while her mouth found his.

Rafe moaned low in his throat and wrapped her in his arms, stroking her back and hair. He kissed her with a passion that only deepened her hunger for more of him. She felt him hard against her and when he bent to kiss her breasts, she arched back opening completely to him. He lifted her, weightless in the water, to set her atop him. As she encircled him with her legs, they began to move together, a secret dance beneath the night-blackened waters of the hot spring, reflections from the stars above glistening like tiny sparks on the water where it broke and splashed around them.

She clung to him and he pulled her hard against him as he lifted her out of the pool and stood, back to a smooth rock, making love to her until all at once their bodies found the same sweet moment of pure union and with a mutual cry of shared pleasure, they tensed, every fiber of their bodies becoming one in that ancient, mystical instant that binds two people, body, heart and soul.

"I feel so—good." The word sounded woefully inadequate. "That was—"

"Amazing."

They were still joined and she could feel the echoes of their passion deep inside, binding them closer than any physical act. "*You're* amazing," she whispered and kissed him soft and deep before he could tell her otherwise.

Rafe realized they must have fallen asleep because when he opened his eyes it was freezing. The water was warm, but Jule's face felt like ice. "Wake up," he urged softly in her ear. "We're going to freeze to death if we don't get out of here and dry off."

Jule shifted and sat up, rubbing her eyes. "Oh, my gosh, did we actually fall asleep here? We could have drowned."

Rafe was already out of the pool dressing. "Probably not. But we're both going to have a helluva cold if we don't get back and get warm."

He tugged on his jeans and boots and held up a blanket for Jule. When she crawled out of the pool he quickly rubbed her dry and helped her to dress. Relighting their lanterns, Rafe led them on a fast-paced retreat back up the hilly trail to the little village.

He was surprised to see a dim golden light still shone through the front window of the little guesthouse. "Almost there. A warm bed never sounded so good."

"No kidding, although jogging to keep up with you warmed me up. I am exhausted, though."

He knew the feeling. A nap against rock had been more painful than restful. He made it worse by forgetting to duck, smacking his head on the doorway as he followed Jule inside. Distracted, he cursed and rubbed his forehead.

Jule's sharp, frightened gasp put him instantly on guard, pain and tiredness forgotten. Instinctively Rafe knotted his fists and shoved in front of her. Instead of trespasser, though, he found himself face-to-face with his grandmother.

Wrapped in a thick woven shawl, she sat by the fire, watching them with her fathomless eyes.

"I'm sorry," Jule said, "you startled me."

Lolanne gestured at them both. "I know you were not expecting company, especially at this hour. I needed to talk to Rafe before you both left. I was afraid I would miss you if I did not wait for you here."

"Have you been sitting there all this time?" Rafe asked.

"I am old," Lolanne said with a careless shrug. "I can sleep anywhere. Will you walk with me?"

A little wary at the reason for her unexpected request, especially at this late hour, he felt compelled to agree. He nodded. "Go on to bed," he told Jule. "I'll be back soon."

Jule searched his face and for a moment Rafe was sure she was going to ask to go along. "I'll be here," she finally said instead.

"I know." Kissing her lightly, he waited until she'd moved to the bed before following his grandmother outside.

They had walked for several minutes along a small creek that ran beside the guesthouse before she began to speak. "There is something I need to tell you."

"I'm listening."

"It is something I have never told anyone. But you should hear it."

Rafe wasn't sure he wanted to hear it. But he listened as Lolanne began to tell him about how a young Jed Garrett had come to the Pinwa to buy cattle and met Anoki Viarriai, then in charge of managing the tribe's herd. After a time and promises of financial gain, Anoki, bringing along his new bride, joined Jed in building Rancho Pintada into one of the area's biggest and most profitable cattle ranches.

Rafe listened, but when Lolanne had said all she had to say, only her final words struck with lightning ferocity and tore apart everything he'd believed was true.

"Jed Garrett is your real father."

Chapter Seventeen

Jule was dying of curiosity by the time she and Rafe set out on the drive back down to Luna Hermosa the next day. Rafe had been in a dark, almost angry mood ever since she'd wakened, refusing to discuss the conversation he'd had with his grandmother until they were alone. Fully dressed, he'd been up and sitting staring out the window when she'd finally opened her eyes. She guessed he'd never gone to bed.

Refusing the offer of breakfast, he'd told Pay with a few short words he had to get back into town to check on Cort. They'd left abruptly, and Jule hoped his family wasn't offended by Rafe's mood. They hadn't seen that side of him yet, so she'd been left to smooth things over as best as she could, promising to visit again soon.

Now he appeared possessed by his thoughts—obviously not pleasant ones—his foot heavy on the gas pedal as they wound down the mountain. Whatever his grandmother had told him, Jule had to find out, even if it meant risking a confrontation with his foul temper in the process.

"Are you going to make me beg?" she asked finally, breaking the oppressive silence. "You promised to tell me when we were alone. We've been alone for half an hour and you haven't said a word."

Rafe's knuckles whitened where he gripped the steering wheel. "This isn't easy. I don't know who I'm angriest at."

"Just start at the beginning, please."

"Apparently my parents didn't have the perfect marriage I always imagined they had."

"I'm sorry."

Rafe's bark of laughter was short and harsh. "It gets a lot worse and you're going to be a lot sorrier."

Not knowing how to respond to that, Jule tried to ignore the sense of foreboding creeping over her.

"Anoki was in charge of the Pinwa's cattle until he started selling cattle to Jed." He didn't look at her but stared straight ahead. His voice sounded tight and hard, the words forced out. "Jed told him he needed a partner. He apparently offered him the moon to help him get the ranch off the ground. So Anoki and my mother left the Pinwa behind. She was only seventeen."

"I knew the first part, but I didn't know Halona was so young."

"Young, spoiled, sheltered. Vulnerable. She was the baby, and my grandmother's only daughter. Anoki was so busy building up the ranch he ignored her a lot of the time. Halona used to come home crying and tell my grandmother she wished she'd stayed and never married him."

"I had no idea it was like that. It sounds as if your father loved the ranch more than he loved her." The words slipped out before Jule realized their implication.

He shot a hard stare her way. "So it seems." He looked away again, his hands pressing the steering wheel hard enough to leave permanent impressions.

"Rafe, I—"

"Jed married Theresa, but that was a joke from the beginning," Rafe went on, quickly, stopping her from going any further. "My mother said that Theresa was cold and unloving. My guess is Theresa found out sooner rather than later that all Jed wanted from her was her money."

Jule nodded. "I remember my parents talking about that. It was quite a scandal when she finally took her boys and left him when she found out about his affair with Del."

"Yeah, well, it would have been a bigger scandal if she'd known the whole truth. Before Del ever came along, while Theresa was pregnant with Sawyer and Anoki was working his ass off on the ranch, it seems Jed decided to pay some extra attention to Anoki's neglected bride."

Jule's stomach knotted. "Oh, no."

"Oh, yes. Jed and my mother had an affair."

"I can't even imagine— She must have been desperately lonely."

"She said she loved him."

"Loved him?" Jule tried and failed to imagine anyone loving Jed Garrett.

"And that he loved her." He gave a derisive snort. "That I know has to be a lie. Because Jed Garrett never loved anyone."

"Who knew?" Jule asked.

"Only my grandmother. Until now. Now you and I know." Rafe downshifted as they headed into the steep, winding decline toward Luna Hermosa.

"Your uncle and his family never found out?"

Rafe shook his head. "My grandmother never told them. It would have been too humiliating for Anoki and Halona. It would have dishonored their names."

"But your father didn't do anything wrong, except neglect his wife."

"He sacrificed his marriage for the ranch."

Jule was so stunned to hear him say that, she was momentarily wordless. Was Rafe imagining history could repeat itself with him?

"I know what you're thinking," he said, "but don't worry,

there's no danger of that happening to me now. I always believed that because my father started the ranch with Jed that there was a chance I'd have a half claim to it. But that's another lie."

"Why? Halona didn't leave Anoki. They stayed together."

"Yeah, probably for my sake. And to spare Anoki the humiliation."

"Of his wife's infidelity?"

With a swiftness that had Jule catching her breath, Rafe hit the brakes and jerked the truck to a stop at the side of the road. He fisted his hands on the steering wheel and rested his head against them for a moment. "I wish that were it," he muttered.

Jule touched his shoulder. He flinched away. "Tell me."

The bleakness in his eyes when he looked at her frightened her. "She stayed with Anoki so no one would know he was raising a bastard son."

Suddenly she wanted to take back her plea. She didn't want to know. It was like watching a rock slide tumbling toward her and being unable to run away.

"Jed Garrett is my father, Jule. My real father."

All she could do at first was stare at him. The words reverberated in her head until they were just sounds that couldn't have meaning. Ignoring the way he stiffened, she reached out and put her arms around him, her cheek against his shoulder. "I can't believe it. I just can't believe it."

"Believe it," he ground out. "My grandmother told me enough details to convince me it's the truth. My mother made my grandmother promise to hide it from everyone to protect Anoki's name. I guess in her way, Halona loved him, too."

"But after they died, I would have thought your grandmother would have wanted to bring you home."

"No, because my mother wanted me to stay on the ranch." He shook his head, his mouth twisting. "She believed Jed loved her and would take care of her son. She told my grandmother that one day I'd own half the ranch. She said if anything happened to her and Anoki, my best chance for a future was staying at Rancho Pintada with my *father.* My *real* father."

Jule didn't want to make things worse but she was desperately trying to justify Halona inadvertently consigning her son to the life Rafe had had with Jed. "In some ways that's probably true," she said carefully. "I'm sure your mother only wanted what she thought was best for you. I'm just surprised no one ever suspected you were Jed's son."

"No one knew they'd been lovers. And, except for my height, I don't look like Garrett. But I'm his blood. Which means I never had a claim to half the ranch and never will." With a savage twist of the key, he restarted the truck.

"But you *are* his son. That should count for something."

He glanced at her in disbelief. "You believe that? After the way he's treated Sawyer and Cort?" He cut her off before she could answer. "No. This ends whatever hopes I had of proving I had a half claim. I don't have a right. I can't pretend to be something I'm not. Even if it meant sticking it to Jed. I'm not Anoki's son. My share in the ranch is exactly the same as my brothers'."

Jule sat back, still reeling with shock. Mulling it all over she muttered, half to herself, "I can't believe Jed doesn't know."

"He doesn't." Rafe shifted into high gear and punched the gas hard. "But he's about to find out."

After a quick visit to the hospital where Cort was still unconscious and listed in critical condition in ICU, Rafe found Jed, his feet propped up, a cigar in one hand, whiskey glass in the other, lounging in his oversized den watching his oversized TV.

"I need to talk to you."

Jed glanced away from the television back over his shoulder at Rafe. "Did we have a meeting today? Don't recall one. Unless you've got some news on your brother."

"Nothing you haven't heard. Or probably care to hear."

"Then the game'll be done in thirty minutes. I'll talk then."

Rafe strode over to the coffee table Jed was using as a footstool and grabbed the remote, punching the power button. "We'll talk now."

Del scurried into the room, still wearing her pink robe and house slippers though it was late afternoon. Her pet poodle squirmed in her arms. "What's going on? Rafe, we weren't expecting you today. Jed's restin'."

"Go away, Del. I have to talk to him alone."

"I will not! I—"

"Go on, the boy's got something eatin' at him and he needs to vent on the old man. I can take it."

Del scowled at Rafe. "Don't you upset him. You hear? I'll be in the sunroom if you need me, honey. You just use that little walkie-talkie gadget I bought you, and I'll be here in a flash."

Rafe followed Del, pulling the heavy pocket doors to the den closed behind her. Looking down at Jed, still smug despite his age and ill health, he didn't know whether to feel rage or pity.

"Stop staring and spit it out, boy. I want to see at least the last quarter of the game."

Rage, Rafe thought. *Definitely rage.* "I don't know what lies you told my mother to get her into your bed, but for whatever reason, she believed them. But I thought you'd like to know, you didn't leave her with nothing. You did give her me."

"You?" Jed's cigar fell out of his mouth into his lap. Stunned, he slapped at it until the red glow turned black. "What the hell are you talkin' about, boy?"

"*Your* boy," Rafe snarled at him. "I'm your son."

Rafe told him then, everything his grandmother had said, and watched as the truth sank in.

Jed's ruddy face went pale and he grabbed for his whiskey. When he'd swallowed it in one gulp, he looked ten years older. "You…" He shook his head, staring at Rafe as if he'd never seen him before. "Your mama was a beautiful woman, a good woman," he said, his voice low and shaky. "She deserved better than Anoki."

Rafe scoffed, pacing away from Jed. He hadn't expected to hear—he didn't want to hear—something that sounded almost like tenderness from Garrett at the mention of his mother. "Well, she sure as hell deserved better than you. You were married to Theresa. She was pregnant with Sawyer. I'd ask what you were thinking, but I'm guessing *thinking* didn't come into it."

"Theresa was a razor-tongued, cold-hearted bitch."

"With family money you didn't hesitate to use."

"She got half of everything I'd built up in this place when she left. I might have used her money to make somethin' out of this godforsaken spread, but she made money divorcing me."

"And what did my mother get for bedding you? Besides a bastard son?"

Jed's eyes narrowed. "You were never a bastard. I adopted you because that's what she wanted. She told me that if anything ever happened to her and Anoki, she wanted you to stay here, on the ranch with me. I promised her."

"I'm supposed to believe that was the only reason?" Fists clenched, Rafe swung away from Jed and then whipped back to face him. "Anoki was your partner. His son would have been able to claim half the ranch. You made sure that couldn't happen."

"You've got no proof Anoki was ever a partner," Jed snapped back. He'd regained some of the composure the news had knocked out of him and sat up straighter in his chair. "You're just speculatin'."

"I'd say it's a pretty good guess."

"Doesn't matter either way now, though, does it?" Jed said, his arrogance back in full swing. He picked up his cigar and lighter and blew smoke Rafe's way. "Whether you're adopted or my blood, you only get what the others get. I've treated you all the same."

Rafe laughed bitterly. "Yeah, you have, haven't you?" He picked up the remote and snapped the game back on. "You ought to go to your grave feeling just great about how you've treated us all."

* * *

Rafe had insisted on dropping Jule at home before confronting Jed and she waited there now, worrying and wondering, half angry at him for shutting her out.

She'd argued to stay and wait for him at his house, but he'd flatly refused. He'd withdrawn completely from her, the way he always did when he was hurting. Like an animal retreating to its cave alone to heal its wounds—that had been Rafe's defense from the first abuses Jed inflicted on him.

Catalina had tried to get her daughter to talk, then pressed her to eat, but the thought of food was enough to send Jule's stomach reeling. Instead she had retreated to her bedroom, where she paced restlessly, anxious for some word from Rafe.

Finally, her cell phone rang, jarring her out of her thoughts. "Are you okay?" she asked, breath held.

"Yeah. Fine."

"And?"

"And I talked to him. He didn't deny it. But it doesn't make any difference to him—so he says—that I'm his blood son instead of his adopted son."

Jule sat down on her bed. "I guess I'm not surprised to hear that, but I wonder how true it is. I'm sure he's doing some heavy thinking."

"Don't count on it. What he's doing is some heavy drink-ing."

"Oh, Rafe—"

"There's nothing you can do. About any of this."

"I could come over and—"

"No. I need some time to myself."

"Don't do this. Don't shut me out. Not now. Not after we've come so far."

"Have we? Why, because we made love a couple of times? Don't get me wrong, it was great and I meant every moment of it. But that doesn't give us a future, does it?"

"It gives us a start."

"On what? How can you expect me to think about starting

anything? I didn't have much to build on before, but I sure as hell don't have anything now."

"Because you're Jed's son?" She understood Rafe feeling anger, disappointment, disillusionment, shock at the news. But she suddenly realized what was eating at him was more than learning the truth about his father. "No, it's not that, is it?" She didn't let him answer. "It's because you don't have enough of the ranch to make you feel like you have anything to build on." Frustration began to rise in her, mounting from all the months of hearing about the ranch, only the ranch. Never about her. Never about them. "It's all about that isn't it? It's never been about us, it's always been about the ranch."

"That's only part of it," he ground out.

"I don't want to hear it." She stood and stalked back and forth across her bedroom. "Anoki might not be your father, but you're just like him. I thought maybe you'd learned something from his mistakes with your mother, but evidently not." Her temper was taking over like a rushing tide mounting to a wave that was about to break wide open.

"Every hope I had that half the ranch was rightfully mine, every hope for my future—it's all changed. I need time to think."

It was almost a plea. If she hadn't been so angry with him, with herself for believing that because he'd told her he loved her and the ranch wouldn't matter anymore, she might have weakened. Instead, months, years of frustration exploded, and the words spilled out before she could measure the consequences.

"Fine, you want time to think, you've got it," she snapped. "All the time in the world. But when you're done and you want to talk, I won't be here to listen anymore. I'm through, Rafe. Through waiting, through being patient, through believing we have something worth fighting for. And mostly, I'm through believing in someone who won't believe in himself."

She broke their connection before he had a chance to respond.

Chapter Eighteen

"Something is wrong with him. You can see that. You just aren't trying to understand him."

Anna Sanchez, her plump hands trembling, pointed to the gray parrot in his cage, alternating between frowning at Jule and bestowing mournful glances at the parrot that suggested she expected him to drop dead in front of her at any moment.

Jule resisted the urge to sigh. "Mrs. Sanchez—"

"You can see how irritable my poor Pedro is."

This time Jule held her mouth tightly shut and tried hard not to show it. *"Poor Pedro" is right. If I had to live with you, I'd be irritable, too.*

"Now if your father were here—"

"He'd tell you Pedro is fine."

Startled, Jule whirled to see her father standing in the door of the examining room. He leaned on a cane and he still looked too thin, but he was upright, with a familiar glint in his eye and bringing a feeling of renewed energy into the room.

Delighted to see him on his feet, Jule gave him a quick hug. "This is a surprise."

"I got tired of your mother's hovering," Abran said with a wink before turning to Mrs. Sanchez. He limped over to give Pedro a quick once-over. "That's Pedro's only problem. Too much fussing. Take him home, ignore him once a while."

"But, I couldn't—"

"Yes, you can," Abran interrupted firmly. "Men don't like too much fussing, Anna. They like to be left on their own every now and then. You trust me."

He walked Mrs. Sanchez out, listening to her continuing stream of concerns and offering a few soothing, noncommittal phrases, while Jule stayed behind to tidy up. For some reason, her father's words stuck in her head, playing over like a stubborn fragment of song. Well, she'd left Rafe alone, hadn't she? She'd told him she was through with him.

Unfortunately, in the last three days, she'd had plenty of time to regret everything she'd said and done. The question was, did she regret it enough to try again, or was she better off letting him go and saving herself the worse pain of having him tell her to her face it was over?

The trouble was, she didn't have an answer.

Hearing her father come back down the hallway, Jule shook off her distraction and used the side door to meet him in his office.

"You've only been home a couple of days," she chided him as he settled into the chair behind his desk and she took the seat across from him. "I didn't expect you to be back at work for several weeks at least. And I know you're not supposed to be driving."

Abran waved a dismissive hand. "You sound like your mother, always fussing. Felix Ramos gave me a ride. I just stopped by to see how things are going." Glancing around the room he added, "I'm thinking by next month, I'll be ready to come in mornings."

"Maybe, but there's no way you can make the outside calls so don't even think about it. You know I'll be here to help."

"For a few more weeks, maybe a month, that's all. I'm going to look for a partner," he said, his expression thoughtful. "I don't see myself doing this full-time any more. It won't be too much longer before your mother will insist on me retiring anyway."

Jule had a growing suspicion that wasn't all her mother had been pressing him on. "A few months ago you wanted *me* for a partner. This is because of Rafe, isn't it?"

"Why should it be about Rafe Garrett? I thought you would be ready to move on by now, get back to your own plans. I never expected you'd stay permanently."

"That's exactly what you expected, and you know it." Irritation spiked through her as suspicion solidified into certainty. Her mother had told him Jule was involved with Rafe again and now her father was doing everything he could to stop it. Not that Jule was sure that saying she and Rafe were involved was accurate any more. And if it was over, this was her chance to leave Luna Hermosa and put him behind her. Her parents would no longer be a reason to stay. The only reason would be Rafe.

Suddenly, despite all the anger, harsh words and things unsaid left hanging between them, Jule knew if she left, it wouldn't be because of her family or his. Not again.

"If this is your way of getting me out of town and away from Rafe, it's not going to work this time. It wouldn't have worked before if Rafe hadn't insisted."

"And you're so sure he won't do the same thing again," Abran said flatly. "Apparently things aren't as good between you as you'd like me to believe."

Jule cursed her mother's habit of revealing every detail to her father. Obviously Catalina, sensitive to Jule's emotions, knew she'd been distracted and unhappy and guessed at the cause.

Her father's words hurt because she feared he'd hit on the truth. But she wouldn't let him see that. "Whatever is between Rafe and me is our business. I know you'd like it to be nothing, but it isn't. I love him."

She hadn't meant to say it straight out and she half expected surprise or protest from her father. Abran, though, only looked resigned.

"This is not what I wanted for you. You deserve so much more."

"I know it's not what you wanted," she said softly. She came over to kneel by his chair and took his hand in hers, willing him to understand. "But it's what I want. And it's what I deserve—someone who loves me as much as I love him. He's trying, Dad, he's always been trying to make himself worthy of me because he knows you and Mom and just about everyone else in this town thinks he doesn't deserve me. But I love him and he loves me, and that's enough. That's all that matters."

Saying it aloud made it real again and filled her with new resolve. She'd teetered on the edge of giving up and letting Rafe go again, convincing herself he'd never be able to break free of his past or of his misguided obsession with linking his self-worth and self-esteem to a piece of land.

Yet if she could walk away then she was convincing him of the same. That he wasn't good enough for her. That she didn't believe they were worth fighting for.

He loved her; she knew that as surely as she knew she would take another breath. She had to try one more time to convince him he was all she had ever wanted or ever *would* want, no matter who his father was, with or without any part of Rancho Pintada. It was a huge risk. He could choose not to believe her.

She could walk away now, move away. But if she did, she would go on wondering what would have happened if she'd only tried one more time to make him believe they would never be whole without each other.

Rafe released the last bison calf he'd been checking, watching as it trotted back to its mother, when the sound of a vehicle coming up the road to the barn turned his head. For one moment, his heart caught, half anticipating it was Jule, at the same time as he told himself he was a damned fool for even thinking it could be after the way they'd left things.

Instead, Sawyer's truck stopped just outside the corral, and his brother walked over to the corral fence to wait while Rafe let himself back outside.

"Is something wrong?" Rafe asked, his first thought that Cort had taken a turn for the worse.

"I don't know. Is there?" Sawyer leaned back against the fence, eyeing Rafe closely. "If you mean Cort, no, there's no change. He's still unconscious, still in ICU, although they've taken him off the critical list. But you'd know all that. The nurses said you'd either been there or called to check every day. So you tell me—what's wrong?"

Everything. "Nothing. I've just been busy."

"Now tell me something I believe. Look, Jule stopped by the clinic the other day and Maya could tell she was upset. She wouldn't say why, but I'd bet everything on it being something to do with you. Even Josh hasn't seen you for the last three days. It's beginning to look like you've decided to push everyone away again."

"That's not it." What he wanted to push away was the truth. No, he wanted to obliterate the truth, go back to believing he was who he'd thought he was. Even if that hadn't been easy to live with, this new thing he'd become was a lot harder.

"What is it then?" Sawyer asked. "Is it Jule?"

"No. Not Jule." He turned away, fisting his hands over the wooden railing. "I love her. But I'm not sure she feels the same anymore. I'm not sure she can."

He didn't need to see his brother to know Sawyer was confused. "It's obvious to anyone with eyes she loves you. I can't imagine what could change that."

Rafe gave a huff of bitter laughter. "No, you probably can't."

"Are you going to enlighten me or do I have to stand here all day guessing?"

Turning on him, Rafe said bluntly, "I'm Jed's son. Not because of a piece of paper. Because I am."

Sawyer stared at him blankly as if Rafe's words hadn't made any sense. "How's that possible?" he finally asked.

"The usual way. He and my mother were lovers." He told Sawyer the rest of it, starting with his grandmother's confession through his confrontation with Jed, only leaving out the part at the end where he'd managed to screw up things with Jule. "You see how it changes things," he finished and waited for Sawyer to agree.

"No," Sawyer said slowly, "actually, I don't."

It was Rafe's turn to stare. "Did you hear any of this?"

"All of it. And I'll admit it's a helluva shock. Or maybe not, considering Jed's habit of bedding every woman who came his way. But none of that will make a difference to Jule."

"It should," Rafe said, turning back to stare again at the vista of land stretching out in front of him.

"Why? It doesn't change who you are. The only difference now is we both have to live with being related to the sorry bastard." Sawyer grasped his shoulder to bring Rafe around to face him. "We've always been brothers. Adoption or blood, it doesn't matter. To me or to Jule."

"And this?" Rafe gestured out at the land. "I can't offer her this any more. I don't have the right."

"Maybe not, although you've got this bad habit of giving up too easily when things don't go your way," Sawyer said, smiling to spite Rafe's scowl. "If I were you, right now I'd forget about what's right or wrong about your claim on the ranch and focus on making things right with Jule. Without her, the rest of this doesn't really matter, does it?"

Rafe didn't answer. He knew what he wanted to say.

But he'd spent nearly all his life convinced he needed the ranch to make himself into someone she deserved.

Now, faced with losing her again, he needed to believe he

could be that man just by loving her. Because loving her was all he had to offer.

Jule had a weird sense of déjà vu driving up to the ranch. It felt like that day, all those months ago, when she'd come back and knew she'd be seeing Rafe for the first time after the years apart. Her stomach clenched, nervous anticipation skittered through her, and a small voice called her the same kind of fool for doing this again.

But she was doing this again because no matter what she'd said or what she'd tried to make herself believe, she couldn't give up on Rafe without trying one more time to save them both.

She was nearly to the barn when she met him in his truck on the way out. Recognizing her, he stopped, looked at her, then waved her on ahead, turning around to follow her back in the direction he'd come.

He met her halfway, at the corral fence. She stopped an arm's length from him, not sure where to look or how to interpret his awkward shifting or the way he stood facing the corral, looking sideways at her instead of head-on.

"I was coming to see you," he said. "You beat me to it."

"I hadn't been here for a while. I mean, to check on the bison. I thought I would today. Check on them." Jule stopped before she sounded any stupider or made that any more of a lie.

Rafe rubbed at the back of his neck. She studied the tops of her boots.

Glancing at her and catching her looking at him, Rafe made a move in her direction, checked himself and quickly fixed his eyes back on the bison.

"Jule—"

"Rafe—"

They both started at the same time then stopped. He gestured for her to go ahead.

Jule cleared her throat and moved to stand beside him,

holding onto the fence as if it might ground her. She nodded toward the few bison grazing in the distance. "They seem to be doing well."

"Yeah, fine."

The conversation, if you could call it that, was so banal Jule considered throwing herself at him and begging him to let her in, to confide in her what was he was really feeling. To tell him that she loved him, needed him and she wasn't willing to move forward without him. But it sounded so melodramatic and desperate she couldn't bring herself to say it and at the same time couldn't think of anything else to say that came close to what she wanted him to know.

Rafe leaned his forearms on the fence, following her gaze to the bison. "I'm thinking of expanding the herd this spring. The market seems good and now that we've gotten the problems under control, I've got a good chance of making it pay." He didn't look at her when he added, "Might do some work on the house, too. Fix a few things, add on a room or two. What do you think?"

"What do I think?" Where was he going with this? And why? "I don't understand."

In one motion he straightened, turned to her and took her hand, bridging the distance between them. "Before, you wanted to know if I was serious. I am. And I'm asking now. Will you stay with me?"

"Stay—why? Why are you asking? What's changed?" Jule threw his own words back at him. "What's different?"

"I'm different. It's taken me too long but I'm hoping you'll have me, because of who I am, the person you've known since we were kids, the man who's loved you since you were a little girl, not for any other reason. I can't offer you any more than my heart."

Jule could hardly speak. "And everything else—the ranch, Jed…"

He straightened his shoulders, shaking his head and Jule saw there were shadows in his eyes that might never be completely banished. "I'm not at peace with that, maybe I never will be. And I'm not ready to give up on this place. But none of it matters if I have to go on without you." She could see his struggle to find the words he wanted. "I don't have anything to offer you but myself. I hope that's still enough for you. Because you're the only thing I need."

It was a long speech for Rafe and it moved Jule to tears. She didn't bother to try to stop them even when he gently reached up with his fingertips to brush them away. "You've always been the only thing I needed. I love you. More than you'll ever know."

Pulling her close, he kissed her, an achingly tender caress that was both a testament and a vow. When it finally ended, Rafe reached between them into his jacket pocket and drew something out. He opened his hand to her and Jule recognized the pink quartz heart hanging from its silver chain, the necklace she'd left behind all those years ago. In a way, it embodied the heart she'd left behind. The one she'd given to him.

"You left this before," Rafe said as he fastened it around her neck. "I hope this time you'll be one the staying behind." With something akin to reverence, he touched the heart where it lay in the hollow of her throat, his eyes never leaving hers. "I love you, Jule. Marry me."

Love and happiness flooded through her, taking with it all the doubt and fear, and, laughing and crying, she kissed him. "Yes," she promised him, "yes," then caught her breath as he spun her around, scooped her into his arms and started striding off in the direction of his house. "What are you doing?"

"Taking you home."

"Home?" The word tasted sweet and she held it close to her heart as tightly as she held to him. "And what then?" she asked, smiling to herself because she already knew the answer.

"I've got thirteen years of catching up to do. I figure I'd better get started."

"Thirteen years *is* a long time," Jule said slowly, pretending to think it over. "This could take a while."

"Years."

"Forever."

Rafe kissed her, hard and long, and she could hear him smiling, feel it against her mouth. "I'm counting on it."

Epilogue

Julene Santiago stepped into the sanctuary, breathing quickened, heart pounding. Not because of the surroundings; she'd been here countless times, though not like this, walking slowly up the center aisle, with everyone watching her. The heady mix of love, anticipation and excitement making her smile glow and her body tremble was because of Rafe.

She would never leave Luna Hermosa again, not without him. He'd told her he'd never let her out of his sight again and she'd listened with her heart—she always had with Rafe. She always would.

They'd been waiting, not patiently, but willingly, for this day for the last four months. Her mother had protested a March wedding (too cold, too snowy, too gray). But that had been more of a last effort to convince Jule that she should think longer and harder about marrying Rafe Garrett than because of some objection to the month itself.

For Jule, she couldn't have wished for it any harder and it

had been too long already. She had been ready to marry Rafe the day he'd asked her; he'd insisted they wait until all his family could be there.

So they'd waited, until after Maya and Sawyer had welcomed Nicolas Cortez Morente into their family, and until Cort, after nearly two months in the hospital, was recovered enough to attend his brother's wedding.

Father Biega didn't kick them out of the church this time, she wasn't wearing overalls (although she'd been sorely tempted), and they weren't alone—it seemed as if most of Luna Hermosa had shown up—but Jule remembered that other long-ago ceremony in this same sanctuary and thought the past and today meant just as much.

When Rafe slipped the ring on her finger—a ruby heart, set in gold, with a bright-blue rubber band twisted around it—she raised Father Biega's eyebrows and smiles from Sawyer and Maya by laughing.

Then Rafe kissed her for the first time as her husband and the tears came at the rightness and the power of it. It wasn't perfect, it never had been, but it was right.

And this time, Jule knew it would last forever.

Because forever had started the day her dad had let her tag along on his visit to Rancho Pintada and she'd earned her first smile from the scowling ten-year-old boy she'd found working in the barn.

Since then, even apart, they'd been inseparable.

Always.

* * * * *

Award-winning author Stevi Mittman delivers another
hysterical mystery, featuring Teddi Bayer, an irrepressible
heroine, and her to-die-for hero, Detective Drew Scoones.
After all, life on Long Island can be murder!

*Turn the page for a sneak peek
at the warm and funny fourth book,
WHOSE NUMBER IS UP, ANYWAY?,
in the Teddi Bayer series
by STEVI MITTMAN.
On sale August 7*

"Before redecorating a room, I always advise my clients to empty it of everything but one chair. Then I suggest they move that chair from place to place, sitting in it, until the placement feels right. Trust your instincts when deciding on furniture placement. Your room should 'feel right.'"

—TipsFromTeddi.com

Gut feelings. You know, that gnawing in the pit of your stomach that warns you that you are about to do the absolute stupidest thing you could do? Something that will ruin life as you know it?

I've got one now, standing at the butcher counter in King Kullen, the grocery store in the same strip mall as L.I. Lanes, the bowling alley cum billiard parlor I'm in the process of re-decorating for its "Grand Opening."

I realize being in the wrong supermarket probably doesn't sound exactly dire to you, but you aren't the one buying your father a brisket at a store your mother will somehow know isn't Waldbaum's.

And then, June Bayer isn't your mother.

The woman behind the counter has agreed to go into the freezer to find a brisket for me, since there aren't any in the case. There are packages of pork tenderloin, piles of spare ribs and rolls of sausage, but no briskets.

Warning Number Two, right? I should be so out of here.

But no, I'm still in the same spot when she comes back out,

brisketless, her face ashen. She opens her mouth as if she is going to scream, but only a gurgle comes out.

And then she pinballs out from behind the counter, knocking bottles of Peter Luger Steak Sauce to the floor on her way, now hitting the tower of cans at the end of the prepared foods aisle and sending them sprawling, now making her way down the aisle, careening from side to side as she goes.

Finally, from a distance, I hear her shout, "He's deeeeeeaaaad! Joey's deeeeeaaaad."

My first thought is *You should always trust your gut.*

My second thought is that now, somehow, my mother will know I was in King Kullen. For weeks I will have to hear "What did you expect?" as though whenever you go to King Kullen someone turns up dead. And if the detective investigating the case turns out to be Detective Drew Scoones…well, I'll never hear the end of that from her, either.

She still suspects I murdered the guy who was found dead on my doorstep last Halloween just to get Drew back into my life.

Several people head for the butcher's freezer and I position myself to block them. If there's one thing I've learned from finding people dead—and the guy on my doorstep wasn't the first one—it's that the police get very testy when you mess with their murder scenes.

"You can't go in there until the police get here," I say, stationing myself at the end of the butcher's counter and in front of the Employees Only door, acting as if I'm some sort of authority. "You'll contaminate the evidence if it turns out to be murder."

Shouts and chaos. You'd think I'd know better than to throw the word *murder* around. Cell phones are flipping open and tongues are wagging.

I amend my statement quickly. "Which, of course, it probably isn't. Murder, I mean. People die all the time, and it's not always in hospitals or their own beds, or…" I babble when I'm nervous, and the idea of someone dead on the other side of the freezer door makes me very nervous.

So does the idea of seeing Drew Scoones again. Drew and I have this on-again, off-again sort of thing...that I kind of turned off.

Who knew he'd take it so personally when he tried to get serious and I responded by saying we could talk about *us* tomorrow—and then caught a plane to my parents' condo in Boca the next day? In July. In the middle of a job.

For some crazy reason, he took that to mean that I was avoiding him and the subject of *us*.

That was three months ago. I haven't seen him since.

The manager, who identifies himself and points to his name-plate in case I don't believe him, says he has to go into *his cooler*. "Maybe Joey's not dead," he says. "Maybe he can be saved, and you're letting him die in there. Did you ever think of that?"

In fact, I hadn't. But I had thought that the murderer might try to go back in to make sure his tracks were covered, so I say that I will go in and check.

Which means that the manager and I couple up and go in together while everyone pushes against the doorway to peer in, erasing any chance of finding clean prints on that Employee Only door.

I expect to find carcasses of dead animals hanging from hooks, and maybe Joey hanging from one, too. I think it's going to be very creepy and I steel myself, only to find a rather benign series of shelves with large slabs of meat laid out care-fully on them, along with boxes and boxes marked simply Chicken.

Nothing scary here, unless you count the body of a middle-aged man with graying hair sprawled faceup on the floor. His eyes are wide open and unblinking. His shirt is stiff. His pants are stiff. His body is stiff. And his expression, you should forgive the pun—is frozen. Bill-the-manager crosses himself and stands mute while I pronounce the guy dead in a sort of *happy now?* tone.

"We should not be in here," I say, and he nods his head emphatically and helps me push people out of the doorway just in time to hear the police sirens and see the cop cars pull up outside the big store windows.

Bobbie Lyons, my partner in Teddi Bayer Interior Designs (and also my neighbor, my best friend and my private fashion police), and Mark, our carpenter (and my dogsitter, confidant, and ego booster), rush in from next door. They beat the cops by a half step and shout out my name. People point in my direction.

After all the publicity that followed the unfortunate incident during which I shot my ex-husband, Rio Gallo, and then the subsequent murder of my first client—which I solved, I might add—it seems like the whole world, or at least all of Long Island, knows who I am.

Mark asks if I'm all right. (Did I remember to mention that the man is drop-dead-gorgeous-but-a-decade-too-young-for-me-yet-too-old-for-my-daughter-thank-god?) I don't get a chance to answer him because the police are quickly closing in on the store manager and me.

"The woman—" I begin telling the police. Then I have to pause for the manager to fill in her name, which he does: *Fran*.

I continue. "Right. Fran. Fran went into the freezer to get a brisket. A moment later she came out and screamed that Joey was dead. So I'd say she was the one who discovered the body."

"And you are…?" the cop asks me. It comes out a bit like who do I *think* I am, rather than who am I really?

"An innocent bystander," Bobbie, hair perfect, makeup just right, says, carefully placing her body between the cop and me.

"And she was just leaving," Mark adds. They each take one of my arms.

Fran comes into the inner circle surrounding the cops. In case it isn't obvious from the hairnet and bloodstained white apron with Fran embroidered on it, I explain that she was the butcher who was going for the brisket. Mark and Bobbie take that as a signal that I've done my job and they can now get me out of there. They twist around, with me in the middle, as if we're a Rockettes line, until we are facing away from the butcher counter. They've managed to propel me a few steps toward the exit when disaster—in the form of a Mazda RX7 pulling up at the loading curb—strikes.

Mark's grip on my arm tightens like a vise. "Too late," he says.

Bobbie's expletive is unprintable. "Maybe there's a back door," she suggests, but Mark is right. It's too late.

I've laid my eyes on Detective Scoones. And while my gut is trying to warn me that my heart shouldn't go there, regions farther south are melting at just the sight of him.

"Walk," Bobbie orders me.

And I try to. Really.

Walk, I tell my feet. *Just put one foot in front of the other.*

I can do this because I know, in my heart of hearts, that if Drew Scoones was still interested in me, he'd have gotten in touch with me after I returned from Boca. And he didn't.

Since he's a detective, Drew doesn't have to wear one of those dark blue Nassau County Police uniforms. Instead, he's got on jeans, a tight-fitting T-shirt and a tweedy sports jacket. If you think that sounds good, you should see him. Chiseled features, cleft chin, brown hair that's naturally a little sandy in the front, a smile that…well, that doesn't matter. He isn't smiling now.

He walks up to me, tucks his sunglasses into his breast pocket and looks me over from head to toe.

"Well, if it isn't Miss Cut and Run," he says. "Aren't you supposed to be somewhere in Florida or something?" He looks at Mark accusingly, as if he was covering for me when he told Drew I was gone.

"Detective Scoones?" one of the uniforms says. "The stiff's in the cooler and the woman who found him is over there." He jerks his head in Fran's direction.

Drew continues to stare at me.

You know how when you were young, your mother always told you to wear clean underwear in case you were in an accident? And how, a little farther on, she told you not to go out in hair rollers because you never knew who you might see—or who might see you? And how now your best friend says she wouldn't be caught dead without makeup and suggests you shouldn't either?

Okay, today, *finally*, in my overalls and Converse sneakers, I get it.

I brush my hair out of my eyes. "Well, I'm back," I say. As if he hasn't known my exact whereabouts. The man is a detective, for heaven's sake. "Been back awhile."

Bobbie has watched the exchange and apparently decided she's given Drew all the time he deserves. "And we've got work to do, so…" she says, grabbing my arm and giving Drew a little two-fingered wave goodbye.

As I back up a foot or two, the store manager sees his chance and places himself in front of Drew, trying to get his attention. Maybe what makes Drew such a good detective is his ability to focus.

Only what he's focusing on is me.

"Phone broken? Carrier pigeon died?" he asks me, taking in Fran, the manager, the meat counter and that Employees Only door, all without taking his eyes off me.

Mark tries to break the spell. "We've got work to do there, you've got work to do here, Scoones," Mark says to him, gesturing toward next door. "So it's back to the alley for us."

Drew's lip twitches. "You working the alley now?" he says.

"If you'd like to follow me," Bill-the-manager, clearly exasperated, says to Drew—who doesn't respond. It's as if waiting for my answer is all he has to do.

So, fine. "You knew I was back," I say.

The man has known my whereabouts every hour of the day for as long as I've known him. And my mother's not the only one who won't buy that he "just happened" to answer this particular call. In fact, I'm willing to bet my children's lunch money that he's taken every call within ten miles of my home since the day I got back.

And now he's gotten lucky.

"*You* could have called *me*," I say.

"You're the one who said *tomorrow* for our talk and then flew the coop, chickie," he says. "I figured the ball was in your court."

"Detective?" the uniform says. "There's something you ought to see in here."

Drew gives me a look that amounts to *in or out?*

He could be talking about the investigation, or about our relationship.

Bobbie tries to steer me away. Mark's fists are balled. Drew waits me out, knowing I won't be able to resist what might be a murder investigation.

Finally he turns and heads for the cooler.

And, like a puppy dog, I follow.

Bobbie grabs the back of my shirt and pulls me to a halt.

"I'm just going to show him something," I say, yanking away.

"Yeah," Bobbie says, pointedly looking at the buttons on my blouse. The two at breast level have popped. "That's what I'm afraid of."

ATHENA FORCE

Heart-pounding romance and thrilling adventure.

A ruthless enemy rises against the women of Athena Academy. In a global chess game of vengeance, kidnapping and murder, every move exposes potential enemies—and lovers. This time the women must stand together... before their world is ripped apart.

THIS NEW 12-BOOK SERIES BEGINS WITH A BANG IN AUGUST 2007 WITH

TRUST
by Rachel Caine

Look for a new Athena Force adventure each month wherever books are sold.

REQUEST YOUR FREE BOOKS!
2 FREE NOVELS PLUS 2 FREE GIFTS!

Silhouette®

SPECIAL EDITION®
Life, Love and Family!

YES! Please send me 2 FREE Silhouette Special Edition® novels and my 2 FREE gifts. After receiving them, if I don't wish to receive any more books, I can return the shipping statement marked "cancel." If I don't cancel, I will receive 6 brand-new novels every month and be billed just $4.24 per book in the U.S., or $4.99 per book in Canada, plus 25¢ shipping and handling per book and applicable taxes, if any*. That's a savings of at least 15% off the cover price! I understand that accepting the 2 free books and gifts places me under no obligation to buy anything. I can always return a shipment and cancel at any time. Even if I never buy another book from Silhouette, the two free books and gifts are mine to keep forever.   235 SDN EEYU 335 SDN EEY6

Name _____ (PLEASE PRINT)

Address _____ Apt. _____

City _____ State/Prov. _____ Zip/Postal Code _____

Signature (if under 18, a parent or guardian must sign)

Mail to the **Silhouette Reader Service™**:
IN U.S.A.: P.O. Box 1867, Buffalo, NY 14240-1867
IN CANADA: P.O. Box 609, Fort Erie, Ontario L2A 5X3

Not valid to current Silhouette Special Edition subscribers.

Want to try two free books from another line?
Call 1-800-873-8635 or visit www.morefreebooks.com.

* Terms and prices subject to change without notice. NY residents add applicable sales tax. Canadian residents will be charged applicable provincial taxes and GST. This offer is limited to one order per household. All orders subject to approval. Credit or debit balances in a customer's account(s) may be offset by any other outstanding balance owed by or to the customer. Please allow 4 to 6 weeks for delivery.

Your Privacy: Silhouette is committed to protecting your privacy. Our Privacy Policy is available online at www.eHarlequin.com or upon request from the Reader Service. From time to time we make our lists of customers available to reputable firms who may have a product or service of interest to you. If you would prefer we not share your name and address, please check here. ☐

SSE07

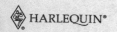

COMING NEXT MONTH

#1843 PAGING DR. RIGHT—Stella Bagwell
Montana Mavericks: Striking It Rich
Mia Smith came to Thunder Canyon Resort for some peace and quiet, but with her recent inheritance, other guests took her for a wealthy socialite and wouldn't leave her be. At least she found comfort with the resort's handsome staff doctor Marshall Cates, but would her painful past and humble beginnings nip their budding romance?

#1844 THE BILLIONAIRE NEXT DOOR—Jessica Bird
The O'Banyon Brothers
For Wall Street hot shot Sean O'Banyon, going home to South Boston after his abusive father's death brought back miserable memories. But Lizzie Bond, his father's sweet, girl-next-door caretaker, was there to ease the pain. It was instant attraction—and then Sean found out she was named sole heir, and he began to wonder what her motives really were….

#1845 REMODELING THE BACHELOR—Marie Ferrarella
The Sons of Lily Moreau
Son of a famous, though flighty artist, Philippe Zabelle had grown up to be a set-in-his-ways bachelor. Yet when the successful software developer hired J. D. Wyatt to do some home repairs, something clicked. J.D. was a single mother with a flair for fixing anything… even Philippe's long-broken heart.

#1846 THE COWBOY AND THE CEO—Christine Wenger
She was city. He was country. But on a trip to a Wyoming ranch that made disabled children's dreams come true, driven business owner Susan Collins fell hard for caring cowboy Clint Skully. Having been left at the altar once before, would Clint risk the farm on love this time around?

#1847 ACCIDENTALLY EXPECTING—Michelle Celmer
In one corner, attorney Miranda Reed, who wrote the definitive guide to divorce and the modern woman. In the other, Zackery Jameson, staunch supporter of traditional family values. When these polar opposites sparred on a radio talk show, neither yielded any ground. So how did it come to pass that Miranda was now expecting Zack's baby?

#1848 A FAMILY PRACTICE—Gayle Kasper
After personal tragedy struck, Dr. Luke Phillips took off on a road trip. But when he crashed his motorcycle in the Arizona desert, it was local holistic healer Mariah Cade who got him to stop running. Whether it was in her tender touch or her gentle way with her daughter, Mariah was the miracle cure for all that ailed the good doctor.

SSECNM0707